# The Reckoning
Linda Tweedie
Kate McGregor

Published by Fledgling Press 2015
www.fledglingpress.co.uk

ISBN 9781905916108

Printed by Bell & Bain Ltd, Glasgow.

# Acknowledgements

The Reckoning, the third book in the Coyle trilogy, was written by Linda Tweedie in partnership with Kate McGregor.

Once again we acknowledge the help and assistance of Clare Cain, our understanding publisher. Her patience with two insecure divas who missed countless deadlines, knew no bounds. She cajoled, bullied and threatened (in no particular order) but eventually got results.

Thanks to Graeme who again got the cover just right. And to Paul, who got the book out there.

Finally, thanks to Linda's beleaguered husband of forty plus years, David, who refuses to ever eat another take-away!

# Acknowledgements

# Prologue

Violence and torture, in their warped psyche, was beyond exhilarating; better than sex, they both agreed. Anyone could have sex but not everyone could inflict or prolong torture the way this pair could.

Genaro Cortellessa and young Davey Thomson had been best pals since primary school. The fact that their fathers were two of the main players in Glasgow's underworld had never, during their formative years, been cause for disharmony or jealousy between the two lads. If anything it made their bond stronger.

Both were motherless and reared in households with no female influence. From an early age the two recognised the exhilaration that cruelty and inflicting pain brought them. The boys were about seven when they experienced their first high. Playing in the woods behind their school, they had come across a bag caught on a branch swinging over the stream. The contents of the bag were obviously meant to depart this world, but certainly in a more humane way than the two youngsters put into practice.

Smashing the bag with dozens of huge boulders, the boys then used it as a football. Thankfully the litter of newborn kittens lasted only a short time. However, the high-pitched squeals of the young animals and the shrieks of delight from the perverted twosome brought a number of their schoolmates to the scene.

Even the hardest bully was sick to his stomach at the mangled, bloodied contents of the Nike holdall. But Genaro and Davey were delirious. To inflict pain and suffering was now their raison d'être. But, judging the reactions of their contemporaries, there could be no more public displays of such wanton behaviour. In future they would take their pleasure in secret. No one else could share their pastime, except of course, their victims, and they would share the experience right to the death.

Here they stood, several years and victims later, at the request of not only their fathers, but the Big Man, Paddy Coyle. The man they both hated with a vengeance. The man who ruled the biggest turf in Scotland, the man who had no right to be in this position, the man who stood in their way. It was their birthright and no one would deny them.

# New Beginnings

"**Y**ou're what? At your age?" Lizzie Coyle leapt off her chair. The chair she'd barely moved from since the day she'd buried her son, Sean. As she hugged Paddy and her daughter-in-law, she could hardly believe their news. "Bridget, pregnant! Would you believe it?"

"Yes. I can hardly take it in myself," smiled Bridget. "I presume you're happy at the news?"

"Happy? I'm feckin' delirious," shouted the old lady gleefully. "Well, you certainly must have settled your differences," she chuckled. "Good God, pregnant after all this time. It's a miracle, that's what it is, a bloody miracle."

"It certainly is, Lizzie, and after everything we've been through in the last year, it's about time we had something to celebrate."

"What? You mean every family doesn't experience murder, kidnapping and imprisonment?"

"That's putting it mildly, but hopefully, that's all behind us now," answered Bridget.

"What's Erin got to say about this? Where is she, by the way?" Lizzie had only just realised her granddaughter and great grandson were missing.

"She's still in Spain," Paddy informed his mother.

1

"Still in Spain? Whatever for?"

"It's a long story, Ma, we'll tell you later."

"No you won't, you'll tell me now. Is she and the wee lad okay? I take it they're safe, or you wouldn't be standing here."

"They're fine, Ma, she's met someone."

"Holy Mother of God, she's been on the pull while her bairn has been kidnapped? Well, that takes the bloody biscuit," Paddy's mother exploded. "We're all worried sick about her and she's getting her end away."

"That's not how it was." Bridget jumped to the defence of her daughter.

"No?" queried Paddy.

"Look, everything's fine. Don't let's spoil this news by arguing over Erin's decision. She's a grown woman and quite capable of making her own choices. What does a mother-to-be have to do to get a cup of tea in this house?"

Still grumbling, Lizzie went off to make tea for her visitors.

"Hey, Ma, what's happened here?" Paddy called through to his mother as he spotted the kitchen window boarded up.

"Bloody kids, that's what. It's the second time in a week it's happened. If I catch the little feckers, I'll tan their arses, so I will."

"Second time?" Paddy repeated. "It would have to be kids, there's no one brave enough around here to take you on."

"A gang of youngsters have taken to hanging about outside. Drinking and carrying on, and when I chase them, I just get a load of abuse."

"What does our Errol have to say about it?"

2

"Nothing, he's very quiet. In fact, I think he's a bit scared."

"Rubbish, there's not an ounce of fear in that lad. There's more to this than meets the eye."

"I'm not so sure. You know he's never been right since his wee pal went missing." Lizzie had never been told about her dead son Sean's involvement in the boy's disappearance and Paddy aimed to make sure she never did.

"Bridget, I've got some business to see to, so you stay with Ma for a bit and I'll catch you back home."

As he left his mother's house Paddy was aware of half a dozen youths loitering on the corner.

"Fuck off you lot, and don't let me see you hanging around here again. Now move." He made to walk towards the group.

They dispersed in different directions, shouting abuse and laughing. All except one. The boy Riley swaggered towards Paddy.

"Is there a problem, Mr. Coyle?" the cocky young lad called out.

"You'll have a problem, ya cheeky young cunt, if I catch you hanging around here."

"It's a free country, Mr Coyle."

"Not where my family are concerned, it's not. Now fuck off before I get serious."

Paddy Coyle couldn't believe he was engaged in an argument with a two-bit street dealer. "Now I won't tell you again, piss off."

With the same insolent air, Tommy Riley swaggered off down the road towards his pitch.

Given the circumstances Paddy was prepared to overlook the incident, but, brother or no brother, this would be Tommy Riley's last chance.

Errol saw and heard the altercation between his uncle and his best mate's brother as he watched from his bedroom window. He knew, as well as the protagonists, that his family had had something to do with Billy's disappearance. He was sure his uncle Sean had been responsible, but Paddy and Michael had covered for him, so they were just as bad. He watched as his uncle drove off, and for the first time ever, he hadn't pestered him about the new car.

The less he had to do with his uncle, the better. What he didn't know, he couldn't tell.

# Denial

"Who the fuck, do you think you are?" Paddy Coyle roared at the two men facing him across the desk in Marie's office. "Get the fuck out of here before I shove that piddling pea-shooter up your nasty Russian arse."

The fucking nerve of them, coming into his club and brandishing a weapon. As if that would scare him. He turned to his brother, Michael, "Get rid of them before I get really angry."

"You heard what Mr Coyle said, gentlemen. It's time to leave, and you understand we are not interested in your business proposals."

The two Russians stood up, bowing to Paddy and Michael. Ivan, the bigger of the two, and they were both well-built guys, faced the brothers and addressed them in perfect English. "Let's hope, Mr. Coyle, you do not live to regret this decision. We came to you with a reasonable business proposition and you throw it back in our face. In the future when things change, and they will, you'll remember this conversation."

"Are you fucking threatening me?" Paddy growled at the man. "Get out of here while you can still walk."

The Big Man was incensed that this pair of Russian

mongrels thought they could threaten him: telling him that from now on they would be his main supplier. He could only presume they had been sampling the gear they were trying to punt.

As Michael escorted the two men off the premises, the smaller of the two, who had left most of the talking to his compatriot, turned to Michael saying, "We will meet again soon, Mr Coyle. You can be sure of that."

An icy chill gripped Michael's gut. They meant business that was for sure.

"What the hell is going on, Michael? Who are these fuckers, anyway? I can't believe they would think they can come in here and dictate terms to us. They're taking us for a couple of mugs. How did this happen?" Paddy ranted at Michael.

"They've been around for about a year or so, Paddy, edging their way in. But for the past few months they seem to be everywhere. More than a few dealers have disappeared."

"Why the fuck do I not know about this?" Paddy accused his brother. "How could these bastards get an 'in' without my knowledge?"

"You haven't been here, Paddy. You've spent more time in Spain, over the past few months, than at home. Not that I'm blaming you. You needed to be with your family, but it has left us wide open. Believe me, it's not just the Russians sniffing around, a few of the other families have been chancing their luck. Nothing serious, and they have been dealt with, but those two are another story altogether."

"Well, I'm back now and they'll all know soon enough

that nobody steps on our toes and lives. I should have just taken them out there and then and be done with it."

"Don't underestimate them, Paddy, their reputation is brutal."

"And mine isn't?"

# Lamb to the Slaughter

It had been so easy. In fact, it was almost criminal; the stupid bitch had never thought for a moment she was walking into a trap. It never entered her pretty little head to question why two strangers would approach her in the street with a message from her fiancé. Who but the most pathetic, naive airhead, would believe anyone outside the family would be entrusted with her safety? She deserved all that was coming to her and, like a lamb to the slaughter, she had trotted behind them to the waiting car. Her fate already sealed.

Margee was surprised to be stopped on her way home. Why Michael hadn't just phoned, or sent someone she was familiar with, was certainly a puzzler, but she was such a trusting soul. She had accepted without question that these two extremely good-looking, personable young guys would have nothing other than her best intentions at heart.

Her suspicions were first aroused when she saw the route they were taking. And when the car drove into an empty shed, down by the old Renfrew Ferry, she was panic-stricken.

"What are we doing here?" she squealed. "Where's Michael? I don't believe he sent you for me. He'll kill you if any harm comes to me," she screamed as she tried to get out of the car.

The first blow smashed her perfectly reconstructed nose. The second shattered the fantastic bridgework carried out by the city's most expensive orthodontist. She was a fighter alright, the two sadistic mates discovered, as they played cat and mouse with her. They inflicted excruciating, unbearable pain on the young woman as they systematically broke almost every bone in her body. Margee fought back, clawing and scratching at her captors, which only made their job even more exciting. She was subjected to the most horrific abuse, violated in ways that would defeat any woman. Each time she lost consciousness they brought her round by drenching her in filthy, ice-cold water.

Finally young Davey finished her off, laughing hysterically as he liberally tossed acid over the once beautiful face of Michael Coyle's intended.

"This must be what being chasing the dragon is like," he said, languishing against the wall smoking a cigarette.

Cortellessa was so sublimely out of it he couldn't speak. Up until that point the two had only practised on stray cats, dogs and the odd rent boy, but nothing like this; this was orgasmic.

They had indulged in a frenzy of pure evil, and now it was time to deliver the message.

# Challenged

Paddy was greeted warmly by Michael as he arrived at the scrapyard. "We didn't get round to it yesterday. Congratulations, so you're not firing blanks after all?" he jested.

"Seems not, but don't expect a brood over the next few years. One more is enough at my age."

"For God's sake, Paddy, you know what they say – life begins at . . ." The conversation was halted by the sound of shots ringing out.

"What the fuck was that?" roared Paddy, fumbling with the catch of the gun cupboard.

As quick as they could, he and Michael tooled up and crashed out of the cabin, just as a blacked-out 4x4 reversed out of the gates. Random shots fired from the passenger window and a large object, wrapped in an old tarpaulin, was thrown out of the vehicle as it sped off in the direction of the city.

"Jesus Christ, what was that all about?" shouted Paddy, as he vaulted the steps into the yard towards the object.

Tentatively, the Big Man pulled back the covering to reveal the battered, unrecognisable body of a woman. She had been beaten so badly it was impossible to identify her and, just to finish off the job, they had poured acid over her face.

"Dear God, Paddy, what the hell's going on? And who is she?" Michael asked as he backed away from the corpse.

"I've no idea," Paddy replied, inwardly giving thanks that this bloody mess wasn't one of his women.

Bridget and his mother were safe indoors, Erin was in Spain and he had just spoken to Marie, not five minutes since. So who was she? Why had she been dumped in their yard, and by whom?

Michael spotted the ring on the corpse's left hand and let out a horrific howl, like a wounded animal, as he fell to the ground, rocking slowly back and forward, sobbing. It was Margee, his fiancée, his beautiful girl; the girl he had only just asked to marry him.

What could anyone have against her? She stayed well out of the business. She had no involvement in his work, so why?

Maybe the Coyles had become a bit complacent, thought Paddy. Maybe they hadn't had their eye on the ball, with all that had been going on over the past year. How the fuck was he going to get Michael through this? How would *he* deal with it, if it had been Bridget or Erin? Revenge, that's how. He would find the culprits, whoever they were, he vowed as he held his brother. He would wipe them and their families off the face of the earth.

The sound of sirens heralded the arrival of the filth, but for once the Coyle brothers welcomed their presence.

# Enemies

"The Horseshoe Bar, ten a.m.," Paddy barked down the phone to Davey Thomson, his counterpart in the north.

"Okay," replied Davey. "I'm sorry for your loss, Paddy. Give my condolences to Michael. She was a lovely girl and this is well out of order. Women and kids were always a given."

Paddy made a number of other calls and received similar responses. He wasn't interested in condolences, he wanted revenge. Hey, it was a no-brainer. Paddy didn't believe in coincidences, and it was no coincidence that only twenty-four hours after their run-in with the Russians, they were about to arrange a funeral.

Lizzie was beside herself with grief and worry; grieving for the life of such a beautiful girl and worrying how this dreadful deed would affect her son. Michael was the quiet one, the thinker. She knew he would always have his brother's back, but losing Margee so soon after the death of his twin was bound to affect him. God alone knew how he would survive this tragedy.

Bridget and Marie had loved the poor girl like a sister. Unlike them, she had taken no active part in the business, but she was most definitely a big part of the family. The women were struggling to help Michael deal with this terrible loss. The police had been all over the scrapyard, setting up an incident room in the cabin. But Paddy and Michael had no faith whatsoever in their enquiries. They seemed more concerned with the daily workings of the yard than investigating the murder. It was obvious it was up to the family to bring the culprits to justice.

The brothers left the Funeral Directors, having made what arrangements they could. Nothing could be finalised, of course, until the body was released, and no one knew how long that would take.

As they walked along the street they could see a long line of vehicles already outside the pub. Their contemporaries, it seemed, had all responded to the summons.

Just as they were about to enter the bar, one of the city's many homeless persons approached them, blocking Michael's way, begging for money. Quick as a flash, Michael took the man down and proceeded to punch him relentlessly.

"For fuck's sake, Michael, get off him!" Paddy tried in vain to separate the two men.

Michael paid no heed and struck blow after blow.

"You'll fuckin' kill him," Paddy roared at his brother.

It was only with the intervention of two waiting drivers that Paddy managed to prise them apart. The beggar was in a pitiful state. Not wishing to draw attention to the incident, Paddy pulled out a bundle of notes and stuffed them in the man's pockets with the warning of worse to come if he didn't take the money and scarper. The battered beggar limped off, unaware of who he had just encountered and not knowing how lucky he was still to be breathing. As far as he was concerned he had just hit the jackpot.

"Jesus Christ, Michael, what are you thinking? In broad daylight too? That poor bastard did nothing wrong."

Shrugging off Paddy's arm, Michael marched into the back room where Glasgow's top men and their lieutenants were assembled. Genaro Cortellessa accompanied his father, Mario, the Italian. The dapper old man had recently been diagnosed with lung cancer, thanks to the extravagant Cuban cigars he smoked incessantly. So it was that Genaro took his father's place. A different cob altogether from the old man, an oily-looking cratur, thought Paddy, with a limp handshake and an effeminate way about him. "I wouldn't trust that geezer as far as I could throw him," he reflected to Michael.

Davey Thomson, reckoned to be the most dangerous man at the table, introduced his son, young Davey. This newcomer was, if rumour was to be believed, as unpredictable as his father. He could be engaged in the most amicable conversation and then suddenly pull a gun. It was these random acts that had secured his reputation. He did not, however, scare either Paddy or Michael and both father and son Thomson knew this. The last, Garry McIntosh, the out-of-towner, together with three of his henchmen, made up the numbers.

"I'm sure you gentlemen know why I called this meet," Paddy addressed the gathering.

Murmurs of condolences swept the room.

"Thanks on Michael's behalf, but that's not the reason I called you here." Slamming his fist on the table, he roared at the assembled crowd, "What the fuck is going on? How did these animals infiltrate our city? Why have we let them get such a foothold in our businesses?"

There was a deathly silence as no one answered.

"So none of you have had dealings with members of the Russian mafia?"

"We've all had dealings with them, Paddy. I've lost three houses and they've taken out six of my best men," ventured Davey Thomson. "Fuck sake, you know me, I'll take on any bastard but this lot are invincible. We've all been approached individually with what seemed to be a good business deal. They offered to supply anything we required at half the price we were paying. They supplied me with girls at a price I couldn't refuse, sex workers from the Soviet bloc. Once they get their fucking feet in the door and suss out how things work, well, it's all over."

"What?" snarled Paddy? "You're telling me these bastards just took over? You just lay down and let them walk over you?"

"They shafted me over shipments from Columbia." Mario explained. "I paid for a consignment, direct from source at an unbelievable price, which as you can guess never arrived. They've squeezed me almost dry while their guys are still out there punting. Like Davey, I can't get to them. They go to ground and then spring up on someone else's turf, causing all kinds of aggro.

"For fuck's sake, do you mean to tell me these mongrels are controlling the city and you idiots are letting them away with it?" Paddy faced the toughest men in Glasgow. "I can't believe what I'm hearing."

"Sorry, Michael, for what I'm about to say," McIntosh turned to Paddy. "Look what happened to Margee, and that was your first encounter. Make sure Bridget and Erin are safe because they will go after them."

"Over my dead body," Paddy Coyle roared at the assembled company. "Over my dead fucking body," he repeated.

"Well that might just be the case, Big Man. Let's face it, Paddy, where the fuck were you when we needed back up? Sunning yourself in fucking Spain, that's where!" McIntosh bit back at the Big Man.

"Cheeky bastard. Sunning myself in Spain? You all know fine why I was out of the country. Anyway, not one of you asked for my help, am I fucking psychic?"

"No, Paddy, but there was a time when if someone sneezed, you would know who, where and why. Be truthful, mate, you've had your eye off the ball for quite a while now. You're fucking lucky you've got a business to come back to."

"Lucky, did you say? Aye, we're really lucky." Michael spoke for the first time during the proceedings, causing a few shamed faces. "Well *their* luck just ran out. I want every damned one of them. By the time I'm finished there won't be one of the bastards left."

"Michael's right," replied Paddy. "It stops here. We're taking back what's ours, and by God they'll pay for what they did to my family. They can forget Glasnost and fucking perestroika, the Cold War's back on. So, are you with us or not?" Paddy Coyle's piercing blue eyes swept the assembly.

First to speak was Davey Thomson. "Look, Paddy, we've had our differences over the years, and we've settled them man to man, but these fuckers, well they're a whole new ball game. For a start there's fucking hundreds of them. They're like those fucking dolls they all have, every time you get rid of one, another pops up. I'm sorry, but I'm not willing to go toe to toe with them

16

for anyone. As far I'm concerned I've got things on an even keel and though I'm not happy, I'm not taking any chances."

"Mario, do you feel the same?" Paddy questioned the Italian.

"Paddy, I'm sorry, I don't have the strength to go against them. And my boy, good though he is, doesn't have the experience, he's too young. I suggest you make a deal with them."

"What about you, McIntosh, what have you got to say on the matter? Are you willing to take crumbs from their table or stand alongside me?"

"No, I'm on the outside looking in on this one. Good luck, pal, you'll need it."

"Well, if you miserable fuckers are not with me, then take the consequences of being against me. Because believe me, I'll sort the buggers out once and for all. Just make sure you don't get caught in the crossfire. Mario, you I can understand, but the rest of you, be warned."

"What a bunch of cowardly wankers," Michael snarled at the departing guests. I propose, Paddy, not only do we get rid of the Russians but we put these cunts out of business as well."

# Protection

Business had been decidedly slow that morning and Tommy Riley was watching the two geezers hanging around the next corner. Big buggers, they sounded and looked foreign but they were too far off for him to hear properly. They'd been around for a while yesterday but business had been brisk so he'd not paid that much attention.

"Oi, Tracy," he called to one of his regulars passing on the other side of the street. "Your usual?"

"Naw, thanks all the same, Tommy. I'm sorted for today."

"Eh? What do you mean you're sorted? Who've you been buying off?"

It wasn't like Tracy to go elsewhere; she knew Tommy would always see her right if she was a bit short. So much for fucking loyalty, he thought.

"Couple ae guys round the corner. Ah think they're Polish, giving away freebies. C'mon Tommy, I couldn't turn that down now, could I? See you tomorrow, pal, unless they're still there."

"Fuckin' liberty," Tommy Riley muttered to himself. He'd have to find out what was going on and put a stop to it.

He walked down the road, totally pissed off to see most of his regulars hanging around. This was unheard of, it was get your gear and fuck off. No one hung around like a Sunday social. But there they were, chatting and socialising.

"Hey, Tommy, you here for a freebie?" shouted one smart-arse.

"Don't think you can collect today and sell it to me tomorrow," shouted another.

"Shut up, ya cheeky cow." He couldn't believe his eyes. Here were his customers, standing patiently in a queue for their free baggie. What the fuck was going on?

The guy dishing out the bags was a big bugger and on seeing Tommy he burst out laughing, "You want free bag?" he challenged the dealer.

"Fuck off now," Tommy faced him up. "This is Coyle's territory and you better shift." He'd staved off threats from bigger and harder arseholes than this pair of foreign wankers. Usually drawing his gun was sufficient to put paid to any dissention, but not so this time. Riley paled at the size of the weapon produced by one of the look-outs. It was like a fucking rocket launcher. Tommy didn't hang about; he took off back down the road a damn sight faster than he'd come up it.

He could hear the Russian shouting after him. "Yeah, you run, boy. Go on, you fuck off, bring *all* the Coyles. This is our turf now, only Mr Coyle doesn't know it yet."

Not one of his customers came to his assistance.

The following morning Tommy hung about, watching all his punters heading for the Russian dealers who were blatantly handing out gear to all and sundry.

What the fuck was he going to do? He'd queered his

pitch with Paddy Coyle, there was no chance the Big Man would come to his rescue, not after their last encounter. "So what?" Tommy muttered to himself. Russians or no Russians, he wasn't backing down to Paddy Coyle. He'd get a hold of Errol, who'd help him or else.

# Happiness

How was it possible to feel so happy, yet so awful and miserable at the same time? It had been hardly any time since her mother had gone back to Scotland, leaving her and Ryan with Nick. It was, without doubt, the happiest time in her life. He was absolutely everything she could ever want in a man. She was deliriously happy, and to top it all her mother had called her from the airport, imparting the news that she was pregnant after all these years. Paddy, her father, had seemingly been strutting about like the cock of the walk and then the bomb fell. Margee, Michael's fiancée, the loveliest and kindest of people, had been brutally murdered.

Poor, poor Michael, thought Erin. Her first instinct had been to fly straight back to her family in their hour of need, but Nick had forbidden her departure, with Paddy's consent apparently. In fact, her attendance at the funeral seemed to be the subject of great discussion. Regardless of the outcome, her mother and gran were being shipped out to Spain.

"What's this all about, Nick? I've never known my father to be in such a state. Is it because Mum's pregnant and he wants her to be stress-free? That's understandable, but why can't I go to the funeral? And why are my gran and Errol being shipped out here? It doesn't make sense."

"Honestly, Erin, I don't know all the ins and outs. All I do know is that your father is engaged in something big, seriously big, and if you lot are out here, then it's less for him to worry about. I agree with him. As far as I'm concerned, I don't want you anywhere near the place. Remember, I've already been through this shit with my wife and I sure as hell don't want to live through it again. I don't intend to let you out of my sight. From now on, whenever you leave this house you'll have someone with you."

"For God's sake, Nick, who the hell are we dealing with? The KGB or CIA?" Erin joked.

"I wish it was that simple."

Erin felt an ice-cold sensation grip her stomach. Surely not again? "Do you really think it's that serious?"

"Well, your father does, and with damned good reason. What those bastards did to Margee was inhumane. For nothing more than pleasure, they tortured and murdered that poor woman, just because they could. What do you think they would do to you, Bridget or your gran? Life is the cheapest commodity to these men, it has no worth. It doesn't matter how many bodies it takes to get what they want or to make a point. This is the way they operate, they have no conscience and they are spread throughout the globe. So make no mistake, none of you are safe anywhere, but there are places less dangerous than others and here, under my protection, is one of them. You need to take this seriously."

# All Aboard

Erin was strolling along the beachside with Ryan snoozing in his buggy in the warm air, and two gorillas by her side. What an incongruous sight they looked. It was difficult to believe that some warfare in Glasgow could reach her out here. But she only had to think about why her man was in Spain to make her realise the world was a small place.

She had taken to spending time on the cruiser, under the tutelage of Simon, the skipper, and proved to be a natural. She loved being aboard even when the Lady Di was moored. And today she was ready for her first trip out.

"Cast off," shouted Erin. She took charge of the helm and the launch moved expertly out into the open sea, leaving her two bodyguards open-mouthed on the quay. Erin, Ryan and the skipper spent the next two hours sailing round the coast, in and out of the myriad of deserted coves and bays. By the time the cruiser returned to dock, Erin felt competent enough to bring the large vessel alongside.

There on the quay, with a face like thunder, stood Nick and the two bodyguards.

"What the fuck were you thinking? Did you not pay attention to anything I said this morning?"

"Jesus, Nick, how much danger could I be in with Simon here? Anyway, we had arranged this before you said anything about Russians chasing after me."

A strange look passed over the skipper's face, unnoticed by the others

"For God's sake, be quiet," he snapped as she and the baby trundled down the gangway. "Don't go shouting our business to all and sundry!"

"Okay, okay, c'mon, I'm starving," she threw over her shoulder as she marched on ahead.

This was going to be much harder than Nick had bargained on. Delightful though she was, she was still young and wilful.

Settled in a shady, beachside restaurant an unrepentant Erin prattled on about her sailing lesson. "I can handle it Nick, seriously, I was well in control."

"Yes, but the sea was like plate glass. Wait till you get further out. The Med can change in minutes. You need a bit more practice before you can take charge, but when you take to the high seas, my lady, you take the boys with you. They can't protect you standing on the quay."

"Protect me from what? Pirates?" she laughed.

"Make no mistake, that's exactly who."

"Long John Silver and Captain Hook watch out." Before he could reply, she continued, "Have you heard any more from Paddy concerning the funeral? I am going, by the way. No matter what he or anyone else says, I'm going back home. I'll do it in a day if you're so worried, but I am going to that funeral. Margee was like a sister to me so there will be no more argument about it."

Just as the food arrived there was a fracas further along the beach. Two burly, foreign-looking men were manhandling a tall blonde, who was giving as good as she was getting.

24

"Nick, that's Sam, I'm sure it is." Erin grabbed the empty wine bottle and took off. Leaving him and the baby, she raced towards her friend who was apparently in trouble.

"Hey, leave her alone!" she yelled at the two men.

By now a small crowd had gathered as Erin hurled herself between her friend and the two attackers. Taken completely by surprise, and aware of the growing audience, the two heavies threw Erin off and turned to Sam, making some threats in a foreign language before beating a hasty retreat.

"Shit! What was all that about?" Erin laughed at her mate. "It's usually you rescuing me. Who were they?"

"Christ, I need a drink. What the devil are you doing here? I thought you went back home with Bridget and Paddy."

"I was going to phone after I had a bit of him-and-me-time before going public."

"Public with who?" queried her friend, shelving the episode with her two attackers for the moment.

By now the pair had arrived back at the table where a furious Nick had been left literally holding the baby. "What are you playing at, girl? You could have been seriously hurt, barging in like that. Don't you think *I* would have been more use?"

"Sorry, I didn't think. I just saw Sam and ran. You're right. It was stupid, but it worked," Erin burst out laughing.

"God, did you see their faces when you appeared from nowhere, brandishing a bottle? Hi, Nick, sorry about all that, it was just a misunderstanding," Sam said sheepishly.

"Some misunderstanding. Spit it out, what trouble are

you in with those guys? 'Cos they meant business."

"It was nothing, honest. A deal gone belly-up. I'll sort it. How about buying me a beer? I could murder one." It was obvious they were getting nothing further out of Sam.

Sam had been in the resort for five or six years, working as a holiday rep. That was until the night Erin Coyle was kidnapped and her life changed. She had been well compensated by Paddy Coyle for her assistance and silence. Then again, her help in securing Ryan had not gone unpaid.

What was she involved in that merited those two thugs roughing her up? What if she and Nick hadn't been in the right place at the right time? Erin was determined to find out; after all, she owed not only her life, but her son's life to this woman.

# Help

"Who is it?" Lizzie called at the top of her voice. She'd been warned by Paddy that under no circumstances was she to open the door unless she could identify the caller. Lot of bloody nonsense, she thought to herself, but to keep the peace she carried out his instructions.

"It's me, Mrs. Coyle. Tommy, Tommy Riley, Billy's brother."

Without hesitation she opened the door and ushered the young lad in. "Hello, son, what can I do for you?"

She'd always had a soft spot for the two brothers. She knew well enough how Tommy made his money, and much as she disapproved of his trade, she could hardly take the moral high ground when it was her own sons who supplied him.

"I need a word with Errol, Mrs. Coyle. Is he in?"

"He's still in school, son. He won't be back till after three, but what would you want with Errol, Tommy? He better not be mixed up in any of your dealings." Errol's grandma said. "I mean it, if you've got him involved in any shenanigans there'll be blue murder."

"No, it's nothing like that, honest. I just need him to do me a wee favour."

"What kind of favour would that be?" Lizzie was not letting him off the hook.

"I want him to speak to his uncles for me."

"What about, son? Why can't you speak to them yourself?"

"We had a bit of a misunderstanding, Mrs Coyle."

"Well, if that's all it is, I'll speak to Paddy. Let's keep Errol out of this. Leave it to me, son. The boys will be here shortly and I'll make sure somebody comes to see you."

Fuck, thought Tommy, that made things even worse. Paddy Coyle was hardly going to take the news that a dealer called at his mother's house to have another dealer sorted out. Fuck, that would *really* go down well. What the fuck was he going to do?

"No, it's okay, Mrs Coyle. I'll sort it out myself, don't bother them."

There were no flies on Lizzie Coyle; she knew exactly what Paddy would do if he thought this lad had brought trouble to her door. "Look, son, there's lots of ways to skin a cat, if you know what I mean?"

What the fuck was she on about? mused Tommy.

"I'll just tell him I'm worried about you, or that your mum asked me to have a word. He'll be fine, don't worry. What is the problem anyway?"

"Honest, it's fine, don't go bothering him."

"Tommy, do you think I'm blind, or daft, or both? I know exactly what you sell, down the way. I've also seen those big buggers hanging about the last two days. Is it them?"

Tommy barely nodded his head. What the fuck had he come here for? He was in the shit right up to his neck.

"Well, off you go and leave it to me. How is your mother, by the way? I've not seen her for a while. Tell her I'm asking for her, and don't worry, the lads will sort it out."

# Drawing a Blank

Thanks to the massive amount in payouts, and palms being well and truly greased, Margee's body was released for burial sooner than normal. During this time the Coyles' enemies appeared to be running amok. Several dealers had either disappeared or been hospitalized, and there had been a number of serious incidents in the club. There were also countless demands for protection money throughout the city, with no reprisals. This news had every division in the Glasgow constabulary on high alert

The glass carriage containing the coffin was drawn by a team of black, plumed horses, followed by a cortege of stretch limos. The procession was being led the short distance from Lomond Crescent to St. Jude's by the funeral director, walking in front, resplendent in his morning suit and top hat.

"There will be no money spent on a wedding, so she'll go out in style," Michael informed his mother as he helped her into the leading car, along with Marie, Paddy and Bridget.

Erin, despite being absolutely forbidden by both Paddy and Nick, had flown home from Spain to attend the funeral. She followed in the second car alongside Margee's only relatives, two elderly aunts who were completely overwhelmed by the occasion. Also in this car was her cousin Errol, who was not coping well with the situation; much to the disapproval of both his mother and Uncle Paddy.

'Time to man up,' they kept telling him. He couldn't. Things were changing in his life and two people he loved were gone. He hoped against hope that Billy would return, but there was no such hope for Margee.

The church was packed to the rafters and the Requiem Mass, a sad and desolate service, was conducted by Father Jack.

The immediate family occupied the first two pews. The Cortellessas and the Thomsons, as befitting their place in the criminal hierarchy, were seated immediately behind: the sons of whom found the whole situation highly amusing.

The wake had been arranged in the club, where Margee and Michael had first met. It seemed as though every villain in the country was in attendance; they had all come to pay their respects.

As the afternoon stretched on and large amounts of whisky were consumed, the company got more and more raucous. Old scores were rearing their ugly heads. Michael Coyle had been in a ruck already and looked determined to start another. The man was roaring drunk, which was completely understandable given the circumstances. However, Cortellessa and young Davey had their surprise timed to a tee, and Michael Coyle was in danger of scuppering things. Somehow they had to put him out of action.

Watching from the sidelines, the two mates saw Michael head for the gents toilets. Following the grieving fiancé, Genaro quickly rendered him out of action and stuffed him into a cubicle, out of harm's way. It was time, and they made for the exit, respectfully bidding their farewells to Paddy.

Just as the two mates and their fathers approached the exit, two masked gunmen burst through the doors. Pushing the old men out of harm's way and before either gunman fired a shot, Genaro and young Davey gunned them down, making them the heroes of the hour.

"I knew it," yelled Genaro to his father. "I knew it! I said to him," he pointed to his mate. "I knew those Russian fuckers would try something."

"That's why we were tooled up," young Davey explained to Paddy as he kicked a body over onto its back.

"Anyone know them?" Paddy asked the assembled crowd.

"No, but look at the weapons they're carrying. No prizes for guessing which camp they came from," volunteered Genaro.

The incident had happened so quickly that few of the guests realised what had gone down. The ones who had witnessed it realised that something had to be done about those Russian bastards and Paddy Coyle was just the man to do it.

# Safe as Houses

"They do have shops in Spain, Lizzie. If you've forgotten something, we can buy it," Bridget cajoled her mother-in-law. "As long as you have all your pills and your passport, we're fine. Same goes for you, Errol."

"I've not got pills," the young lad answered back sharply.

"You know fine what I mean. Let me have your passport for safekeeping," his Aunt Bridget stood, hand outstretched.

"Why do I have to come?" grouched the youngster. "Nobody is going to come after me."

"No, I don't suppose they will, but Uncle Paddy and Uncle Michael would feel much happier if you were safe with Nick and Erin. Just think of it as an extra school holiday in the sun."

"I don't want to come. I want to stay here and help. Anyway, who's going to look after my mum?"

"Sorry, son, this one's a bit too dangerous for you, but I promise you, when it's over, you and I will have a wee chat. In the meantime, you look after your granny and the rest of them for me, and I'll look after your mum. I'm counting on you." Paddy hugged his nephew.

"Erin, Lizzie, make sure she rests and take good care of her," he kissed his wife goodbye.

"I'll ring you tonight."

"Take care of Michael, son. He's in a bad way."

"Of course, Ma, but I have to let him have his way, he's owed that."

By the time Paddy arrived back at the club, his family were well on their way, courtesy of Ritchie, an old buddy of Paddy's and owner of a chartered flight company, who'd come to their rescue in the past.

It had been decided that Lizzie, Bridget and Errol would take up residence in Diane Mack's apartment. Since no-one knew how long the family would be in residence, it seemed the obvious solution and there was less chance of them being spotted. The luxurious beachfront apartment had been left to Ryan as part of his father's estate.

"She certainly liked her comfort," Lizzie commented on the lavishly-furnished apartment.

"She did. It was a shame she didn't live long enough to enjoy it. C'mon, I'll show you to your rooms," offered Bridget. "It's been a long day and I think we could all do with a bit of shut-eye."

Each one knew there would be little chance of that tonight.

"Well, did you miss me?" Erin asked as she snuggled up on Nick's lap.

"Not a bit," he joked. "Did you get the guests settled in their new abode?"

"I did, and my gran thinks it's far too flash and there's not a comfortable bed in the place. It wouldn't be her if there wasn't something wrong," laughed Erin. "Tell me truthfully, do you really think we are in any danger? I presume my dad told you what happened at the wake?"

"He did, and you have no idea how lucky you were. Thank God the Cortellessa lad and Davey Thomson's son were on the ball. As far as you being in danger, I don't know. I think you're all as safe as it's possible to be, but these guys are everywhere and past masters at networking. I wouldn't be surprised if they know you're back already."

"Well, in that case, we'd better not lose any more time." Erin headed for the bedroom, thanking her lucky stars that her mum had offered to keep Liam overnight.

There was precious little sleep either for those two, but neither had any cause for complaint on that score.

# Double Whammy

*The bodies of two, as yet unidentified males, have been discovered in woods on the outskirts of the village of Beith. A spokesman for Strathclyde Police Force say they are treating the incident as suspicious and are appealing to anyone with any information to contact them or their local police office.*

Genaro and young Davey had hurriedly picked up the bodies of the two gunmen and dumped them in the boot of the 4x4 parked outside the club. Cortellessa and Thomson had recruited the men on a recent drugs run to Liverpool. Charlie Karpatchi and Ted Polski had been selected because of their Slavic appearance and their ability to get their hands on Russian-style weapons. It was money for old rope as far as the two Liverpudlians were concerned. They hadn't, of course, taken into account that their newfound friends were setting them up and there was no way the bounty would be paid.

The twosome were again delighted with the outcome. Just like the girl, this was too easy. Surely it couldn't be this simple to take their birthright? Paddy Coyle, The Big Man, was almost eating out of their hands, and the moronic Russians had no idea that most of the discord in Glasgow was being laid at their door.

When they went into the 'meet' the next day, Genaro Cortellessa and Davey Thomson were treated to a standing ovation. Paddy and both fathers had been singing their praises and extolling the virtues of both young men. Their level-headedness and quick actions had saved lives. The fact that only the gunmen had lost their lives was an absolute miracle. Then the disposal of the bodies, quickly and without drawing attention to the situation, merited gratitude from the present assembly.

The two were preening. This was exactly how things should be. This respect was what they were born to experience and with luck, the next few days would cement Paddy Coyle's downfall.

# Out in the Cold

Disconsolately, Tommy kicked the empty Tennent's can back and forth. It rattled up and down the street on what used to be his patch. So much for the back up promised by the Coyles, he thought. He was beyond anger; he was desperate. Yet again they had let him down. It had been over a week since he had called on old Ma Coyle. A week since she'd promised to get things sorted. She was just like her sons, all talk.

He'd not seen sight nor sound of any of them since the funeral. At worst, he had expected Paddy to come after him for having the audacity to speak with Lizzie. There had been nothing, not a cheep from anyone. He really was out in the cold and it didn't look like there was any chance of him recovering his wage without some serious back up. The Russians had taken over completely; there were always three of them, all armed, and he was certainly no match for them. In the past, the fact that he was one of Paddy's dealers had been threat enough for any interlopers, but not now. It actually looked like the Russians were taunting the Coyles, enticing them to have a go. The Big Man was more than conspicuous by his absence and Tommy, like many other of Paddy's street traders, looked like he was being hung out to dry.

He needed a plan, he told himself. He couldn't just hang around waiting for things to happen. First of all he needed a new pitch, but more importantly he needed a new supplier. For the past few days he had been hanging around the Grammar School but business was grim. He was forever standing on someone else's toes; crashing in on someone's patch, no matter where he set up. He'd taken a few beatings into the bargain. To make matters worse his ma had gone on the trot again. Since young Billy had gone missing Sandra had taken to disappearing for days on end, only returning home when whatever money she had was gone. Each time she came back she was worse than the time before: filthy, bruised, battered and suffering from the D.T.'s. She would imagine bugs were crawling out of the wallpaper; mind you, from the state of the house they might not all be imaginary. The place was disgusting and the smell was becoming overpowering. She would never have won housewife of the year, but things had never been this bad.

Life hadn't always been a bed of roses for the Rileys but they certainly had never plummeted to these depths before. Giving the can one more good kick, sending it clattering down the road, Tommy wiped away a tear. For the first time in his young life he was beat. He had no idea how to get out of this mess, but one thing he was sure of – he'd get Paddy Coyle back if it was the last thing he ever did.

# Life of Luxury

Lizzie Coyle strolled along the beachfront, enjoying the morning sun warm on her face. Loath as she was to admit to her daughter-in-law or her grandchildren, Lizzie loved Marbella and everything about it. The weather was amazing for a start. No dull ache in her bones because of the damp, dreich Glasgow weather. The apartment was luxurious but still comfortable and homely. And best of all, she didn't have to lift a finger; there were maids who came in every morning. Imagine her with a maid, she chortled to herself. Mary, Mother of God, Theresa would have a fit. It was a shame she couldn't have had a wee holiday with her, but her friend wouldn't leave her bedridden husband. The lazy good-for-nothing was no more bedridden than she was, but he had played the part for so many years it was taken for granted now. Still, it would have been nice to have a bit of company and she would have had quite a laugh with Theresa, especially at the sights and boy, there were some sights to behold.

Lizzie had established a pleasant, daily routine since arriving in Marbella. She'd begin her morning with breakfast on the balcony, a pleasant stroll along to the marina, stopping for a cafe con leche. Hark at her speaking Spanish. She hadn't worked out yet how to ask for extra milk, but she'd only been here a little over a week, she'd soon master it. A gentle stroll back, indulging in a bit of window shopping, just in time for lunch. Bridget had been right; the shops were wonderful, so full of bright colours and fine materials. No good for a September in Glasgow, but she could look, couldn't she?

She already recognised a few faces, mainly retired couples, out like her for their morning constitutional and one or two nodded hello to her in the passing. Talking about sights, approaching her on the other side of the road was a remarkably odd-looking pair. An elderly black gentleman, dressed in the most outrageous technicoloured Hawaiian-style shirt and a peculiar pair of shorts. Lizzie, laughing to herself, couldn't make up her mind if they were long shorts or short longs. His companion was a middle-aged woman, as drab as he was colourful. Grey hair, grey complexion and grey clothing. Lizzie smiled at the picture they made. There was something vaguely familiar about the couple, but Lizzie couldn't for the life of her put her finger on it. She was sure she wouldn't have forgotten such a striking pair. The couple passed on the opposite side of the street, unaware of the amusement they had caused.

As much as Lizzie loved Marbella, Imelda Gavin hated it. She hated the hot sun burning her fair Irish skin. She hated the apartment she shared with her brother. She hated her clothes; clothes that had been bought for the damp Irish mists and cold Glasgow winters which were totally unsuitable for the hot, dry climate she now found herself in. But it was her duty and when her beloved brother had informed her of the death of Bobby and

Dianne Mack, Imelda had boarded the next flight to Malaga and taken up residence.

She had been in Spain for the past three months, during which time she had been unable to coax Francis to leave the safety of his apartment. The death of Bobby had devastated the old priest and he had called on his sister to come to his aid; the only person aware that he was still alive.

"It's a glorious day, Francis, why don't you come with me to collect the mail?" cajoled Imelda.

"I don't know if I'm up to it yet, my dear. I'll just sit for a while out on the balcony."

"Please, Francis, just twenty minutes. You promised yesterday and the day before. What do you think is going to happen if you leave here? I'll look after you."

"Don't be stupid, woman, I just don't feel up to it. I'm not well and I'm an old man, leave me be."

But Imelda knew if she didn't shift him soon he would end his days in this small apartment.

"Well, if you're not going to move, Francis, I'm sorry to say this, but I'm back off home to Galway. There's far more important work to be done than me babysitting you in this godforsaken place. So make up your mind, either you come for a stroll with me, or I leave you to get on with things. I can arrange for someone to come in and see to you, but it's your choice."

"Tomorrow, I'll go with you tomorrow. Just let me stay here today and I'll go with you in the morning."

"If you're going to be fit tomorrow, then you're fit to go today," his sister insisted and before he had time to change his mind Imelda had propelled him out of the apartment and into the lift.

He was back in the real world; albeit reluctantly.

# Sam Scam

"C'mon then, tell me, what was yesterday all about?" Erin questioned her lunch companion.

"It was nothing serious," replied Sam. "It's all taken care of now, don't worry."

"Hey, it's me you're talking to. Do you expect me to believe that two guys jumping out of a moving vehicle and trying to bundle you into said vehicle is nothing? It's not serious? Well don't call on me when it is. Listen, Sam, if you don't want to talk about it that's fine, but you have to assure me something like that is not going to happen when I'm with my son. He has to be safe." Erin looked straight into her friend's eyes. "I'm serious."

"Honest, it's fine. It was all a misunderstanding. A touch of mistaken identity."

"So who did they mistake you for?" Erin laughed at her friend who stood tall, at just a little over six feet. "Tell me, how many are there like you, here in Marbella?"

"They mistook me for a mug, that's who."

"Okay, spill the beans. Maybe I can help."

"I've been working for the past few months with a property developer, selling to mainly the English market. I was doing really well, making good money, on paper that is."

"What do you mean on paper?"

"Just what I said, on paper. I never got paid. They owed me thousands in commission and I never saw any of it. There was always a problem. The banks were holding cheques and so on. But I knew how much was being paid into the bank in deposits. Then we were being bombarded with calls from buyers who'd paid serious money and their property wasn't built. It was then I realised it was a scam."

"But why were they after you if they owed you? It doesn't make sense?"

"Well, I resigned."

"Okay, but that looked like a pretty poor leaving do, so what else happened?"

"For a start, I paid myself what I reckoned I was owed."

"Fair do's. And?"

"I emailed every one of their clients, telling them what was happening."

"Jesus! So how do you reckon it's sorted and they're not still after you?"

"They were arrested this morning, along with the mayor and half the town council."

"Shut up!" laughed Erin. "You were responsible for all that? No wonder they were after you."

"Don't be daft," snorted Sam. "That was nothing to do with me, it was pure coincidence. Thank goodness I took my money in cash yesterday or there would have been no chance of my being paid."

"So how come you know they got arrested?"

"After the shenanigans at the beach I thought I'd better pay them a visit and see if I could sort things out. After all, I don't want to have to leave town."

"Seems reasonable; so what's that got to do with the mayor? He's Ryan's godfather, you know."

"Of course I know. When I arrived, the place was crawling with cops. Apparently someone they had conned was a Spanish big-wig, who didn't take kindly to being done out of his dough."

"So why was the mayor arrested?"

"It seems the whole of the council have been involved in land racketeering. Selling off green belt land and issuing building permits to all and sundry, making a fortune."

"Were your two involved in this racket?"

"It looks like every builder in Marbella was in on it. But they scammed the wrong person and got caught in the net."

"Shame!" said Erin sarcastically.

"One of the Gardaí Civil on duty recognised me; I had to call them in one time when an investor got a bit troublesome, so I got talking to him about what was going on."

"And what was going on?"

"They were searching the office and, believe it or not, asked me if I knew the combination to the safe."

"Tell me you didn't tell him."

"Don't be fucking stupid, of course I didn't. Anyway, they took a few papers, locked up and left."

"You're joking!" exclaimed her friend. "They just left? Didn't put a guard on the door till they got a locksmith?"

"It's Spain. Of course not."

"Was there much in the safe?"

"Plenty, but at the time I was only interested in what I was actually due. I wouldn't risk turning them over, those guys are heavy duty."

"It's a shame you didn't know what was going to happen, or you could have paid yourself a little bonus, if you get my drift," Erin gave her friend a sly nod.

"Erin Coyle, you devious monkey. I did think of it, and I still have the keys to the office."

"Are you thinking what I'm thinking?" whispered Erin.

"Only if you're thinking what I'm thinking." sniggered Sam.

Throwing twenty pesetas on the table the two ran out of the restaurant.

"Taxi," called Sam.

# The Start

The club was closed as a mark of respect.

The Coyles had brought together their entire workforce. Although most were legitimately employed as security guards or doormen, they were all capable and willing to stand alongside the brothers whatever the circumstances.

Banging his fist on the table, Paddy brought the room to an immediate silence. "You all know why we're here," he addressed the assembly. "Tonight is payback time, tonight we take revenge for what that trash had the nerve to do to one of our own."

Michael stood ramrod straight beside his brother as Paddy delivered his message. The once jovial, happy-go-lucky brother was gone. In his place was a man of stone, a man devoid of feeling and lusting for blood.

"By this time tomorrow," continued Paddy, "there will be either no Russians or no Coyle crew left in this city. It will be one or the other, and I don't intend to lose. They know we're coming for them, but they don't know when. Make no mistake, this is no walk in the park, these buggers fear nothing. It will be them or us. The plan is simple, and if each of you does what's asked, it's a no-brainer. The timing is crucial. We'll hit each target at exactly the same time. This will make sure they have no time to contact anyone. Take absolutely no prisoners, with the exception of the two main men, they are to be brought back here alive."

"There's a five-thousand-pound bonus on each of their heads to the crew who bring them in," Michael spoke for the first time. "Remember, I want them alive."

"Does anyone have any questions?" Paddy asked his audience.

"What about the filth?" asked Tiny, one of the Coyles' most loyal and long-serving lieutenants.

"Don't worry, they'll be taking the night off."

"Christ, Paddy, you can't control the whole of the city," the man replied.

"Says who? Don't worry about Glasgow's finest. You'll all have to work fast as you'll only have fifteen minutes to carry out the raid, secure each gaff and get away."

"Okay. Anything else? No? Well let's get this show on the road."

A convoy of vehicles left the car park, speeding off in various directions, seen only by a single scout who had been in position for the past twelve hours. Paddy Coyle wasn't going to have it all his way.

# Spy in the Camp

"They've just left, Davey. Twelve cars and two bikes. The club is locked and alarmed."

"Thanks, Tommy, good lad. Call round tomorrow and we'll sort you out." Young Davey ended the call to his latest recruit, Tommy Riley. The lad had come to see him earlier in the week, looking for help, and although the two had known each other for years, it had taken some balls for Tommy to approach him. Riley had always been most definitely a Coyle dealer and the fact that his pitch was right under the Big Man's nose spoke volumes.

This tip-off alone had more than covered the loan Davey had furnished the young dealer with.

Having someone able to operate freely on Coyle turf would give Cortellessa and Thomson access to information they could not have gained in any other way. Davey had every intention of keeping the lad sweet.

Stopping his car at the nearest public telephone, the chosen way to communicate without calls being traced, Davey dialled the mobile number.

"I've just heard from my informant. They're on the move. It's time you left."

"We can take them out no bother," answered the Russian.

"Don't be stupid, you're outnumbered, and this will hurt Coyle far more than any bullet. Think what a mug he's going to look. Lie low for a couple of days, let him stew. It will make him reckless and that's when we'll strike."

"I still think we should stay and fight it out. We could finish Coyle for good. Russians never walk away from a fight. It is the Cossack blood."

"Listen up, my friend, sometimes you can win the battle but lose the war. Trust me, lie low. It's you the Big Man is after. Why risk what you have built up?"

"Okay, point taken," came the curt reply.

Genaro signed to his mate, thumbs up. "They've taken the bait and are going across country."

As crew after crew returned to the club, Paddy Coyle was beside himself with anger. He had already smashed a marble table in the foyer and it looked like a demolition squad had hit the bar.

"How the fuck did they know?" he screamed at his men. "Tell me! How the fuck did they know? Somebody tipped them off and I want to know who it was!" His face was purple with rage. "Some cunt sitting at my table, eating my bread, is a Judas. And God fucking help them when I find out who it is."

Around the club, man after man protested his innocence.

"It wasn't me," shouted one. "I don't even know what the fuckers look like."

"Nor me," answered another.

"Somebody could have been on the look-out."

And so it went on among the crew members.

"You know, Paddy, there's not a man here that doesn't

owe you or Michael, so it's not come from here," ventured Tiny. "Those Russians aren't stupid. They've been on high alert for weeks so it stands to reason they'd be well aware of our movements."

"We looked like a bunch of muppets," yelled Paddy. "The whole city will be taking the piss, laughing at us. I can't believe it, not a fuckin' gaff open. Every single one closed for the night, tucked up ready for bed while we're all standing outside like a squad of 'Wee Willie Winkies'. I have never been so humiliated."

Paddy stormed out of the club in desperate need to vent his anger which was held in check only by the look on Michael's face. Fuck, he had to calm down for his sake. Paddy had promised his mother he'd look after his brother. How was he going to live this night down?

# Retail Therapy

Erin and Sam stopped the taxi a block or so away from their destination and strolled casually past the building in question, making sure there were no police on duty or any suspicious-looking characters hanging about. In fact, they were probably the most dubious-looking. All the other pedestrians were going about their business as normal.

Fumbling for the keys in her voluminous tote bag, Sam checked once more that the coast was clear as the two intruders entered the office. It was obvious the place had been turned over. The office looked like it had been hit by a tornado: papers and documents were strewn everywhere. Crossing into the smaller office Sam quickly punched in the combination to the safe and the door swung open.

"Don't touch anything," ordered Sam. "There would be no reason for your finger prints to be in here, but there'll be no problem with mine."

"Oops," giggled Erin, hastily dabbing everything she'd touched with the hem of her dress.

Stuffing the contents of the safe into their tote bags took only a few minutes.

"What about that?" asked Erin, pointing to a hand gun and a box of ammunition.

"Take it, you never know," With raised eyebrows Erin buried the weapon at the bottom of her bag.

"C'mon, that's everything, let's get out of here."

Sam opened the door cautiously and checked to make sure there was no-one about. They were locking up just as a taxi drew alongside them.

"Good luck or what?" muttered Erin.

A tall, mean-looking guy got out and paid the driver and the two girls jumped in the back.

Erin gave the taxi driver her address and turned to her co-conspirator, "Nick's out all day. We need to see what we've got and what we are going to do."

"You can do what you like, but I'm off for some serious retail therapy," answered Sam.

"Of course, me too, but let's be sensible about this. We don't know how much we've got or what the documents are all about. Let's go back to my place first and take it from there."

Ten minutes later they were closeted in Nick and Erin's bedroom with the contents of the bags upturned on the bed.

"Christ, that's some haul," laughed Sam. "Fifty-fifty split?"

"Agreed," said Erin. "We'll have to be careful about the foreign currency. If we suddenly start flashing billions of roubles, or try to exchange them, word might get around and God help us then because somebody is going to be looking for this."

"These documents look like property deeds, but I need to study them properly," Sam answered, flicking through the pile of official-looking papers. "How much did we score in pesetas and sterling?"

Erin began separating the currency into piles. "There's

four hundred and fifty thousand in pesetas, a hundred thousand in sterling and a shitload of roubles, but I don't know how much that would be worth. Why don't we split the pesetas and leave the rest for the moment until we know the score? They could be out on bail already and let's face it, you are going to be their number one suspect when your employers find the cupboard bare."

"You're right. Anyway, I can't walk about with all that money. You'll have to keep it here for the moment. I'll take some now and meet up with you later."

"You're very trusting, Sam. Who's to say I won't just disappear and leave you to face the music?" Erin asked.

"It's not a matter of me being trusting. There's no way Paddy Coyle's daughter would shaft me. Not after all we've been through. So, do we agree? The money and the documents stay here for the moment?"

"I need to put it somewhere Nick wouldn't think of looking and I don't really know the house that well."

"Hide it amongst the baby's things. He's not likely to go snooping there, is he?"

"No, but I'll need to watch out for my mum and granny. They're into everything, nosey buggers."

"Right, that's settled for now. Let's have a bit of retail therapy before you go and pick up your son and heir."

Half an hour later they were entering the fragrant premises of Gucci in Puerto Banus.

As the twosome headed into town, a furious Russian had been faced with an empty safe, no money or documents and the likelihood that he'd be blamed for the disappearance.

Who could have robbed them? Who could have acquired the goods? he mused. No way was it the Gardaí; they didn't know the combination and there was no way this particular safe could have been breached without it.

What should he do? What *could* he do? If he reported the loss he would more than likely be shot. If he didn't he would still be shot. Who could have done this? What about the two women who had got into the cab, could they be the culprits? He didn't think so, but it was all he had to go on.

Fortunately for Alexei Petrov, he always used the same taxi company. Mainly because they had a Russian-speaking operator. The driver who had delivered him to the office confirmed he had picked up two other passengers. Alexei immediately ordered a cab to take him to the address he was given.

There was no sign of life, but this was his only clue. The problem he was now facing was even more curious. This was the address of Nick the Greek, a face well known to this member of the Russian Mafia. Why on earth would Nick the Greek rob his employers? He was in partnership with them. He needed guidance on this.

# Unholy Communion

I could get used to this, thought young Errol as he sipped the most delicious chocolate shake he'd ever tasted, baking in the late afternoon sun. Gran seemed to like her drink too, the large tot of brandy floating at the bottom would help.

The two had developed a comfortable routine. Lizzie would walk down to meet Errol from school; close but not so close that she embarrassed him in front of his new friends. They would then stop off for a drink and some cake before tackling the steep hill up to the apartment. They'd always had a good relationship, since it was Lizzie who had brought the young lad up, Marie never having been the slightest bit maternal.

For the first time in as long as he could remember, he didn't feel anxious, he didn't have that permanent knot in his stomach, the feeling he'd always had in the early years when it was all about his colour. Gollywog and Paki were some of the more pleasant names he had had to endure. Glasgow wasn't the most tolerant of cities. Firstly, he was illegitimate, secondly he was mixed race and thirdly he was a Celtic supporter.

Being a Coyle meant he was expected to be tough, expected to be able to handle himself and fight himself out of any corner. He was challenged, almost on a daily basis, to defend something or someone, especially by 'the big boys'. The sad part was, that like his uncle Paddy, he really could fight. It came as naturally as breathing to the young boy, but it also gave him the reputation of being a bully and he hated that. He hated drawing blood; he hated the daily chant in the playground of 'fight, fight' and the tribal gathering to see someone being beaten for no real reason.

Here in Spain he was anonymous; the playground culture was entirely different. The fighter was not the hero, in fact quite the reverse; scholars and sportsmen were the most applauded, and as for colour, there was every shade imaginable. Most of the residents aspired to be as golden brown as him and spent hours by the pool or the beach to achieve it. He had never been much of a scholar but he excelled at all sports and here he was enjoying his moment in the sun.

Errol was ashamed to admit that he been neither homesick nor missed his mother. Marie's lifestyle was such that the youngster spent most of his time with Lizzie and saw Marie fleetingly. He would give anything to stay out here permanently but he knew that was most unlikely. Although she wouldn't come right out and say it, he knew Gran was in her element too.

With Auntie Bridget having a new baby, she would definitely want to go home and Gran, of course, would want to be with her. There was always Erin. Maybe he could stay with her and Nick? But, reluctant mother or not, Marie would never let him stay.

They finished their drinks and Lizzie gave her grandson the money to pay the bill. As Errol was waiting at the counter he noticed the old couple sitting inside in the gloom. This was not unusual, most elderly Spaniards preferred to be out of the fierce heat. Errol paid no attention to the couple as he waited to pay, however, when the elderly gentleman rose to leave, he stumbled and fell onto the hard, tiled floor. His wife struggled to help him up and Errol and the waiter raced to help. The man, although unsteady on his feet, was emphatic that he wouldn't need a doctor and would be fine.

Errol looked sharply at the old man. He knew that voice. How many times had he had his knuckles rapped for not paying attention or failing in his duties as an altar boy? But this old geezer was black, it couldn't be him, and he couldn't have a wife, he was a priest. Then it dawned on him, she wasn't his wife, she was the chapel housekeeper. It was definitely her. What the devil was going on here?

"Missus, hey, missus, don't I know you?" Errol called after her as they hurried into a waiting cab.

"Thank you for your help," the woman called back. "No, I don't think we've met," she added as the cab sped off.

"What the devil was all that about?" Lizzie asked as he returned with the change.

"Granny, I've just seen Canon O'Farrell and he's black."

"He's what? Black, did you say?" His granny roared with laughter. "Jesus, son, by this time he'd be black alright, he's been dead this past year."

"The woman was the horrible one that looked after him and Father Jack. Honest, Gran, it was them. And they knew who I was, that's why they bolted."

"It could have been anyone. A relative perhaps, but it definitely wasn't Canon O'Farrell, no matter what colour he's turned."

"How many black Irish priests do you know? I'm telling you, Gran, it was them."

"I think you've been out in the sun too long, my lad," smiled Lizzie.

Errol wouldn't let up and by the time they reached home, Lizzie was fast running out of patience.

"God almighty, laddie, give it a bloody rest, it's not possible. The man is dead so whoever you saw was *not* Canon O'Farrell."

"I'm telling you it was and I'll prove it," shouted the youngster as he rushed into his room, banging the door behind him.

"What's biting him?" Bridget asked her mother-in-law. "It's not like him to throw a tantrum. Do you think he's missing home?"

"No he's bloody not, he's been having the time of his life until today."

"So what's wrong?" asked Bridget.

"We stopped on our way home for a drink and some cake as usual and he got it into his head he saw a ghost."

"A ghost?" laughed Bridget. "Well that's original. There's not many ghosts spotted in bright daylight drinking coffee and eating cake."

"He's convinced it was Canon O'Farrell and that bloody sister of his and, wait for it, the Canon is now black. What do you make of that?"

"We've all seen him and it's true, he does look like the old priest, but you can assure Errol it's not."

Errol stood listening to the conversation from behind his bedroom door. He was right, he knew he was and somehow he'd prove it.

# Back in Business

"Could things get any worse?" Tommy Reilly muttered to himself. He was exhausted and bone-weary, having been up all night, once again, searching for his mother. He'd hit every crack house he knew of in the flats, but no sign of her, and if he was to believe any of these spaced out imbeciles, she'd been seen everywhere from Paddy's Market to being in the company of some Sheik looking for a bit of rough. He had to get some sleep, he was so weary and disillusioned, there was no telling what he might do if things didn't improve.

Tommy hadn't set eyes on Sandra, his mother, for over a week. He was really beginning to worry. She'd never been away this long before and he dreaded what state she'd be in. Every time his mother returned from one of her sojourns, she was worse than the time before, so fuck knew how bad she'd be this time.

Walking past Ma Coyle's abode, he wondered what was happening there. With the exception of Paddy and Michael, there had been no sign of any of the family since the day of the funeral. Even Theresa, Lizzie's best pal and confidante, had no idea where they were. If she didn't know, then no-one did. He glanced down the street toward his old pitch and his interest was piqued. There was no sign of the Russians and a few of his old regulars were hanging about as if waiting for someone.

"Tommy," shouted Tracy. "Tommy, got any gear?" the stupid mare shouted from the other end of the street.

"Shut up, ya bampot," he yelled back. "Why not ring the polis while you're at it? Where's Rasputin and his sidekicks? I thought they were your bessie mates?"

"C'mon, Tommy, it was just business, they were giving the stuff away for nought. You'd take it an' all. Well, they've scarpered. A couple of Paddy's crew came calling yesterday and two of them are now holidaying in the Southern General hospital. The other one could try out for the Olympics, he moved that fast."

"What's that got to do with me?" Tommy felt a stirring in his gut, maybe things were on the turn.

"I told them all you'd be back, Tommy, didn't I folks? Tell him, I said he'd be back."

Before he could answer, a blacked-out vehicle drew up alongside him.

The fucking arrogance of the man. Who did he fucking think he was? Nothing, not a cheep, no contact, being left to deal with those Russian bastards all on his own and now, up rolls the courier asking if he wants his usual amount.

His fucking usual amount? Tommy could barely answer the man. His usual amount? He hadn't had a customer for weeks, he'd had to go to another family for help putting food on the table and this fucker asks him if he wants his usual amount.

The effort it took to stop Tommy from shoving his piece down the man's throat and pulling the trigger was immense. The lad didn't know he was capable of such anger. Where did these fuckers get off? He aimed to show Paddy Coyle he couldn't take the piss out of the

Rileys any longer. Oh, he'd eat humble pie for now, but the first chance he got he'd make them pay. Make them pay for his little brother, for the state his mother was in, if she was still alive, and the beatings he had taken over the past few weeks, somehow, he'd get his own back. But for now he was back in business and he'd make bloody sure he couldn't be turfed out again.

"You in the market or not?" The guy was pushing Tommy. "C'mon son, I've got other customers anxious for their gear."

"Fuck them, I've not seen you for weeks, you weren't so anxious then." Tommy faced up to the courier.

"Look, son, either you want the merchandise or not. It's up to you but I'm not hanging about arguing with a two-bit street dealer," he made to drive away.

"I didn't say I didn't want it, but I'm short, I haven't had an earn for the past three weeks."

"Before you ask, son, this isn't the fucking credit union, payment in full or ye get nothin'."

"Look, I've got half now, I'll pay the rest tomorrow. C'mon, you know me, when have I ever welched on a deal? Here, take this," he stuffed a bundle of notes in the courier's hand. "There's £250, you'll get the rest tomorrow. Ask Paddy, he'll vouch for me."

"It's Mr Coyle to the likes of you. I'm warning you, screw me over and you're dead." The courier handed over the package.

Tommy was back in business, but by Christ he wouldn't forget the fuckers who deserted him when he need them most.

Sandra Riley had no idea here the hell she was or how long she'd been there, but she did know she needed to score. This was the worst comedown she'd ever had. She hadn't eaten in days and had been out of her face continuously on a cocktail of White Lightning cider and anything else she could cajole out of her companions. She'd taken speed, smoked crack and had a bit of KitKat. Dear God, she was going to die, the pains were everywhere: her joints, her legs and her back; her kidneys were excruciating and she had the shakes so bad. She had to get home, home to her boys. They would forgive her, they loved their mum. Tommy was a good lad, always looking out for his little brother, making sure he was fed and off to school on time. She knew she could count on him. This was it, never again, she told herself, never again. She would stay at home and be a good mum.

But there was something not right although she couldn't quite remember what it was. Her head was spinning – she needed to score, but there was definitely something not right. It was something to do with Billy, her youngest. What was it? What was she not remembering? Then it hit her like a thunderbolt – her Billy was gone. Her boy had disappeared over a year ago and no-one knew where he was or what had happened. Tears streamed down her dirty cheeks. Her boy, what had happened to him, what terrible, terrible fate had befallen her laddie?

Tommy had not been the same since Billy went missing. He blamed the Coyles and nothing would dissuade him from that belief. Paddy had always seen them alright, surely he couldn't be responsible? As for Sean, poor bugger, well he'd got a quick one. Probably how I'll go, she mused.

The shakes were bad, worse than usual and she needed a fix, she had to have one and *now*. For all her faults, Sandra had never gone to score off her son. She'd always kept well away from Tommy, but she was way past that pride now. Moving as discreetly as she could, stepping over bodies, who might or might not be alive, she headed for the door.

"Where the fuck do you think you're sneaking off to, lady?" demanded a bear of a man, blocking her way.

"I've got to get home to my sons, mister," she whispered.

"Your sons? You've never bothered about your sons since you got here. Taking everything we've got, bragging about your supplier. Telling us you can get anything and any amount. Yet here you are, pissing off now we're cleaned out. No chance, lady. Wherever you're going, I'm going too." And he pushed her out the door.

Sandra suddenly recognised where she'd spent the last few days; in fact, she could see her Tommy down at the corner. She was only yards from her home, but how was she going to get rid of this maniac without taking a beating? Fuck, she wasn't up to this; every nerve in her body was jangling. She needed to sort herself out fast then deal with this moron. She couldn't let this fucker know the dealer was her son.

As soon as Tommy saw her he cottoned on right away. At least she was alive.

"Hello, Sandra, you've been on the missing list for the past few days. I thought you'd deserted me." Tommy forced a smile across his face as he checked her out. She didn't seem too bad.

"You know me, son, wherever I lay my hat as they say. I need a fix, Tommy, enough to straighten me out."

"What about me?" Her companion butted in. "She needs more than a fixer, sonny, or I'll be fixing things."

"Who the fuck died and made you the boss? Listen,

pal, I'm not here to deal with your domestics. Sandra's a good customer, but you, who the fuck are you?" Tommy blagged his case. "You can get to fuck right now or you'll be the one needing fixed. Now fuck off." He pointed his trusty firearm at the growling junkie.

# On The Warpath

"They're back on the scene. I've had reports from all over the shop," said a furious Paddy. "The fuckers knocked off two bookies yesterday – one in Pollockshields and the other in the Gorbals. In both cases they held up the staff, emptied the safe and then trashed the place."

"Was it definitely them and not some cunts taking advantage?"

"Hey bro! Outside this room, who'd be brave enough? There wasn't enough cash to make it worthwhile. No, this was definitely to let us know they're back."

"We've hit every gaff they were operating from and they're either shut or 'under new management'. All we've actually accomplished is to chase away a few dealers."

"Who the fuck is the 'new management'?" asked Paddy.

"The word on the street is that it's either Cortellessa or Thomson, depending on the territory. For my money, I'd say it's both. And the fuckers are collaborating with our friends."

"No way! Christ, if it hadn't been for the sons at the funeral there would have been a massacre."

"They were fuckin' well prepared, Paddy," ventured Michael.

"Thank God."

"No. I mean they were really well prepared. Think about it, two masked guys burst in the door and within seconds they're on the deck with not a shot fired. I don't care how alert those lads were, to react in seconds isn't possible. They had to know there was going to be an attack. Think about it, think about where they were positioned, where the fathers were positioned. Lucky or what? This has bothered me from day one. Funny how I was out of commission, out cold in the lavvy. When have you ever known me to pass out? Never."

"Michael, you were fucking roaring drunk."

"So what? I had a lump the size of a fucking ostrich egg. Where did that come from?"

"The state you were in, God knows how you got it."

"Paddy, think. What about the clean-up? The two of them were up and away within minutes. Christ, half the mourners didn't even know something had gone down."

"Like you said, they were well prepared, but surely they were just looking after their own?"

"Paddy, their own were never in any danger and now they're bragging that they have taken back what was theirs to begin with."

"Do you mean to tell me that those two pups have the balls to take on us?"

"If they had the backing of the Russians, then yes, they would have."

"You know what this means? It's an all-out war, Michael, and we might not come out on top. We need to have a little chat with Cortellessa and Thomson Junior, just to make sure."

"The minute you call them in, they'll know the game's up. I propose we go look for them and pick them up without any warning. Let's face it, where you find one, you usually find the other."

Mario Cortellessa Senior lived in the Newton Mearns district of the city. A very up-market suburb with predominately detached villas, occupied by well-heeled members of Glasgow society.

Turning into the drive, Michael and Paddy were surprised at the number of cars parked there. It was obvious that something was up. Through the window of the lounge, Paddy and Michael caught sight of Genaro being comforted by the guests.

"Jesus, Paddy, I think the old man's copped it," spoke Michael.

"I think you're right. This can wait," said Paddy, just as their quarry appeared at the front door.

"Paddy, Michael, what can I do for you?" the young man nodded at them.

"It's your father we came to see, lad."

"I'm sorry, you're too late. He passed away this morning," the young man answered, tears in his eyes.

"We knew he was ill but didn't realize it was so serious. Sorry for your loss, Genaro. He was a fine man and he'll be sorely missed."

"Thank you. He *was* a good man and he would want me to carry on as usual. So, what did you want to see him about?"

"Nothing important, son. We'll come back when things settle down."

"Thanks. If you'll excuse me, I have to go and see to the family," Genaro closed the front door.

Paddy turned to his brother, "This changes nothing, Michael. If anything, it's all the more reason to make a move. He's not much more than a kid and he certainly doesn't have the nous to run the business."

"Paddy, you were years younger than him when you took over."

"Things were different then," Paddy smiled.

"Were they? I'm not so sure, but he and his sidekick are loose cannons. We can't let them run wild. You know, Paddy, I've got a feeling in my gut that won't go away, there's something about those two. I don't trust them and more to the point, I don't like them."

"It'll be interesting to see what happens over the next few days. We need to be vigilant, I don't think young Cortellessa was quite as upset over his father's passing as he would have us believe."

# Bearing Gifts

"**G**ood God, lassie, is there anything left in the shops?" Lizzie asked, seeing the pile of glossy bags.

"They're not all mine, Gran. *She* can shop for Scotland as well," Erin turned to her friend. "Don't worry, there are a couple of nice pieces in there for you."

"That's okay then," smiled her gran.

"What about me?" laughed her mother. "I can't get into anything. I feel so fat."

"You are and you love it," Erin handed her a large pink bag, with the name of the most expensive shop in Marbella emblazoned on each side.

"Of course I didn't forget you," she kissed her mum on the cheek. "I didn't forget you either, wee man," she plonked a large wooden train down on the floor next to her son, who was squealing with delight. "In fact, I didn't forget anyone," as she handed a huge box to Errol, who was hovering on the sidelines in anticipation.

"Gee thanks, Erin," Errol ripped the paper to reveal just what the young lad was desperate for; a top of the range skateboard. "Thanks, it's brill, just what I wanted. Is it okay if I go over to the park, Gran? I'll be back for tea."

"Off you go, but mind the time and be back for six."

The boy was off before Lizzie had finished.

"Oh, Lizzie, that'll look lovely on you." Bridget admired the stunning day dress Erin had chosen for her gran. "Honestly, it'll take years off you," she felt the fine texture of the dress. "You'll look like one of those rich matriarchs we see every morning."

"Wait till you see the other one. They're beautiful, dear, thanks, but you shouldn't have."

"Of course I should have. You've been a great help with Ryan. None of us know what we'd do without you, go and try them on."

Bridget's dress was a mixture of pale, muted, summer colours; a wraparound style which would grow with her expanding waistline.

'Oh, it's lovely, darling, but like your granny says, you shouldn't have. You can't go around spending Nick's money on us, it's not right."

"Who said anything about Nick's money? Remember, I'm a woman of means now, and really, gimme a break. When was the last time I bought anything? The sales were on and I just felt like indulging us a little, we haven't exactly had the best year."

"What about you, madam? You look like you've been keeping up with her." Bridget turned to Sam.

"Commission cheque, *and* I'll be eating beans for the next month, but it was worth it," she replied, pulling dress after dress out to show her admiring audience.

Later that evening, when Ryan was in bed fast asleep and Nick and Erin were on their own, she confessed, "I had a bit of a shopping spree today."

"Good for you, just don't break the bank," he laughed.

"I didn't use your money. I wouldn't do that without permission."

"You don't need my permission. Buy what you want, I just want to see you look beautiful."

"Maybe so, but I have some money of my own."

"Look, Erin, I don't want your father supporting you or the wee fella. You're my responsibility not his, and I would rather you didn't take money from him."

She decided to let Nick continue to think the funds had come from Paddy. She would conceal the remainder of their loot on the cruiser. No-one except the skipper had access. It was the perfect hiding place, she thought.

# Russian Roulette

"You're telling me the safe door was open and the contents gone?" Sergei Romanov was not a man given much to conversation.

He was sitting at a huge, highly-polished desk, hands outstretched. Behind him stood his two bodyguards, from whom he was never apart. Rumour had it they were his brothers, but no-one knew for sure. All that was known was, if Sergei didn't like the answer to any question he posed, one or the other would shoot the messenger.

"So, you do not have what I sent you to collect?" The big Russian splayed his fingers out in front of him.

"No." Petrov replied nervously. "I'm telling you, I couldn't collect the merchandise. The safe was empty, someone got there before me."

"You should have been quicker," the oligarch replied.

"Sir, I went straight from here. I could not have reached my destination any quicker."

"That is not my problem. You were sent to collect and you failed."

"I know who has your property, but it is a complicated situation. I did not know what to do, so I came straight back."

"This had better be good. You know the punishment for failure. Go on, tell me who stole my property and what is complicated about the situation. You either have it or your do not. See? Not complicated in the least."

"When I arrived, two women got into my taxi cab. I didn't see from which direction they came, but when I discovered the theft, I called the taxi company and the driver confirmed he had picked up a fare – two women, dropping them at Calle de la Cruz."

"And this is important, why?"

"Calle de la Cruz is the address of your associate."

"My associate? Who?"

"Nicholas Stasinopoulos, sir. The two women who stole your property went straight to his home. I did not wish to confront either them, or Mr Stasinopoulos, without instructions from you."

"You stand before me and tell me my partner is double-crossing me? That I should believe you failed to collect my property and are placing the blame on an honourable man, a man I have done business with for years?"

"It's the truth, why would I lie? Why would I put my life in danger, why would I name such a person if it were not the truth?"

"You have twenty-four hours to recover my property. No-one must know of this conversation, especially Stasinopoulos. Do not fail."

The man was ushered from the room.

Allowing himself to breathe, the locksmith could hardly believe he had got out in one piece. If he managed to pull this off, he would surely go up through the ranks, earning respect, but first, he had to retrieve what had been stolen.

A strange, old black man was waiting outside the office as Petrov left. He heard Sergei greet his next visitor in English.

"Good morning, Father. How nice to see you. You are keeping well?" Sergei took his visitor by the hand, guiding him to a comfortable, well-padded sofa.

"Well, I'm not dead yet," the old man chuckled. "Though there are many who wish I had remained so."

"Well, I certainly would not be amongst them." Sergei shook the old priest's hand in friendship. "Let's have some tea before we get down to what has brought you here. I take it this is not just a social call?"

"You are correct. I do have a small problem, but tea would be fine."

The two men chatted comfortably until the tea things were removed.

"Okay, what seems to be the problem?"

"I have been recognised. I know it's happened before, but this time is different. I had a close encounter with one of the Coyles."

"You've come across them before. Marbella is not a big town, you were bound to come face to face with them at some time. I did warn you."

"I had managed fine up until now. The problems with my skin usually puts anyone off, but not so this time."

"Who recognised you?"

"The boy, Errol, the old woman's grandson. He knew me right away and when he heard Imelda's accent, the game was up. I've seen him a couple of times, scouting about, looking for us."

"So, is it a safe house you need?"

"No, I'm quite happy where I am and I have to consider my sister. She's not that happy here in Spain and a move would upset her even more."

"How can I help?"

"I want rid of him, we can't take the risk of getting caught, not with our backgrounds."

The Russian flinched at the inference. "When you say 'rid of him', what exactly do you mean? I am not in the business of disposing of children."

"You didn't used to be so squeamish," said ex-Canon O'Farrell.

"I will allow you that because we go way back, but Father, do not think for a moment that you can blackmail me over past dealings. I will help because I like and respect you, not because I fear what you know. If that were the case, you would not leave this room."

# Hidden Treasure

"Hi, it's me. I'm going to bury our treasure today. I have the perfect place; I'm going to stow it aboard the Lady Di."

"You sure that's a good idea? What about the skipper and your charters?" Sam didn't sound convinced.

"Good God, I'm not going to be leaving it on the bedside table. Anyway, there are no charters booked for the next few weeks and it will give us breathing space. I spend quite a lot of time down at the marina, no-one will think it unusual. We can spend the morning down there without raising any suspicions."

"Good, we can take a picnic to make it look even more authentic."

"Right. Meet me at the marina at 11 o'clock, Nick has an appointment this morning so he won't be around.

"Okay, see you then."

Erin felt much better knowing that their haul would be out of the house. Nick was certainly no angel, but she didn't want him taking the rap for a shedload of stolen money and possession of a gun and ammunition which he had nothing to do with.

Alexei Petrov waited in the shadows. He was sure

the goods were in this house, but he had no intention of coming face to face with Stasinopoulos; let the boss deal with him. He watched as the Greek sped off in his Ferrari, leaving only the woman and the child. He'd give them a bit longer to leave before entering the house.

Just as he was about to climb the wall, the huge iron gates swung open and out roared a powerful Mercedes, almost knocking him over. It was being driven by the young woman he'd seen only briefly yesterday. He slipped into the grounds as the gate closed behind him. Crime definitely paid, if this villa was anything to go by.

He scouted around the property. There appeared to be no-one else at home, but since he didn't know how long the residents were likely to be away, Petrov wasted no time.

Petrov had been recruited a year ago by Sergei Romanov, having narrowly escaped a prison sentence in his homeland. For most of his working life he had been employed by Moscow's foremost locksmith. There was no lock, he bragged, that he couldn't breach, and his services were always in demand.

However, things changed politically in the mother country and honest, working comrades like himself were seen as fools and treated as such. With a wife who saw her friends sporting furs and jewels, he was lured by the rewards of personal enterprise. There were many safes in the capital, containing riches beyond his wildest dreams. Unfortunately for Petrov, although he could crack any safe, he did not possess the criminal mind necessary to avoid detection and was forced to flee and was now under the command of a harsh and unforgiving master.

The safe in the Stasinopoulos household was surprisingly basic and, disappointingly, displayed its contents without any real effort required from Alexei. It held nothing of any importance: a couple of high end watches, some lady's jewellery and a few thousand pesetas. Certainly much less than one would expect a 'Face' of Nick's standing to contain. Unlike Alexei Petrov however, Nick had an exceptional criminal mind and kept nothing which could incriminate him anywhere near his home, certainly not in his personal safe.

Nothing, absolutely nothing. Where the fuck could it be? Petrov was beginning to panic as he systematically ransacked the villa, hoping against hope that the occupants would be stupid enough to conceal the missing money and documents somewhere in the house, but more importantly, the gun. He had to retrieve the gun at any cost.

Strident screams coming from the ground floor shook him back to reality. Springing to life, he sped through the house, crashing into the source of the noise.

Bea, the housekeeper, had worked for Mr Stasinopoulos since he had arrived in Marbella and she was extremely well-compensated for her trustworthiness and loyalty. But, when she realised the intruder was still on the premises, and dealing with him was way off her remit, without hesitation and still caterwauling, she locked herself in the cloakroom until she was sure he had gone. No sum of money was worth facing any intruder.

This was not a situation for the police. Mr Stasinopoulos would not wish it to be made public. She had to get in contact with him immediately.

*

Erin and Nick arrived back at the house within minutes of each other.

"Dear God, what's happened?" Erin was shocked at the state of the beautiful villa.

"We had a visitor," snapped Nick.

"Was anything taken?" She was thanking her lucky stars she'd moved their haul this morning.

"I'm not sure, I don't think so. I think perhaps he was looking for something, but for the life of me, I don't know what. I've never kept anything at home that could incriminate or jeopardise me. The safe is open, but the money and jewellery are still inside," observed Nick. "The way the place has been ransacked certainly makes me think this wasn't a regular burglary. I'm going to check the CCTV, there's bound to be footage. I'll find out who was responsible."

Erin felt an icy, cold hand grab her insides. Walking out to the hall, she was pretty sure this break-in had something to do with her and Sam's escapade, but how had they been traced so quickly?

"I'll get my mum and gran over to help Bea. It's not the first time our house has been turned over. It's usually by the cops, though."

She was going to have to own up, but what would Nick think of her? A common thief, perhaps. That was a bit like the pot calling the kettle black, but these guys were funny when it came their women. Look at her mum and dad, they might be living off the proceeds of crime, but no-one ever voiced it.

She needed to talk to Sam, but first she had to get her family over to put things right. None of them would be shocked or judgemental. Hell, it had happened to them countless times.

# The King is Dead

Mario Cortellessa was laid to rest with as much pomp and ceremony as befitted any Mafia boss. In life he had been a flamboyant, immaculately-dressed man about town, never without his trademark Cuban cigar. In death, he was equally pretentious. He was sent to his maker in the most expensive casket, amidst the most magnificent floral tributes and with hundreds of mourners. The funeral guests were treated to a scrumptious repast in the city's only five-star hotel. All this was on strict instructions from the man himself, in the hope that if people didn't remember him in life, they would certainly remember him in death. Everything about the ceremony and the feast reeked of money. Mario had hoped it would be an indication of his wealth and stature. He had failed to take into account one thing: the fickle nature of man.

Mario Cortellessa had arrived in Glasgow at the end of the war, penniless. He operated for years out of the south side of the city, making his money from a string of betting shops, a casino, (the first in the city) and personal protection to all who felt they required such a service. The city boasted a large Italian contingency and he, courtesy of his connections, was the main supplier of the narcotics that found their way into the veins or up the noses of the drug-taking population of Glasgow. There was no arguing with Cortellessa. He had the backing of one of the oldest societies known to man –the Cosa Nostra – and no-one messed with them.

"Are you sure you can pull this off?" Michel questioned his brother. "It seems too easy and you know what happened the last time something was simplicity itself."

"This is different. By all accounts there's no love lost between the boy and his father's men. We've already seen some defections. I have it on good authority there are a couple of splinter groups ready to challenge him, and the majority think he's nothing but a useless prick who spends more time with Davey Thomson's lad than is healthy."

"Well, I can't argue with that sentiment. I told you before, there's something about that pair that makes my skin crawl," answered Michael. "Still, getting a crew to change sides is risky, these boys go way back."

"Aye! Way back with the father, not with that bum-kissing tosser. We'd never stand a chance if Mario was still alive, but it's a different ball game now and let's face it, Michael, Mario was a tight-fisted bastard, not renowned for his generosity. If we lay our cards on the table and offer them all a decent wedge, I think most of them will bite our hand off."

"On the other hand, you could start the biggest turf war since the eighties, and no-one wants to go back to that," Michael pointed out. "Don't forget, you've got those fucking Ruskies in the mix now."

"Trust me, they won't be a problem. The Eyeties fucking hate them. It was becoming a problem when Mario was alive and his men won't entertain them now, not with him gone. We put it to them, either make the change now, with no aggro, or fight it out for the next six months, and we pick up the pieces. The outcome is going to be the same, whatever they choose.

"For me it's a no-brainer," replied Michael. "The kid can't run the show on his own and, as you say, there are going to be problems in the future. Word on the street is that a couple of his top men are ready to challenge the leadership already, and the poor bastard isn't cold yet."

On the eve of the funeral, just as Mario's remains were being brought into the cathedral, Paddy and Michael Coyle, together with a dozen or so of their top men, entered Black Jack's, the casino run by the Cortellessa family. Setting off the fire alarm, the brothers emptied the salon, leaving only the staff. It took very little persuasion to sway most of them when Paddy made them an offer they couldn't refuse. The gambling venue changed hands without as much as a blow being stuck.

On the morning of the Requiem Mass, their betting shops changed hands in a similar manner. Genaro was left with nothing.

As the priest was conducting the final prayers, Paddy and Michael were given the signal that the takeover was a fait accompli. They offered their condolences and shook hands with the son who, unknown to him, had just been quickly and efficiently deposed, and who had been the unsuspecting victim of a successful coup.

"What the fuck do you mean I can't come in?" Genaro shouted at the doorman. "I own the fucking joint." What the fuck was going on? Maybe he'd mixed too much coke and Jack Daniels and he was hallucinating? "Get out of my way, you stupid bastards." Genaro made to push his way past the burly doormen.

"Sorry, sir, we have strict instructions from the owner not to permit you, or any of your guests, to enter the premises," said the senior of the two barring Genaro's way.

"What are you talking about? I am the fucking owner, you arsehole. Get out of my way!"

Enjoying the altercation to the hilt, having been subjected to many a humiliating encounter with this ignorant smart-arse, the two doormen ceremoniously dumped the Italian ponce on his arse, onto the pavement.

By now Genaro was in a purple rage. He'd seldom, if ever, been denied anything in his young life, certainly not entry to his own property. And it *was* his now. The eldest son inherited everything in Italian culture.

A familiar figure appeared at the top of the steps leading into the casino. "Problems, boys?" Paddy Coyle enquired.

"No sir. This gentleman appears not to understand his membership has expired," replied the doorman.

"Membership. What fucking membership? Paddy, tell him who I am, for fuck's sake."

"It's Mr Coyle to you, laddie." And turning to the two doormen, Paddy, grinning from ear to ear, said, "Boys, this here is Genaro Cortellessa, son of Mario Cortellessa, deceased. One-time owner of this club."

"What do you mean 'one-time owner'? Get out of my way, you fucking idiot."

By now the rest of Genaro's party were receiving similar treatment and young Davey Thomson was more than ready for a set-to.

"Where the fuck did they come from?" Davey quizzed his mate later. "There were fuckin' hunners of them." He was referring to the number of security guards who had appeared from nowhere to assist in the expulsion of the two mates and their party. "Most of them seemed to be your guys. What the fuck's going on?" He yelped as the nurse finished stitching him up. He certainly had come off second best in the night's free-for-all.

"We need to have a word with your dad," said Cortellessa as he waited to be sewn up. "Let's face it, your lot could be next."

"No chance," replied his mate. "No fucking chance."

# Old Pals Act

"Listen, you stupid, thick fucker. Your loyalty is first and foremost to this family, not to your bum chum." Davey Thomson had his son and heir by the scruff of the neck, whilst systematically slapping him around the ears.

"He's my mate, Dad. I have to help him, he would do the same for me," whined Davey.

"Don't be so sure. Anyway, what's it to me if Paddy Coyle is operating the Italian's territory? From what I heard, Coyle just walked in and took over. Your pal has to be man enough to take it back in order to keep it. That's the law of the jungle, boy, and there's nothing we can do. I'm fucking sure I'm not going into battle against the Coyles. They can keep it as far as I'm concerned, and the same goes for you."

"But Dad . . ."

Junior was interrupted before he could put his case forward. "But Dad nothing. You'll stay out of it, or else," threatened Thomson Senior. "What the fuck do you two ninjas think you can do anyway? Ride into battle waving your light sabres and take on two thirds of the city? Fucking halfwits," Thomson shook his head wearily.

"Light sabres are *Star Wars*, not *Ninja Turtles*," the son muttered, under his breath.

"I couldn't care less if you had *Dr Who* and the fucking Daleks backing you. Stay out of it, or you'll have me to contend with. And I'm worse than the whole fucking lot put together."

"What am I going to tell him, Dad? He's counting on us to help."

"Tell him what the hell you like. He's got only one chance, and that's no chance. Cortellessa will only come out on top by taking Paddy Coyle on personally. And unless he's got a death wish, that's never going to happen. We're not getting involved, it's not our fight. Why should we put our men in danger and then hand the whole fucking shebang over to that sleazy pup? Get a grip, son."

"But Dad," whined the son.

"No. I'm not interested. Now fuck off and give me peace." His father returned to reading the morning paper.

"He won't see you," Davey told his best mate. "He's not interested. Says you have to sort this out yourself, it's the only way your troops will respect you. Miserable old bastard."

"That's okay," grimaced Cortellessa. "I kind of expected that. My father would have said exactly the same, but I've got a plan that will put the Coyles out of action for good."

"You have?" replied his mate, somewhat bewildered.

"Yep. Mr Paddy Coyle's days on this earth are numbered, mark my words," pronounced the Italian, mysteriously. "And it's so easy, it's criminal," he laughed.

# Lights Action Camera

Nick had been in his office, viewing the video tape, for the past twenty minutes or so. Rewinding it time and time again. Back and forth to the spot where Erin could be seen leaving the property, driving her Mercedes. It was at that point the camera picked up someone sneaking onto the drive, making for the house. The various cameras showed the intruder checking for an entry point.

"He'd been watching the house since around eight o'clock this morning," said Nick. "That's me leaving to go into town and you driving off about an hour later." He showed Erin the footage. "You didn't notice anyone hanging around, did you?"

"No, but truthfully, I wouldn't have been paying any attention. I was running late."

"I suppose not," agreed Nick.

"Do you recognise him?" she asked

"Nope, could be anyone. There's only one clear picture, but he doesn't look at all familiar. I've put the word out," Nick said, replacing the video tape. "I don't suppose there's much point in putting this in the safe. It didn't stop him the last time."

"Change the combination anyway, he might just have got lucky," offered Erin.

"I don't think so, but what I *am* going to do, is have cameras installed inside. I thought having them on the exterior was deterrent enough, obviously not. Don't worry, this place will be as safe as Fort Knox before the day is out. It was probably just an opportunist, but I'm not taking any chances."

"Heavens, Nick, I'm not easily scared. Paddy insisted on me having judo lessons when I was a kid and taught me how to use a gun when I was sixteen. Honestly, I'm fairly well able to take care of myself. But I agree, if you did have cameras inside, we would probably be able to identify this scum. I hate the thought of him going through our things."

"Where were you rushing off to anyway, this morning?" Nick asked her.

"To pick up Sam. As I said, I was running late. We were meeting at the marina and I hate anyone waiting for me, but," she pointed to her son, "his lordship was playing up something awful this morning."

"I'm sorry I've spoiled your day, but when Bea couldn't get me at first, she automatically called you."

"No need to apologise. Of course I came straight back. Surely this concerns me as much as it does you?"

The sound of Erin's relatives arriving cut off any further conversation between the couple.

"You both all right?" Lizzie enquired.

"Yes, we were out of the house when it happened," Nick assured her. "It was Bea who disturbed him."

The housekeeper was still quite shaken by the episode and Lizzie took it upon herself to send the poor soul off home, assuring everyone that she and Bridget would have the house shipshape in no time at all.

Mother and grandmother set about their task. "It's

been a long time since we've had to do this," Bridget commented to her mother-in-law.

"Aye, the one benefit of being poor is that it doesn't take long to put the house back together. I remember one time when the twins were young and Marie was still a toddler, the house got raided. We had so little, we were glad the buggers had planted evidence," laughed Lizzie.

"Daft old bugger," smiled Bridget. "I've got to say though, Lizzie, I'm not happy about Erin and the wee lad staying here if he can't look after them."

"She's fine. That girl's a lot tougher than you think, and there's no way she'd put Ryan in any danger."

"You're right, but I still worry."

"You've no need," said Nick as he entered the room. "It's all in hand. I've just had the same conversation with Erin and she's okay about staying here. Ladies, I have to go out for a while, but I'll be back as soon as possible. There are two of my boys patrolling until I get back, so don't worry."

"Come in, Nicolas my friend. Come in, sit down. Let me get you a drink," said Sergei Romanov. The oligarch prided himself on always observing the social niceties.

Nick apologised for calling off their meeting earlier that day. "Thanks, Sergei. Sorry about this morning. I was on my way here when I got a call from my housekeeper. She disturbed an intruder."

"No-one was hurt?"

"No, but the house was ransacked. He was obviously looking for something."

The Russian studied his business partner's face, "What makes you think that? What could he have been after?"

"I have no idea. Like you, I never keep anything in my home. Never more than a few thousand pesetas. Certainly nothing that could ever incriminate me or anyone I am associated with. I managed to catch him on camera, but I don't recognise him."

"Let me see it, maybe I can help?"

"Thanks, I will. Now, what was it you wanted to see me about?" Nick settled back in his chair.

"It's okay. I had a problem with the recovery of some property, but I have it under control now. I am more concerned with your problems, my friend. There are very few who would attack your home, especially with your reputation."

"I know. Maybe it was only a chancer, an opportunist."

"What opportunist would be able to crack a safe and having done so, leave the contents intact? It doesn't make sense."

"I know, but there is nothing else I can think of."

"What about the girl?"

"Erin?"

"Yes."

"What could she have to do with this? If it was a kidnap attempt, why would he wait until she'd left the house?"

"You're right, my friend. I am merely making suggestions."

"Well, I've upped my security. If I can think of anything, I'll be in touch."

"Remember to send me a photograph of this man. You never know," Sergei said enigmatically.

"Look, it's the safest place to hide the stuff." Sam was emphatic that they should return their haul to the house.

"There's no way anyone will break in again with all the new security that's been put in place."

"No, I'm not incriminating Nick in any of this. I wish to God I'd kept my mouth shut. This is getting way out of hand."

"It's okay for you, you live with a guy who's minted. And Daddy-dear is not exactly short of a bob or two. I, on the other hand, am skint."

"I know," Erin consoled her friend. "I know, and I'm equally to blame. But for me it was about the initial excitement and that's worn off now. I'm scared this will affect my relationship with Nick. What's he going to think of me?"

"He'll think you're brave, ballsy and not afraid to seize an opportunity when it arises."

"Or just a common thief," Erin moaned to her friend.

# Status Quo

"More tea, Paddy, Michael?" Theresa waved the teapot at her charges. Since Lizzie's defection to Spain, Theresa had taken on the role of head-cook and bottle-washer at 28 Lomond Crescent.

Michael had returned to their mother's house shortly after Margee's death, unable to stay in the home they had made together. Paddy moved in with the excuse that he would keep his brother company while Bridget and the family were in Spain.

"No, you're fine, missus, that was grand."

Clearing away the breakfast dishes, Theresa chattered twenty to the dozen, most of which Paddy and Michael completely ignored, but now and again something would trigger a response.

"What was that you said about Sandra Riley?" Paddy asked

"She's been on the lash and God knows what else for the past while. Young Tommy has been worried sick. She's prone to go walkabout since their Billy disappeared, but never as long as this. I know he's no better than he should be, but he's a nice lad and by heaven, that family haven't had their sorrows to seek," the neighbour prattled on.

"Is the mother back now?" enquired Michael.

"As far as I know, she's back for the moment, but I wouldn't hold my breath on her staying put for long. She gets hammered and then sets out looking for her son. Honest, Michael, the poor soul will never know peace till she finds out what happened to her laddie and she has a body to bury."

"Is there anything we can do, Paddy?" Michael looked over to his brother, who seemed engrossed in the morning paper.

"Don't know what, the boy's a fucking menace. Sorry, Theresa. I've had a few run-ins with him over the past couple months and trust me, if it weren't for his loss, I'd have tanned his arse."

"I know he can be a bit brazen, but it all stems back to Billy disappearing. Let's face it, your Errol's not been the same since then either. He and Billy were almost joined at the hip. Errol's never forgiven himself for not hanging around that day, but he knew Lizzie and Marie would murder him for even being near Tommy's pitch. He's convinced that if he had stayed with his mate, Billy would still be here."

"Maybe he would," answered Michael, "but you can't turn back the clock."

"Is there nothing you can do to help them? She's an accident waiting to happen. And I'm afraid if Tommy loses his mother, it'll be the finish of him."

"What do you suggest, Theresa? We're not fucking social workers. Other folk have had losses around here," Paddy glanced at his brother, "and they don't end up junkies or jakies. What exactly do you want us to do?"

"Never mind me, son, I'm just sounding off. I know you'd help if you could. I miss Lizzie and Bridget, they'd have sorted this mess out, easy as pie. Is there no word on them coming home soon?" Tears trickled down the older woman's wrinkled cheeks.

"It shouldn't be much longer. I want them home in plenty of time before the baby's born," said Paddy gruffly.

"Oh, son, I can't wait. A new baby! Now what would you say to a nice bit steak for your tea?"

"I'd say, thank you very much and there's money under the clock. Get your Peter a nice bit of fillet steak as well." Paddy rose from the table, "Right, boyo, let's get to work," he addressed his younger brother.

"Any word on the two fugitives?" Paddy asked his brother.

"Not a dickie bird. Someone's hiding them, that's for sure. And whoever it is will get the same treatment as their guests when I finally catch up with them."

"I don't understand why no-one's come forward, not even the low-lives. The smell of cash always brings someone out, and ten thousand is quite a temptation."

Paddy had been against Michael posting a bounty for the capture of the two Russians thought to be responsible for Margee's death, but it had brought nothing. "The only information I wheedled out of Thomson was that he thought they had left the country. I don't believe it. Those two wouldn't run, they'd fight it out to the death."

"Maybe they're not as brave as they'd have us believe, but if I have to go to fucking Russia to find them, I will," snarled Michael.

# Second Thoughts

"I'm telling you, it's the ideal place, no-one is going to search the house again. Whoever it was won't take the chance. Look at the security Nick's put in place. I just feel it's too exposed on board the boat. If this guy who's looking for it knew where you live, then it's even money he knows about the Lady Di. And it would be a damn sight easier to search a cruiser than a house with occupants and housekeepers."

"No, I'm not taking it back. We'll have to take our chances until we decide how to proceed."

"Would you not speak to Nick, ask him for help? I still think he would be okay."

"Definitely not. If I was going to speak to anyone, believe it or not, it would be my mum."

"Are you mad?" yelled Sam. "Bridget would frogmarch you down to the local cop shop and turn you in personally."

"That's where you're wrong. My mother sails much closer to the wind than people would believe."

"Well, maybe we should have a word with her. I'm not comfortable leaving this lot on board where anyone could swan off with it, but I do understand you not wanting to expose your home."

"Erin, it's Sam. I've just got back and I've also had a visit from our friend. My apartment has been turned over."

"Shit, this is serious. What do we do now? It won't be long before he finds out about the cruiser. Okay, I'm coming over. Let's collect everything and do what we should have done right away – rent a security box at the bank. That way we're not incriminating anyone, and it's safe. I'll pick you up in twenty minutes."

"The scary thing is, he knows what *we* look like, but we wouldn't recognise *him*. He could be watching us from the quay right now."

"Well, let's get going," said Erin, shivering as she retrieved the money, documents and the gun.

"No, leave that, and the ammo."

"Why?" asked Erin. "I would have thought it would be the first thing you'd want rid of."

"No. I have my reasons," the girl replied.

"Surely you're not thinking you might use it?" challenged Erin. "Jesus! Annie Oakley eat your heart out. Listen, Sam, I've had lessons in shooting and I wouldn't go brandishing this about. It should go in the box with everything else."

"No. It's not loaded, but it could certainly be a deterrent," Sam protested.

"Trust me, even unloaded, it's too dangerous. The person you are pointing it at won't know it's empty."

"Maybe, but I want to keep it."

Half an hour later the twosome were sipping a glass of chilled wine in a small bodega across from the Banco de España where their loot had been secured safely. Despite

Erin's protests, the gun and ammunition were still on board the Lady Di for the moment.

"Should we 'fess up and tell them all about your visitor?" Erin questioned her friend. "I think we have to. For a start, Nick is treating this as some sort of challenge to his status, when in fact it has nothing to do with him. And Mum and Lizzie want to ship me back cause some madman is running around."

"Let's give it a few days, see what develops. Maybe he'll give up."

"Dear God, have those few sips of wine gone straight to your head?" gasped Erin. "Give up? He's far more likely to bring in more men. Why the devil would we wait to see what happens next? We're like sitting ducks."

"You're right. Let's go visit Bridget and see what she has to say."

"I have to collect Ryan, so now is as good a time as any."

The two left, followed by a most irritated and disgruntled Russian, who now had to work out how to gain access to a safety deposit box.

# Mummy's Boy

"Where the fuck has she got to this time?" Tommy Riley muttered to himself as he climbed the fourth flight of stairs in the flats behind his 'office'. This was the third time this week she'd gone AWOL and much as he loved his mother, he was coming to the end of his patience.

Kicking the door viciously, he was not surprised to find it unlocked as it bounced back to catch his shin. Yelping, Tommy gave the door yet another kick, only for the same thing to happen. "Fucking dump," he spat. He entered what had once been a family home, but now was nothing more than a hovel: a squat, housing a dozen or so crackheads in various stages of euphoria. The place was littered with the paraphernalia associated with their habits.

"Anybody seen my ma?" he asked no-one in particular.

"Naw, son, she's not been here for a couple days." A bundle of rags answered him back.

The disembodied voice could hardly identify himself in the mirror, let alone Sandra Riley.

"Are you sure she's not been here today?" Tommy asked again. "Do you know who I'm looking for?"

"Aye! Yer ma," said the voice.

"What's her name then?" said Tommy, getting madder. "What does she look like?"

"For fuck's sake, ye'll be wanting a DNA test next. Listen, son, yer ma, whoever she is, isn't here, she's not been here and if she turns up, she'll not get in here. Satisfied? Now fuck off and leave us in peace," the rags moved slightly.

Tommy Riley almost jumped out of his skin as a bony hand grabbed hold of his ankle. "Got any spare, son?"

"Get to . . ." he didn't finish the sentence. The emaciated, poor creature who had hold of his leg, was the person he had spent the last two hours looking for.

"Mum, what the hell are you doing in this shithole? Come on, let's get you back home." The lad gently helped his mother up. What the hell was he going to do? He had to work to keep them alive, but as soon as he left the house she was off. He'd tried locking her in, even paid a neighbour to look after her, but she had turned out to be as bad as his mother with the drink. Tommy was at his wits end; she was going to kill herself.

"I saw Billy today, he was on his bike over at the play park. He's coming home for his tea tonight. I have to get to the shop and get something nice for his tea," Sandra babbled on.

She really had lost the plot. This was all the Coyles' fault, he seethed. All their fucking fault. If it took till the day he died, he'd pay them all back for what they had done to his family.

She needed to be sectioned, but he couldn't get her to a doctor and the ones round his way were a bunch of fucking quacks, as much good as a chocolate teapot, but something had to be done.

"Alright, Tommy?" enquired the Big Man as he made to enter number 28.

"Does it look like I'm fucking alright?" Tommy was struggling as he endeavoured to keep his mother upright. Skinny as she was, she was a dead weight and the poor lad was buckling under her.

Paddy scooped Sandra up, "She needs to see a doctor, Tommy."

"Fucking paramedic, are you? Of course she needs to see a doctor, but none of those bastards will have anything to do with us."

"No? Come with me."

Paddy carried the near-unconscious woman into the surgery and demanded to see a doctor immediately.

Dr Singh, the duty physician came out to the entrance, all bluff and bluster, until he recognised the Big Man. After which, it was a completely different story.

Despite his hatred for Paddy, Tommy had the good grace to recognise that without Coyle's intervention, his mother would likely not have made it through the night. As it was, she was tucked up in hospital, receiving the best medical treatment money could buy.

# Mummy's Girl

"To what do I owe the pleasure?" Bridget was surprised to see her daughter and Sam this early in the day. "I've just put him down for a nap."

"That's okay, Mum. It's you we came to see. We've got a bit of a problem," said Erin, embracing her mother.

"A problem, is it? By the look on your face it's serious. Is it Nick? Have you two split up? I knew it wouldn't last. I was just saying to your granny this morning . . ."

"No, we haven't split up," Erin interrupted her mother, "thanks for the confidence."

"Well, what do you expect me to think? You come here all po-faced, telling me you've got a problem. He hasn't been knocking you about, has he?"

"It's nothing to do with Nick. Sit down, Mum, and let me explain." Erin ushered her mother to the large sofa. "We came into a bit of money recently," Erin began her tale.

"What do you mean, you came into a bit of money? I take it that's the cash you've been flashing about lately?" Bridget commented.

"Yes."

"How did you come into possession of it? I assume it doesn't belong to Nick? I know your dad is generous but not to that extent, so where did it come from?"

"Well, if you'd shut up and let me get on with my story, you would find out. As I said, we came in to a bit of money and now we think the owner wants it back."

"The owner wants it back? Of course he's going to want it back.." Bridget suddenly had a light bulb moment. "Jesus, Mary, Mother of God, that's what the to-do at the house was all about! Here's me thinking that Nick couldn't take care of you and all the time it's you pair of daft buggers bringing trouble to his door. Well, that takes the bloody biscuit. So help me girl, you get more and more stupid the older you get! Go on, tell me how it came about."

"Well," said Sam.

"I might have known you'd have something to do with this, 'cause this one here's got more hair than wit."

Erin blushed to her roots, "Muummm!"

"No wonder. Get on with the tale."

Taking a deep breath, Sam began her story. She explained how she hadn't been paid and had helped herself to the contents of the safe.

"I don't agree with it, but you were well within your rights," commented Bridget. "So how is it that the bloody Russian Mafia are after the two of you?"

Erin continued with the remainder of their story, finishing with their trip to the bank after Sam's apartment had been ransacked.

"What are we going to do, Mum. Should we try to give it back?"

"What?" exclaimed Sam, "No chance, not when we've come this far."

"And how far exactly do you think you've come?" asked Bridget indignantly. "Please forgive me if I don't want my daughter and grandson found floating face down in the pool. 'Cause believe me, that is a very distinct possibility. We have first-hand knowledge of how these guys work."

"Should we go to Nick? After all it was his place that got turned over and he thinks it's him they're after."

"No, he's a good guy and we would never have got Ryan back without his help, but he's too far in with the Russians for my liking. No, I think we leave things just are they are until your dad comes over next week."

"What about Sam? She can't stay in her place on her own," ventured Erin.

"I don't suppose she can, and we certainly don't want anyone else involved. She'll have to stay here, but not a word to Errol or your granny. We'll tell them she's had a fall-out with her boyfriend and he's kicked her out."

"Thanks, Bridget, and I'm sorry we've brought all this trouble to your door, especially in your condition."

"I'm pregnant, not dying," the older woman replied. "Now go and get your stuff while I get a room ready. And by the way, leave the safety deposit key here."

Sam reluctantly handed it over.

# Man to Man

"I'm telling you, it couldn't be easier," said Cortellessa, doing his best to convince his buddy that this plan to dispose of the Coyles, was foolproof. "Listen, it's too easy for words. The two brothers have been staying at their mother's gaff since the family took off for Spain."

Cortellessa outlined his scheme. "They usually come rolling home around two in the morning. So we give them an hour or so then strike. Roast two birds with one match." Genaro laughed at his own joke.

"Sounds kosher enough," Davey Junior replied, "but we're done for if it goes wrong."

"We're done for anyway, mate, if we don't fry them. It's all or nothing, Davey. You want to be El Supremo and I want my turf back, so what else is there? Once the Coyles know for sure it was us and not the Ruskies who executed the bird, we're dead. They'll come after us with everything they've got. Torching the house is the surest and easiest way of disposing of them.

Davey Senior arrived at the Horseshoe Bar alone. No Junior, no lieutenants, no back up. Alone. He had to sort this out, man to man with the Coyles. It was his only chance to save his son's skin and, possibly his own.

If the rumours had reached Thomson's ears, it didn't take a Philadelphia lawyer to work out that the Coyles had heard them too. Yet, despite his warning, Junior had still persisted in throwing his lot in with the Russians.

Davey could understand Cortellessa's situation, but his idiot son? What the fuck was he playing at? What had he to gain? The boy had everything – money, women, fast cars and a lifestyle every young guy in Glasgow would die for, but still the pup wanted more. He was a greedy little fucker. Second-in-command wasn't good enough, no, Junior wanted to be Cock of the Walk, number one.

Thomson recognised his son and his mate were more than capable of removing him and taking over the firm, but he also knew that the subtleties of leadership were way beyond either of them; they wouldn't last five minutes. Everyone knew Thomson was a mad bastard, and, like Paddy Coyle, he was old school; he respected and rewarded his workforce. He knew, without them he was nothing but a back street fighter. He also knew that within days of Junior taking over, the crew would dump him, if he was still alive at that point. The kid had made a lot of enemies; he'd also disrespected a number of influential people who would take great pleasure in seeking their revenge.

The main problem was that both his son and his mate were impatient. They wanted everything and they wanted it now. They were not prepared to wait and learn their trade. Any stupid fool could brandish a gun and shoot their way out of a situation; but the clever man talked his way out. Davey knew the only way his son could take over was by taking him out. He also knew his beloved son would not give that a passing thought. Neither boy had any family loyalty, it was them or him and he knew who *his* money would be on.

105

*

"On your own, Davey?" Paddy remarked. "It's not like you to travel light. I've seen you with half a dozen heavies just to have a pee."

"Walls have ears, Paddy, and there are far too many stories circulating for my liking."

"True, Davey, true. From what I've heard, most of the rumours are about you and yours."

"Really?" Davey Thomson, for once in his life, was floundering out of his depth.

"Yes, really, Davey. Shame you haven't brought Junior along, we could have put all this nonsense to bed, once and for all."

"What's Junior got to do with anything? Last week you were hailing him as the hero of the hour and now you're calling him in? I don't think so! You've no jurisdiction over me or mine."

"True, but when a young pup like Junior and that daft mate of his are taking the piss… Well, what would you do, Davey?"

"I'd leave well alone and let his chief sort things out."

"I couldn't agree more." The Big Man leaned across the table and stared straight into Davey Thomson's face, a gaze braver men than Thomson had wilted under, "But you and I know that's not happening, Davey, is it? You're not sorting things out. Your son, your second-in-command, is parading around Glasgow in the company of two Muscovites, doing all but singing the Red fucking Flag. Am I right, Michael?" Paddy turned to his brother for confirmation.

"You're right, Paddy," replied Michael.

"It seems to me you're losing your grip, Davey. Things are getting more than a bit out of hand. Maybe you're getting past it, mate? Could it be time to hand over the reins?" Paddy asked provocatively

Infuriated by Paddy's remarks, but desperately trying to keep hold of his infamous temper, Davey snarled back at him. "You cheeky cunt, Coyle, who the fuck do you think you're talking to? I was running the biggest firm in the city before you were even born."

"Maybe so, old man, but you're not running it now, are you? Between that stupid cunt of a boy and Ivan the fucking terrible, you've been sidestepped. You've been quite content to sit back, read the papers and let them do the donkey work. Well, they fucked up big time when they took on the Coyles. That includes you. Ignorance, my friend, is no excuse."

No-one had dared threaten Davey Thomson in years and he sure as hell wasn't going to stand for it now. Paddy Coyle or no Paddy Coyle, he pulled out a lethal piece of armoury and, aiming it at the eldest brother, smirked, "Not so cocky now, are we? Any more of your pish and I'll blow your fucking brains out."

Completely unperturbed by the threats, Michael grabbed the weapon from Thomson and yelled. "Have you any idea how many cops are out in the main bar? You idiot," he snapped. "You do know you've just sealed your fate, Davey? No-one, not even a mad bastard like you, gets away with pulling a gun on me. Here's the situation. Unless you hand over Junior, Cortellessa and the whereabouts of those two Russian pricks in the next forty-eight hours, we're coming for you. Understand? Now get out before I get angry."

"So much for sorting things out," Davey muttered to himself as he left the busy bar. Christ, how had it come to this? His fucking temper, that's how. As usual, Davey

Thomson had let his temper get the better of him. He'd fucked up big-style and there was no going back. As things stood, he had forty-eight hours to muster an army, or fly the white flag, and that was never going to happen

Despite his churning guts, Davey Thomson walked out of the meet with his head held high. Those fuckers would never know how worried he actually was.

This was all down to Junior, but he was his son and no-one, not even a Coyle would interfere between a father and son. Fuck it! It was years since he'd had a good fight and he had been one of the best in his day. By God, if he was going down, he'd take a few with him.

"Well, how do you think that went, bro'?" Paddy looked at Michael.

"Exactly as I expected. There's no way Thomson would give up his son. But as for the other dude and the Russians, he'd do it without a second thought, especially if it were to get Junior off the hook, but he's too far up that Russian's arse to plead innocence. No, we've got a fight on our hands and I for one can't wait."

Paddy Coyle had never known his young brother to relish a battle, but he was a changed man.

# Stalker

"I'm telling you, he's been stalking me for days. It was Errol who first noticed the guy. He's convinced he's your ex, the fictitious one, the one who supposedly dumped you."

"Where? I can't see anyone," Sam scanned the marina. "You're paranoid. There's no-one except a couple of crew members and I know them," Sam waved to the persons in question.

"Look, over by the fountain, that's him. The guy wearing the baseball cap."

"Fuck, Erin, how can you possibly identify him from that distance?"

"It's him, and I'm positive it's the guy who was caught on camera breaking into the villa. Who else could it be?"

"You did say your father was having problems back home, hence the reason the family was shipped over here."

"Naw. This too much of a coincidence. We knock off a stash and all of a sudden a vicious-looking Russian is on our tail?"

"We don't know that for certain."

"I don't care what you say, I told you from the beginning we had to keep Ryan out of the picture. I don't give a monkeys about the money. I'm calling Nick and I'm not moving off this boat till he gets here." Erin thanked heaven Nick had insisted she carry a cell phone at all times.

"Nick, it's me. I'm on the Lady Di with Sam and Ryan. I think we're being followed."

"Where's Simon? Nick asked.

"I don't know. I think he had another charter this week."

"So where's the guy right now?"

"Over by the fountain."

"Okay, act naturally. Go into the stateroom and lock the door. I'll be there in five minutes."

The line went dead.

"Did you hear what he said?" Erin asked Sam.

"Yes. Let's do what he says, although I think you're being paranoid. If he turns out to be just someone waiting for a friend, we won't need to tell Nick about the money."

"So we just tell him a lovesick Russian has taken a shine to one of us? Behave yourself girl."

The roar of Nick's Ferrari could be heard approaching the marina.

"Where is he?" asked Nick, jumping out. "I can't see anyone."

"He's gone. If he has been following me, he'd definitely recognise your car and take off."

"Can you describe him?" Nick questioned both women.

"He looked Russian," ventured Sam. "You can just tell. They have a look, if you know what I mean."

"That's not much to go on, especially when there are God knows how many thousands of Russians in town. I better get on to your dad, Erin. He's been worried they would come after you here, although he did think it would be safer than at home. Obviously not. Until I hear from him, it's back to full security, and as for you," he spoke directly to Sam, "you stay around Erin and Errol, no flitting around town until I get a handle on this. It's far too dangerous."

"I thought my dad was coming here at the weekend?" Erin asked.

"Things are hotting up over there and it looks like he's going to have to postpone his trip for a bit."

The two girls exchanged glances, this wasn't good.

As Nick did a quick check round the Lady Di, Erin whispered to her co-conspirator, "Let's speak to my mum and then we'll decide what to do."

Watching from the deck of an unoccupied charter, Alexei recognised Nick the Greek, and no matter what his boss demanded, he was not taking this guy on.

"So soon, my friend? What has happened?" The Russian boss welcomed Nick back into his inner sanctum.

"I've brought the shot of the intruder as you requested, but just after I left here this morning I had a call from Erin and her friend. They were on board the Lady Di and convinced they were being tailed. Erin was sure it was this guy." Nick handed the photograph of Alexei across the table to his business partner.

Watching intently, Nick was sure Sergei recognised the man in the photograph.

"He looks vaguely familiar, but I come across so many faces, I can't be sure. However, we'll circulate this. Someone is bound to come up with a name. In the meantime, do you want me to post security guards?"

"Thanks, but that's all taken care of."

"While you are here, there is the question of the two comrades who were running the sales office. How do we get them out of jail? The office is closed and it is costing us money."

"What do you propose? Can we bail them out?"

"They are both foreign nationals and as such, must stay on remand. It could be months before their case comes to trial."

"Surely if we close down the operation there will be no charges to answer? We can offer compensation to those involved, if they withdraw their complaint. There is more than enough cash to cover such costs."

"There lies the problem, my friend. There are no funds to do as you suggest. The safe was empty."

"That's not possible. I personally did an audit a few weeks ago and there have been no major expenses since then. Those two must have helped themselves to plenty."

"My first thought also, but if that was the case, why would they hang around? They couldn't have predicted they would get caught up in the raid and trust me, they would never steal from me. They know what the consequences would be. It is unthinkable."

"So who else had access to the safe?"

"No-one as far as I know. There was a female sales negotiator and a couple of promoters, but they would not be privy to such information."

"What about the woman, what do we know about her?"

"I was about to ask you the same question, my friend."

"I never met her. I only visited the office out of hours. The fewer people who knew of my involvement, the better."

"So we know nothing of her?" asked Sergei.

"No. She was hired by them and if she's responsible, she'll be long gone. Who in their right mind is going to empty a safe of at least half a million and flash it around town? I hate to say it, but I think we can say goodbye to that little birdie."

"It's not like you to wave goodbye to that kind of money, Nick. I thought you'd be tearing about town screaming for blood."

"Under normal circumstances, yes I would, but there are too many other things going on, and anyone even smelling of corruption is being banged up. I sure as hell don't intend to land in that hotel."

"You are absolutely sure you never saw this woman?"

"Definitely not."

What a pity, my friend, the Russian thought to himself. Either Nick was a blatant liar and had stashed the loot, or he was a fool. Whatever the truth, Nick was finished. Their business partnership, going back at least ten years, was over, and Sergei Romanov would not tolerate failure.

Shaking hands, as Nick rose to leave, the Russian bent forward and kissed his now ex-partner on the right cheek. Nick knew at once he was being warned, but why?

# All Fired Up

Junior, with Cortellessa in tow, was last to respond to the summons from Davey Thomson.

"What the fuck is he doing here?" Pointing at Cortellessa, Thomson challenged his son. "This is family only."

"As far as I'm concerned he *is* family, so give it a rest, Dad."

A few of the men grumbled at the Italian's presence, but most were more anxious to discover why they had been dragged from their comfortable, easy earners.

"I had a meet with the Coyles this afternoon," Thomson Senior informed his soldiers. "It seems they don't like us anymore, just like the Italians," and looking directly at Genaro he continued, "they intend to take us over and have the whole city under their control."

There was no way Thomson could divulge the real reason for the ultimatum, his boy and his mate would be thrown to the wolves without any hesitation.

"We have forty-eight hours to surrender and fly the white flag. No chance. So who's with me?" he challenged his men

"That Paddy Coyle is too big for his fucking boots," remarked one codger.

"Yeah, I agree, but he can back it up. Look at the manpower he controls," said another. "Thanks to that stupid fucker," he pointed to Cortellessa. "You just lay down and let him walk over everything your father worked for."

Thomson surveyed the room with dismay. Christ, it was like *Dad's Army*. Apart from the two sons there was no-one under the age of sixty. They were a bunch of pensioners, not the squad of fearless villains they'd once been. How the fuck were they going to take on the Coyles? They'd be slaughtered.

Oh no, he thought. What the fuck is that numbskull about to embarrass himself with now? as Junior stood up to speak.

"By the end of this week the Coyles will be toast." Junior boasted.

"Toast? What the fuck are you on about, boy?" asked his father. "This is no time for pissing about and fairy tales. These guys mean business. If I don't give in to their demands they'll come after us big time."

"Trust me, Dad, we'll finish them off."

"And how do you plan to do that?" Davey Thomson sneered at the boy standing before him.

"We're going to torch his gaff."

"Who the fuck do you think you are? Fucking Guy Fawkes? Do you really think a couple of fireworks will finish off the Coyles? Go away, son, and let me think."

His face burning with humiliation, Junior marched out of the room, followed by his mate, to the ringing laughter of the old men.

"I'll show him, stupid old bastard," he ranted at Cortellessa. "He's a fucking dinosaur. We'd be as well hanging a white flag out the window now."

"There's no way that bunch of pensioners could take on the Coyles." Cortellessa agreed with his mate.

"What a fucking red face! Showing me up in front of that lot. He'll be sorry, trust me."

"Get hold of that wee drug dealer, the one that works on Lomond Crescent."

"Tommy Riley? What do we want him for?" Davey Junior asked, still seething at his father's remarks.

"He can give us the heads up when the two brothers are in the house. A couple of fireworks, my arse."


Tommy Reilly had spent one of the best afternoons he'd had in a long time. Sandra had been snoozing when he eventually arrived at the clinic. What a journey. It had taken three buses and a two mile walk to reach the place. He almost gave up, but he was desperate to see how his mother was coping.

He had no worries that these people would get his mam off the gear, but could they help her with her demons? They couldn't bring their Billy back and it was that loss that drove Sandra to the dark, dark place.

Watching her as she slept, a single tear ran down Tommy's cheek. For the first time since Billy had gone, she was peaceful. None of the desperate twitching and distress displayed by the drug-crazed soul she'd become the last time he'd seen her. And no matter what he felt about the Coyles, Paddy especially, Tommy knew in his heart his mother would not be alive today if it were not for him. But surely this was only payback? They'd taken his brother from him, so it was only right the Coyles be responsible for keeping his mum alive. One thing he was sure of, until she had completed the programme and was home, he would keep his nose clean, no way would he jeopardise her treatment. What happened afterwards, well only time would tell, but for now, things were on the up. Sandra was clean, optimistic, just how she'd been in the old days, the days before Billy disappeared.

# Decision Time

No matter what Imelda Gavin said, she couldn't get her brother to leave the confines of the small apartment since they had encountered Errol Coyle. She was almost stir-crazy. Between the intense heat and her brother's refusal to accompany her, even to church, she was at her wits end. How she hated this country and longed to go back to Ireland. To the cool, pleasant temperature and the lush green countryside. Not this harsh, dry concrete dessert, with semi-naked women parading themselves all day long. If only she could persuade Francis he would be perfectly safe back home, but he was a determined old beggar and up until now she couldn't budge him.

"Francis, I'm off to mass, won't you come with me? There won't be many about at this time of the morning and certainly none of those Coyles you're so afraid of."

"No, dear, I'm fine. I made my peace with God a long time ago, there's nothing he can do for me now," the ex-priest chuckled to himself.

"Well, why not come and have breakfast down by the marina?"

"No thanks, I'm not hungry. You go and have a nice morning. I'll stay here in the shade."

The shade! It was just after seven a.m. and the temperature was in the mid-eighties. Pulling on a shawl to cover her arms and a wide straw hat, Imelda set off to church, muttering to herself all the way there.

Enough was enough, she decided. She was going home, with or without him. She understood her brother's fear of the Coyles but commonsense decreed they were more likely to capture him here in Spain, than in the wilds of Galway. Just as she made that momentous decision, a youngster on a skateboard came flying round the corner, crashing into her.

"I'm sorry, missus, I'm really sorry," the young lad was trying to help Imelda to her feet, but it was obvious from her screams that something was very wrong.

Within minutes a small crowd of spectators had gathered. However, sussing she was English-speaking, the locals left the ex-pats to deal with the old woman while waiting for the ambulance to arrive

"It'll be here soon," one well-wisher advised.

"What's your name, dear?" asked the man who'd called for the medics.

"Imelda Gavin."

"Are you on holiday?" the man asked.

"Where are you staying?" asked another.

"I'm visiting a relative." The rest of the conversation was cut short by the arrival of the paramedics.

"Those bloody things should be banned," one of the spectators pointed to the skateboard.

Errol, sensing the attention of the crowd turning on him, mounted his board and took off as fast as he could.


"Granny, she told the ambulance man her name was Imelda Gavin and she was visiting a relative. Honest, that's what she said."

"Calm down, laddie. Who said what? And what were

you doing away over that side of the town anyway?"
Lizzie asked.

"Going to meet a mate." Errol lied quite easily to his
granny.

"At this time of the morning? Don't you lie to me, you
little monkey," she said as she clipped the boy sharply
round the ear.

"Ouch!"

"Now, what were you doing in that part of town and
so early?" his granny demanded.

Shamefaced, the boy admitted he'd been trawling the
area since the day he'd first seen the priest and his sister.

"I promise, Granny, I'm not making this up. Why
would I? She told the ambulance man her name was
Imelda Gavin and she talks just like the Canon did."

"So, what do you want me to do? I'm not taking on
the feckin' IRA and Auntie Bridget's in no fit state to be
traipsing round Spain looking for a dead priest."

"Come to the hospital, please. She definitely broke her
leg or hip or something, so she'll still be there. Please,
Granny."

"Errol, I'm not telling you again. There is no way
Canon O'Farrell could have survived. The man you saw,
and we've all come across him, is black, and unless the
Canon has joined the black and white minstrels, you've
got the wrong man."

"But…"

"No buts, my lad. Sit down and eat your breakfast,
I'm off to mass."

Errol pushed the plate away and stomped back to his
room.

"What's up with his lordship?" asked Sam, sitting
down and tucking into the boy's breakfast. "It's not like
him to be moody."

120

"He's not pleased because I won't trek halfway across town to check out that it was Imelda Gavin, the Canon's sister, who was admitted to hospital this morning."

"How does he know she was hospitalised?" Sam queried.

"According to him, he knocked her over with his skateboard."

"Could it be true?" Sam asked Lizzie. "He doesn't seem the sort to make up tales."

"Oh, I'm quite sure he knocked the bejesus out of some poor devil, but it wasn't that Irish harpie."

"How about if I go with him?" Sam volunteered. "I'm not doing anything in particular today."

"Do whatever you like, but I'm damned sure it's a waste of time. There's not many comes back from the dead, and certainly not looking like Al Jolson. Be my guest." And Lizzie headed off to church.

"She's having an x-ray," Sam told Errol, returning from the hospital reception. "So we know for definite that it was Imelda Gavin who was brought in this morning. It says so on the admission form. I doubt there are many Imeldas in Marbella, and certainly not one with a broken leg and other minor injuries. However, we need to get a look at her to confirm she is the housekeeper."

The two set off in search of the X-ray department.

"That's her Sam, definitely," Errol pointed to the sleeping woman on the guerney.

Digging into her voluminous tote bag, Sam produced a small camera and took two quick snaps just as the nurse came to collect her patient.

"We don't need to hang about here," said Sam. "*We* know it's her, but to convince your granny and Bridget we need to get these developed. C'mon, I know where we can have these done while we wait. What's your next move, Sherlock?" Sam teased the young lad.

"I don't know, but I do know Canon O'Farrell is here and he had something to do with my friend Billy's disappearance."

"We have to be careful, mate. If he thinks we've rumbled him, he'll disappear and you'll never find him."

"Should we tell my granny and Auntie Bridget?"

"Let's wait and see. It could turn out to be a false alarm. Maybe there are more brothers and sisters."

"That's what my gran says, but I know it's him. I don't know how he got like that, but I would recognise that horrible old sod anywhere. He was forever trying to touch us. All the altar boys hated him."

"Okay let's go and get these photos done."

Bridget and Lizzie had to admit the image of the sleeping woman was most definitely Imelda Gavin, Canon O'Farrell's sister and housekeeper.

"There's no getting away from it, it's her alright. I'm sorry, lad, it just seemed so impossible. What the hell is she doing here?" asked a disbelieving Lizzie. "Now, don't go jumping in at the deep end. We know it's her but there could be any number of reasons why she's here. I don't know how, but we still have to prove that an esteemed Irish cleric, who was lost overboard all that time ago, has turned up alive and kicking and is as black as the Earl of Hell's waistcoat. It's not possible."

"That's what you said about *her*." Errol pleaded with his gran.

"First things first, we have to find their address," said Sam.

"Go to the nearest Catholic church. What other reason would she have for being out and about that early? She would be on her way to mass when Errol ran her over," suggested Lizzie.

"Of course, let's go." Sam and Errol headed for the door.

The cool interior of the Santo Christo Church was a welcome treat from the scorching midday sun. Mass had just ended and the senior cleric was bidding his congregation adios.

"Father, I'm hoping you can help me," Sam addressed the man in Spanish.

"I'll try, daughter."

"An elderly lady was involved in an accident quite near here, early this morning. We believe she was on her way to mass when the accident occurred."

"Oh dear, is she all right?" The priest enquired. "What can you tell me about her?"

"Her name is Senora Imelda Gavin. She is small, slim, about sixty, grey hair and Irish."

"We have a few Irish ex-pats living around here. Senora Gavin has been a regular for the past few months."

Errol nudged Sam in recognition of the housekeeper's name.

"You wouldn't happen to have her address?" Sam continued. "We need to let her friends know what's happened."

"She lives with her brother in the Amarillo Apartment complex. I'm sorry, I don't know the number."

"Thank you, Father, that's a great help."

"How serious was the accident, was she badly hurt?" asked the concerned priest.

"She'll be fine. Thank you again, Father."

The two went in search of the apartment.

"Dear God," gasped Sam. "It'll take days." She looked at the huge complex. "There must be at least three hundred apartments. Now we know how they preserved their anonymity. How on earth are we going to trace O'Farrell?"

# Throwing Down the Gauntlet

Davey Thomson hadn't seen his son or his sidekick since the meeting the day before. Davey Senior had shipped in a couple of crews from the capital and recruited a fair number of new bodies to act as security. He was well protected, but he knew that to survive this takeover, protection wouldn't be enough. Maybe he'd get lucky and Junior and his mate would succeed in their arson attack, but he wasn't counting on it. Maybe he could renegotiate with the Coyles. There was no way he was waving the white flag, but with a big enough show of strength he could persuade them it wouldn't be in their favour to start a turf war. His men might not be in the first flush of youth, but no way would they lie down like the Eyeties. His boys would fight to the death. Sadly, Davey knew in his heart, that's exactly what it would be, to the death. He was beaten before he started. Did he really want to engage in conflict at his age?

"That little bastard's avoiding us," Junior snarled. "I told him to stay close by the telephone kiosk throughout the day."

"I take it there's still no reply?"

"Now he's back in Coyle's good books, he thinks he can disrespect us. Well, he's got another think coming," replied Junior. "We need this problem sorted out, pronto.

The longer we hang about, the more chance my dad has of fucking it up, or worse, surrendering to Coyle."

"We need to pay Riley a visit."

"What! Are you fucking mad? We can't just march into Coyle territory and capture the wee shit."

"What do you want me to do, send him a fucking letter? I'm beginning to think you're not up to this, Junior. We need to make a stand or forget it."

"Of course I'm up for it, but not a suicide mission. We need to take the Coyles out before we start any heroics."

"How do we get in touch with Riley, then?"

"Send in a couple of runners, get them to pick him up and if he's not around, they can at least do a recce and identify the house."

"As long as we know the address, they can stake the place out."

There had been at least five calls in the past hour; all, he suspected, from Davey Junior. Tommy was well aware of how much he owed him, but it would have to wait. He needed to make himself scarce while Sandra was undergoing treatment at the Coyles' expense. She *had* to finish the programme and there was no way that could happen without Paddy's finance. So, no matter how obliged and grateful Tommy was to Junior, he was staying way out of the picture.

"Are you not going to answer that?" one of Tommy's regulars complained. "Ma heid's bursting," the guy moaned, opening the door of the telephone box to the shrill ringing of the phone.

"Don't you fuckin' dare," Tommy bawled at the complainer. "In fact, piss off, you're getting nothing here."

126

"Sorry, Tommy, I was only trying to help," the customer grovelled.

"Piss off. I mean it. Go and get your stuff from someone who gives a fuck."

"Oh, Tommy, I didn't mean anything bad." Holding out his money he pleaded, "Please, I'm fucking jangling, mate."

Tommy grabbed the money and handed over the goods. It was then that he saw the blacked-out vehicle crawling into Lomond Crescent towards him.

Panic-stricken and amidst an angry hue and cry from his remaining customers, Tommy mounted Billy's trusted BMX and sped off. He had taken to using the bike as a means of a quick getaway, since it allowed him to weave in and out the close-knit streets. He pedalled like fury; no way was he hanging around. This didn't look like a social call.

"Hey, what the fuck's going on?" shouted the woman next in the queue.

"What're you playing at, ya bampot?" called another after him. "When are you coming back?"

Tommy Riley paid no attention.

This bunch of saddos were Tommy's livelihood and under normal circumstances he would have faced Goliath to keep them happy, but Sandra came first. As far as he was concerned the Coyles and the Thomsons could fight until hell froze over, but they would do it without his input. He'd lost one member of his family, he was damn sure he wasn't going to help lose another.

# Changed Days

From his vantage point on the seventh floor balcony of the multi-storey block, Tommy had a bird's eye view. There were several customers still hanging about in the hope he would return and the sinister vehicle had parked further up the crescent.

He had no intention of returning until the coast was clear. He knew it was bad for business, but so was being kidnapped or smacked around the head with a baseball bat. His family had suffered enough; he would sit this one out.

From time to time the vehicle would slowly drive out of the crescent only to return ten minutes later. Tommy was damned sure they were waiting for someone, that someone being him. At just before six p.m., the occupants of the car, obviously not wishing to make the acquaintance of the Coyles, pulled out of the crescent just as Paddy and Michael arrived. The brothers parked up and, as arranged earlier, called into number twenty-six.

"That was a tasty bit steak, Theresa. Don't ever let on to Ma, but it was as good, if not better than her legendary fry-up."

"Aye, she's not bad with the old frying pan is our Theresa." Peter agreed, holding court in the huge orthopaedic bed he had occupied for as long as either Coyle could remember.

"Away you go," Theresa blushed to the roots of her steel-grey hair. "It was nothin', and you're right, don't tell Lizzie, she'd have my guts fir garters," the neighbour chuckled.

Theresa had always considered her cooking to be superior to her old friend's, but she would never have dared voice such an opinion. She was more than delighted that all the men agreed with her.

"They tell me you're after Davey Thomson and his mob," Peter addressed Paddy.

"And who might *they* be?" Paddy answered, none too impressed.

"I have my sources," confirmed the invalid, completely missing the warning tone in Paddy's voice.

"Well, Peter, I suggest you tell your sources to mind their own business and not to meddle in ours," said Paddy threateningly.

"Be quiet, Peter, the lads don't want to hear your drivel," Theresa warned her husband. "Don't mind him, boys, he's full of piss and wind." She gave Peter another glare.

"Thanks, Theresa, that was fit for a king. We'll see you in the morning."

Turning to the man of the house, both Coyle brothers nodded and took their leave.

"You know, if it wasn't for her I'd give him such a dig," said Michael.

"He's a fucking waste of space lying in that bloody huge bed while she still does three jobs to keep them afloat," agreed Paddy.

"There's bugger all wrong with the lazy scumbag, why does she stay with him?"

"The same reason Ma took Da back time after time, it's bred in them."

"Mm . . . Did you clock that motor when we arrived?"

"I did but I didn't recognise it."

"Nor me," answered Michael. "They didn't hang around after we pulled up. Interesting."

Lomond Crescent was decidedly quiet this evening, Tommy thought. A few of his regulars had turned up looking for a fix, but finding Tommy AWOL, they had wandered off elsewhere. No way was he going back out on the street tonight, he'd be like a sitting duck. No, he decided, for the first time since Billy had gone missing, he was having the night off. His ma was in good hands and if he lost customers tonight, so be it, they'd come back tomorrow.

"Fuck it," he muttered to himself, "I definitely deserve a break."

# Nocturnal Pastimes

"**D**on't speak to me, ya stupid old goat. What the hell were you thinking? Paddy and Michael only come about here because they can trust us," Theresa laid into her churlish husband. "They don't want to listen to you blabbing your big gob off about David Thomson as if he's your best pal. What the hell do you know anyway? Lying day after day, festering in that bloody great bed."

"I know far more than you give me credit for. I hear what's said and believe me, not everyone loves that pair of gobshites like you and your daft pal."

"Aye, maybe so, but you'd be far better keeping what you think you know to yourself."

"They'll get what's coming to them one of these days, mark my words."

"Perhaps, but in the meantime you won't be wanting any more of that best fillet steak you threw over your neck earlier?"

"Oh, I won't be rude and refuse their hospitality, but don't think I won't drop the buggers in it the first chance I get."

There was much more Theresa didn't know about her husband of forty years. For example, she didn't know that he wasn't bedridden, choosing to believe her man was a poor victim. She was also unaware that quite often, when she'd retired for the night, Peter had the full run of the house. Even more unbelievable, he would frequently take a stroll down Lomond Crescent into the estate and check out what was going down.

She definitely did not know that he had, on many occasions over the years, taken the bus into town. It was so long since any of his neighbours had clapped eyes on him, he was never recognised. In fact, many of the younger ones didn't believe he was still alive and were convinced Theresa had finished him off and buried the body in the back garden.

Theresa never suspected a thing. When her beloved fancied a night out, he would slip one of his sleeping pills into her evening cuppa and within half an hour she would be dead to the world for at least eight hours and absolutely nothing would wake her.

Furious at being shown up in front of his next door neighbours, Peter vowed he'd show them, he'd get the better of them all. He'd take a trip into the city, have a few drinks and whatever else came his way. But first, he had to see to his wife.

"Fix me up a drink, Teresa, I'm feeling bad tonight, you know I hate arguing," the pathetic inhabitant of the bed complained. "I need an extra painkiller and one of my sleeping tablets."

"I'm sorry, Pete, I don't like it either when we fall out." His wife was feeling guilty. "But you really should be grateful to those lads, they've always seen us alright."

"Don't get me started again, woman. Go and make us both a drink and forget about the Coyles for one night."

Theresa, glad to be back on good terms with Peter, returned a short time later with two steaming mugs of hot chocolate.

"Could I have a touch more sugar? It tastes a bit bitter." Peter got his wife out of the room and slipped the pill into her drink. All he had to do now was wait.

Splashing himself liberally with his favourite cologne, *Eternal* by Calvin Klein, Tommy was ready for the off. He'd always been a sharp dresser and for the first time in God knew how long, he was back in the game; a cocky young dude with plenty of swagger and a few quid in his tail. Hailing a cab, he was on his way. First stop the Provan Mill for a few liveners and then off into town.

"Tommo, long time no see." His schoolmate, Jamie, slapped him on the back.

"Hi, Jamie, yeah, I've been off the scene for a bit. Anyway," he looked around the deserted bar, "where is everybody?"

"Don't know, I just got here. I heard there's something big going down, but I'm keeping well away. I only just got out of the 'big hoose' and I've no intention of going back."

" Quite right."

"Hey, by the way, what have you done to upset Junior Thomson?" his old mate asked.

"Me? I've not done a thing. Why're you asking?" Tommy shivered.

"He just asked if I'd seen you. He didn't look too pleased when I said no."

"When was this?" Tommy asked.

"About ten, fifteen minutes ago."

"I'm sure he'll catch up with me if it's that important."

"Yeah," replied his mate, "no doubt he will." He headed for the payphone. The twenty quid on offer would come in handy.

Tommy had no intention of hanging around and was well on his way to his next haunt before Jamie had finished his call.

He was hardly over the threshold of the next hostelry when he was accosted by one of his better class of customer. "Hey, Tommy, got any gear on you?"

"Shut the fuck up, ya tosser. Why not take out an ad in the Evening Times?" Tommy moved quickly away from the big-mouthed idiot, but not far enough or quickly enough.

"What've you done to upset Junior? He's not at all pleased with you, wants me to phone him if I come across you. What do you think I should do, Tommy?"

"Do what the fuck you like. I'm not bothered by that wanker. Tell you what," Tommy said sarcastically, "I'll phone him and we can split the thirty between us."

"It was just twenty."

"He mustn't reckon much to your chances. He was offering thirty down the road."

Sniggering at the man's discomfort, Tommy headed for the city centre. It was no good hanging about here; he was bound to bump into Thomson or one of his compadres. Some night out this was turning out to be.

Peter, on the other hand, was having a banging night. He'd gathered up his stash; all the loose change he'd pilfered from Theresa over the past months. He was delighted to have amassed nearly twenty-five quid; more than enough for a good drink and a fish supper on the way home.

Cautiously leaving the house, checking Theresa was fast asleep and still snoring loudly, he caught the bus into town.

As he stood at the bar, enjoying his first pint in a long time, Peter soaked up the atmosphere. There was nothing to beat a Glasgow pub on a Saturday night. The noise, the smoke, the banter and the usual squabbles: two old codgers were squaring up to each other over a game of dominoes. There was a leery gang of young chavs, downing their American-style beers, before heading for one of the many night clubs Glasgow was famous for. No doubt most of them would end up in A & E.

I could be doing this every weekend, he mused to himself. Why did he persist with this charade? It had been okay to begin with, but now it was boring; no life at all. It was about time he made a change. Loath to admit, even to himself, how much he'd been affected by the way the Coyle boys had spoken to him – like he was a no-mark. They wouldn't have spoken to him that way a few years ago. No way. The young Peter would have kicked them up and down the street for fun. Now he was the joke and he knew it.

He would have to take it easy, mind. Recover bit by bit, make it believable. He could hardly pick up his bed and, like Lazarus, have a miracle cure. Ordering his second pint, the invalid made his decision. Tomorrow would be the last day he spent in bed. Well, he had to take into account he'd more than likely have a fucker of a hangover, but tomorrow would be the beginning of his fake recovery.

Shit, of all the bars. There, standing only a few feet away from him, was that poxy dealer from down their street; the one whose brother had gone AWOL. Hopefully the lad wouldn't recognise him. Christ, he was too old and too long in the tooth to be playing these daft games. He was right, he did need to sort things out.

What a night this was turning out to be, Tommy thought. He'd have been better staying indoors and watching *Casualty*. Fuck, if Thomson caught up with him he might end up in one of the episodes. Still no sign of any of his mates. There was no-one he recognised in the bar, except for one old geezer sitting over in the corner. He didn't look like one of his customers, but you could never tell what sorts turned up looking for some gear. But whoever he was, he certainly wasn't the company Tommy was looking for tonight.

"That's the second call about our missing pigeon," Junior reported, hanging up from the call. "First he was in the Provan Mill and then he was spotted not a million miles away, in the Caravel."

"Forget him for tonight, we don't need him," replied Cortellessa. "Is everything under control and double-checked?"

"One hundred percent."

"Good. We'll deal with him tomorrow. I've got a nice little surprise planned for that wee fucker."

# Spanish Ayes

It was almost lunchtime and Imelda had still not yet returned from mass. She was probably still sulking over his refusal to accompany her. He had no inclination to go anywhere these days and her constant badgering was becoming intolerable. Until he was sure the boy had been dealt with and was no longer a threat, he was staying put in the safety of his apartment.

"Sam, Sam look at this," Errol pointed to the mail box for apartment 2101.

The two intrepid investigators had spent a couple of hours the previous day checking out the names on the mailboxes in the apartment complex.

"What do you think? A bit of a coincidence, wouldn't you say?"

The name on the box for apartment 2101 read Cleland, the name of Canon O'Farrell's late partner in crime. Like most of the other mailboxes, number 2101 was not particularly secure and easily opened. Flicking through what was mostly junk mail, Sam came across two recent pieces of correspondence addressed to Snr Francis O'Farrell. Without hesitation Sam ripped open one of the envelopes.

"You maybe shouldn't have done that, is it not against the law or something?" Errol asked.

"I don't suppose he'll call the police on us, knowing what we know. Anyway this is just confirming a hospital appointment."

"So it is him?"

"Let's go grab a drink and look at what we know up to now." The two headed for Errol's favourite café.

Once their drinks had arrived, Sam produced a notebook and pen. "We know Francis O'Farrell, or someone who goes by that name, lives in apartment 2101. We also know that the sister of Francis O'Farrell lives in the same apartment. What are the chances of there being another brother and sister of that surname living in the complex?"

"Highly unlikely," answered Errol.

"How likely is it that some random tenants just happened to be in the apartment once owned by O'Farrell's business partner?"

"Highly unlikely."

"What we don't know is how the Canon survived when he was lost overboard. Could he have swum back to shore?"

"Christ, Sam, he must be about a hundred, could someone his age swim that distance?"

"I wouldn't think so, but more to the point, this man is black and no matter what we say, there was definitely not a black priest in Glasgow."

"So is it him or not?"

"I don't know, but the pros outweigh the cons."

"So what do we do now?" Errol asked. "Should we go and knock on the door?"

"That's the one thing we don't do. He is one seriously dangerous man."

"He's ancient."

"Maybe so, but he's an evil man with nothing to lose. So, no heroics, no going off on a mission. We need help with this. I think we need to speak to Erin and Nick."

The boy agreed, but Sam could tell from his appearance he wasn't convinced.

"Don't underestimate this old guy. If we've sussed *him* out, the chances are he's done the same. Think. Who were you with when you first came across him?"

"Granny."

"Exactly, and both the priest and his sister know exactly who she is. We could be putting both her and Bridget in danger."

"Okay, I promise I won't do anything stupid. Uncle Paddy would skin me alive if anything happened to either of them."

"Good lad. We'll get him if we all work together. Now let's find Erin."

The pair would not have been quite so confident had they been aware of who was watching them from a balcony on the second floor.


"Sergei, what the devil is going on? I thought you were going to get rid of the boy?" O'Farrell barked down the line at the Russian.

"It's in hand, my friend. I gave you my word, did I not?" answered the gangmaster, one of the most powerful men in Marbella.

What was wrong with this old man? Had he, Sergei, not given his word that the boy would be dealt with? Yet this nobody, this insignificant cleric, who had more than outgrown his usefulness, dared to question him.

"The boy and his accomplice are outside my building as we speak."

"Have they seen you or traced your exact location?" the Russian demanded.

"I don't think so, but it is only a matter of time," answered the priest. "They're only yards from my apartment. I can't afford for them to get any closer and, as I told you, I certainly have no intention of spending my last days in a Spanish jail."

"Don't panic. Where is your sister?" Sergei spoke calmly and quietly to his caller.

"I don't know. She hasn't returned from mass this morning. I thought she was annoyed with me because I wouldn't accompany her, but now I'm not so sure."

"Pack a few necessities, someone will come to collect you." The line went dead.

There was something in the Russian's tone of voice that set off alarm bells. Sergei wasn't a man to mess with and O'Farrell knew he'd overstepped the mark. He had not shown the usual respect necessary when dealing with these over-inflated egos. Perhaps calling him had not been the best idea.

"Simon, it's Francis O'Farrell here, how are things?"

The captain of the Lady Di and he had been friends for many years. They had enjoyed many a trip in the old days when the Macks had been the darlings of the Marbella set.

"Good God, sir, it's a long time since I heard your voice." Christ, he'd almost said he thought the old man was dead.

"I've been out of circulation for a while, my boy, dickie heart."

"Sorry to hear that. Is there something I can help you with?"

"As a matter of fact, there is. I want to hire the Lady

140

Di for a week or two. I just want to get away for a while to relax."

"You know it belongs to the Coyle girl now? She spends most of her time down here so she might not go for it. I could always rustle up something similar."

"I'd prefer the Lady Di. I know my way around her."

"I'll see what I can do."

"Tell her you've got a last minute charter. She won't suspect a thing. I'll pay the going rate, of course."

"Okay, but I have to be back in port by Saturday, there's a family party organised on board. When can I expect you?"

"Within the hour."


"Boss, it's Simon. I thought you might want to know, I've just had a call from the old priest, Snr Cleland's partner. He wants to charter the Lady Di, says he wants to get out of town for a bit."

"Thank you, Simon, you did right. Keep me posted and don't let him disappear." Sergei hung up.


What was he going to do about Imelda? He couldn't hang around. He had to leave now, time was marching on. No matter what had happened over the years, his sister had always stood by him, had his back, she'd certainly never taken off in a strop. Something had to have happened, but what? Had she had an accident or been taken ill? Whatever the reason, right now he had no choice. If he stayed, either the Coyles or Sergei's mob would catch up with him. It would not fare well for him, whoever found him. Once he got aboard the Lady Di he would work out a plan. It was imperative he leave immediately.

# Old Pals

"**F**uck!" Peter exclaimed. "Look at the time."

"Aye, doesn't it fly when you're having fun?" His old workmate laughed.

He had been so anxious to avoid the wee drug dealer earlier in the evening that he'd walked slam bang into Dougie Wilson, an old workmate from way back.

"Christ, I was sure you'd popped your clogs years ago," Dougie had exclaimed. "Where have you been hiding all this time?"

"I don't keep so well, Dougie. I don't know if you remember I had an accident?" Peter answered in his most solemn, droll voice.

"Jesus, man, you're not still milking that shite? it must be fifteen years since that happened."

"Sixteen, to be precise."

"Didn't you get a decent lump of compensation?"

"It didn't last for long, not with my wife."

"So you've been on the sick? Collecting for all these years? Lazy bastard," Dougie said grudgingly.

The two old mates blethered and reminisced throughout the evening, recounting story after story. Peter had forgotten how enjoyable life could be. The time flew past and the beer went down sweetly. The strident ringing of the bell followed by the barman bellowing

"Last orders," announced closing time.

"Well, Peter, it was good meeting up after all this time. We should do it again soon, with some of the other lads."

"I'm not ready for home yet," Peter moaned, having had his first proper night out in ages.

"Fancy a couple of cans back at mine?" offered his mate.

Double-checking his watch, Peter could hardly believe it was almost two in the morning. He'd missed the late bus and he most certainly couldn't wait for the early morning shuttle. Theresa, pill or no pill, would be up and about before too long, heading for early mass. He was going to have stump up for a cab. Still, he'd had a brilliant night out. Once he got his act together this could be a regular occurrence, as long as he kept her ladyship in order

Peter wasn't the only one having to stump up for a cab home. Tommy, having managed to cop off with a good-looking wee bird, looked like he was on a promise. But she was obviously a veteran at conning blokes into paying her taxi fare because, on arrival at her place, she niftily nipped out of the cab without as much as a snog.

It hadn't been the most successful of evenings, but at least he'd managed to avoid Junior and his mate, he reflected as he stepped out of the taxi.

"Shit," he yelled as he was almost flattened by a speeding car roaring out of Lomond Crescent.

"You alright, son?" The taxi driver asked.

"Only just," Tommy answered.

That was a close shave. Surely they weren't out looking for him at this time of night? He was positive it was the same vehicle that had been parked here all afternoon.

What was that smell? Jesus, Mary, Mother of God, Theresa's house was on fire and the smell of petrol was overwhelming.

Hammering next door, Tommy managed to rouse Paddy.

"What the fuck's going on?" the Big Man roared at Tommy. "It'd better be good, fucking wakening folk up this time of the night."

"Next door is on fire, phone the fire brigade," yelled Tommy.

"What, who's on fire?" Paddy shook his head, still waking up.

"Theresa's. For fuck's sake, man, get a move on."

There was no chance he could get into the house from the front, the door was well alight, the downstairs window had been smashed and the curtains were already ablaze. Fortunately, like most inhabitants of the street, few ever locked their back doors and Tommy gained access through the kitchen.

Soaking a towel at the sink, Tommy covered his head and charged through the ground floor of the house looking for either inhabitant. The big bed was already smouldering, but there was no sign of the invalid. Belting upstairs, he located the sleeping lady of the house.

"Theresa, Theresa!" Tommy yelled at her. "Theresa, wake up! The house is on fire. Come on," he shook the comatose woman. "Theresa, wake up, we have to get out."

"What's wrong?" She muttered, "What's the matter?" She was still well under the effect of the sleeping pill.

"The house is on fire, come on," Tommy encouraged her, "lean on me, you'll be okay."

"What about Peter, did you get him out?"

"Peter's not in the house, I checked."

"He's in the sitting room," she yelled hysterically. "He's in the big bed, he can't walk."

"Honest, Theresa, I checked. Let's get you out and I'll go back and check again."

"I'm not going without him," the older woman screamed at her rescuer.

"I promise, Theresa, but we have to get out now."

Wrapping the wet towel round her head, Tommy managed to half drag, half carry the woman down the stairs and out the back.

"Paddy, Paddy where's Peter?" Theresa clung on to her neighbour. "He's still in there, he has to be, he can't walk. Tommy, go and find him."

Paddy caught hold of the lad, "No, son, wait till the fire brigade get here, you've done enough. You're a brave lad and I won't forget what you did tonight."

The brigade soon had the blaze under control.

"There was no-one else in the house," reported the chief to a hysterical Theresa. "My men have searched the premises from top to bottom and I can assure you, the house is empty."

"It's not possible, Peter hasn't left this house in twenty years."

"Well, he's definitely not in there." The chief repeated.

"They must have kidnapped him," Theresa sobbed inconsolably. "What would they want with my Peter?" she wailed.

The whole street was now out watching the goings on.

"How did the fire start, officer?" Michael asked the chief.

"It was petrol-bombed. Look, you can see the trail from here," the fire chief pointed out traces of petrol. "It wasn't a particularly professional attack," he continued. "If they'd been serious they would have done the back and front and no-one would have got in or out. Thank God the young guy was on his way home. He saved that woman's life, without a doubt. Is there any reason you can think why someone would carry out such a deed?" He asked Paddy because he couldn't get any sense out of Theresa. She still refused to believe Peter had not perished in the fire.

"Come into ours." Paddy tried coaxing his mother's friend and neighbour into number twenty-eight.

"Why, Paddy? Why? What have we ever done to anybody?" Theresa pleaded. "Where's my Peter, what's happened to him?"

"Why don't you ask him?" Paddy watched the man in question alighting from a taxi and staggering his way towards the group of people gathered outside his home.

Fuck, what were all those firemen and cops doing in the street?

Fuck, what was up with Theresa, weeping and wailing? He could hear her from here.

Fuck, it was their house, what happened?

Fuck, how was he going to get out of this mess?

It was after four a.m. before the last of the response teams drove off.

"What are we going to do, Paddy? I've lived in that house for thirty years. Everything's gone all my memories, my things. What am I going to do?" Theresa was inconsolable.

The reality of the situation was beginning to sink in. "Oh God, we'll be moved to heaven knows where, and Peter, what's going to happen to him? The social will crucify him, he'll get done for fraud, oh Paddy."

146

"It'll all look better in the morning," said the Big Man. "Don't you worry, we'll sort things out. Go on up to Ma's room and try and get a bit of sleep."

"I don't think I'll shut my eyes ever again," she wailed as she climbed the stairs to the safety of Lizzie's room. "If only she were here, Lizzie would know what to do."

"You should have gone to get checked out." Paddy told Tommy as he handed him a glass of brandy.

"I'm fine, just singed about the edges."

"Did you see anything, lad?"

"A black 4x4 roared out of the street as I was paying the taxi, fucker nearly flattened me. I'm sure it was the same one that was parked up in the crescent this afternoon."

"Did you see who was in the vehicle?"

"No, it happened so fast. But I did get the number plate earlier."

"Good lad, but I would be surprised if they're not false. Did you see anything else?"

"Nope, sorry."

"Get yourself home and try to get some sleep. As I said earlier, you're a brave lad and I won't forget this night. You saved Theresa's life. How's your ma, by the way?"

"She's coming on fine, thanks. I'll get off home."

All this while Peter had been sitting quietly in the corner, contemplating how he would play the situation.

"Oi, Lazarus," Paddy turned his attention to him. "What have you got to say for yourself?"

"Well, laddie," Peter knew he was taking a big chance here, "we all know this present was delivered to the wrong address. It was meant for twenty-eight not twenty-six. Let's face it, boys, the only Russians me 'n' Theresa ever come in contact with are Comrades Smirnoff and Vladivar and with our income, not very often."

"Maybe so, but if you hadn't been out on a pub crawl, the fire wouldn't have had a chance of spreading."

"And I'd have been burnt to death," the man exclaimed.

"Don't be so fucking stupid, we all know you can walk."

"How long have you kept up this deception?" challenged Michael.

"Years. Well before your Sean passed away. It was his idea. He rumbled me one night, walking about the living room and he thought it was hilarious. He used to take me out regularly, well, until he lost the plot over that wee lad's brother."

He could see he had taken Paddy and Michael aback over his revelations; it was time to play his ace, it was all or nothing.

"Oh, I know most of what happened back then, it would be a shame if Lizzie's memory of her laddie was tarnished even more."

"Don't try blackmailing us, Peter, or believe me, you won't live to regret it."

"Listen, if I was going to shoot my mouth off I'd have done it long before now. All I want is the house fixed and me and the wife can get back to normal. Believe it or not, I'd decided to come clean. I was going to tell her over the next few days."

"Of course you were," sneered Paddy.

"I know you don't believe me, but it's true."

"This conversation is to be continued, but right now, I for one could do with some kip." Michael ushered his older brother out of the room.

"Oh, Paddy, look at the place," the older woman sobbed. "Who would do such a thing? Me and Peter have lived in that house for over thirty years. Now it's all gone. All my things, all my memories. What's going to happen to us? Oh, Paddy, I can't believe anyone would hate us that much. We could have been killed in our beds."

Only one of you, thought Paddy Coyle wryly.

"I know it looks bad, but we've had a talk this morning and Michael has a contact in the council who will get this moving right away. In the meantime, Peter's going to stay with us and you're going with me to visit Lizzie and Bridget."

"That's awful good of you, son, but I can't leave Peter, or you and Michael for that matter. Who would cook and clean? It's nice of you to offer but I have to say no."

"Listen, Peter's fine and we'll manage, maybe not as well as when you and Ma are here, but we'll be fine. Anyway, you'd be doing me a favour. Once word gets out, neither Lizzie nor Bridget will believe you're okay until they see you face to face and I can't be doing with them threatening to come home and kicking up a fuss. So will you come with me?"

"Well, if you put it like that. Are you absolutely sure?"

# Disclosures

"The priest and the money are completely separate issues, Erin," pleaded Sam. "Nick doesn't have to know. It's what we do about O'Farrell that interests me."

"Grow up, Sam, of course he does. If you think for one minute I'm sending my man off to do our dirty work without all the facts, you're worse than stupid."

"You were well up for this at the start. In fact it was your suggestion."

"I'm well aware of my involvement and I can't believe how idiotic I've been but, I told you from the start, the minute Ryan was in any danger it was a different ball game. So, either I tell Nick everything, or you're on your own.

Pacing back and forth on the terrace, running his hands through his hair, Nick Stasinopoulos was completely unable to process the tale his girlfriend and her sidekick had lain bare.

"Have you any idea what you've done, or how serious this is?" he demanded. "For a start, in one fell swoop you've destroyed a ten year business partnership, probably lost me millions into the bargain and made it look like I've betrayed the trust of my friend. How the hell did this happen?"

"It was my fault," volunteered Sam. "I'd been working for a consortium of Russian property developers. I worked my ass off, made loads of sales, but never got paid. Always, it was the bank, or suppliers, excuse after excuse. I knew how much was in the safe, so I helped myself to what I was owed, that was the day Erin came to my rescue."

Good God, he'd actually witnessed the whole episode but, being too interested in Erin's safety, he hadn't paid any attention to Sam's attackers.

"There was a damn sight more than a couple of thousand pesetas in that safe, as well as important documents."

"How do you know what the safe contained?" Erin's ears pricked up.

"Never you mind what I know or don't know."

"Anyway, we went back the next day and emptied the safe."

"Where are the contents now?" Nick asked.

"In a safety deposit box in the Bank de Seville."

"Have you any idea how serious this is?" Nick flopped down on a chair. That's why this place was turned over." he said incredulously.

"My place as well," agreed Sam.

"Christ, it wasn't some crazed boyfriend terrorizing you. By the time this situation plays out you might well hope that it had been. When a contract is put out, the deal is kill or be killed. In other words, whoever is after you knows that if he fails, he will pay with his own life, so he has nothing to lose."

"Would it help if I returned the money personally?" volunteered Erin.

"No, and don't think you can use your father's name.

Paddy has no status here. In fact, it would make me seem even less of a man. In Sergei Romanoff's eyes, if I can't run my home and control those close to me then I do not deserve to be his partner or friend. It's the code they live by and Romanoff has been insulted irreparably."

"I'm so sorry, Nick, I don't know what else to say or do," said a contrite Erin.

"Quite frankly, neither do I."

# Behind Closed Doors

"Hello is that Marie Coyle?"

"Yes, who's speaking?" Marie snapped.

"Listen and don't interrupt. I have a message for your brothers. The two Russians responsible for the woman's death are holed up in Spittle Farm, on the way to Loch Lomond, three miles north of Drymen. Have you got that?"

"Paddy's not here, he's out of the country," answered Marie.

"Well, you better get him back because they won't hang around. . ."

The line went dead and Marie couldn't make up her mind if the call had been genuine or a hoax. It was strange that the caller had made no mention of the reward offered by Michael, which would lead her to believe the call was kosher. What should she do? Paddy had enough on his plate in Marbella, and no way could she give this information to Michael. Although her poor brother appeared to be dealing with his grief, he would be unable to resist going after them, with or without Paddy. This could tip him over the edge. No, she would deal with this herself. For years she had bemoaned the fact that her brothers didn't take her seriously, and since the first contact with these guys, Paddy had upped the security surrounding her to a ridiculous level; she might as well put them to good use.

"The wrong fucking house, you got the wrong *house*? I can't believe it," Davey Thomson doubled over with laughter. "Not only did you torch the wrong fucking house, you even managed to screw that up."

The two conspirators stood shamefaced at the derision levelled at them by Davey Senior.

"Number twenty-six? Everybody and his dog knows old Ma Coyle lives at number twenty-eight Lomond Crescent. Fuck, if you'd asked me, *I* could have told you. But no, you pair of plastic gangsters sit about all day staking the joint and still get the address wrong."

"Da! Give us a break," whined Davey's son. "Anyone can make a mistake."

"Give you a break? What a pair of clowns. You couldn't organise a piss-up in a brewery. Not only did you get the wrong house, you didn't have the nous to do it properly. Any self-respecting arsonist knows to do the back first and then the front of the building, that way there are seldom any survivors. I swear to God, it's Dumb and Dumber. I don't know who's the thickest."

"You wouldn't speak to us like that if you knew . . ."

Cortellessa, concerned Junior was about to blow the whistle on their activities, interrupted his mate, "Sorry, Davey, we cocked up big-time."

"What were you about to tell me, son? What amazing piece of skulduggery have you two performed that will make us all fall at your feet in admiration?"

"Nothing," said his sullen son, backing out of the room.

"That's it, I'm done," Junior ranted. "I can't take any

more from that old bastard, I'm going to finish him off once and for all. Fuck Paddy Coyle, he can wait. I'm not being treated like a fucking idiot by anyone, far less my old man."

"Calm down, Junior, you know what he's like. Remember, he's your da and he's worried about Coyle. Leave him be, he'll cool down."

"No, he's gone too far. I'm taking over. He can go fuck himself – it's time!"

# Change of Abode

"Lizzie, oh, Lizzie, I can't believe I'm here, and in a private aeroplane too. It's so good to see you. With everything that's going on at home, I don't know how I would have coped. You'll never believe what's happened! Me and Peter got bombed."

"What!" both Bridget and Lizzie exclaimed at once.

"Aye, we got bombed and young Tommy Riley saved my life."

"Hey, is that my good frock you're wearing?" asked a peeved Lizzie, spotting her friend's attire.

"I'm sorry, Paddy said you wouldn't mind. It was the only thing that fitted me, all the rest were far too big."

Cheeky mare, thought Lizzie.

"Sit down, Theresa. Catch your breath and let's start at the beginning," demanded Bridget. Turning to her husband, she continued, "And as for you, I spoke to you just this morning and you never mentioned you were coming or that you were bringing a house guest."

"Sorry, it was all done in a rush," answered Paddy.

"Okay, so what happened? And I want the truth." Bridget glowered.

"Unbelievably, number twenty-six was fire-bombed and I've a good idea who was responsible," Paddy began. "I also figured a bit of time with you and Ma would do Theresa the world of good."

"How's Peter coping?" Lizzie enquired.

"Oh, he's fine. I don't know if it was the shock, but he's on his feet and running about like a scalded cat." Theresa boasted.

"Now why doesn't that surprise me?" Lizzie muttered. "Why on earth would anyone want to do you harm?"

Bridget and Paddy exchanged knowing glances. Paddy knew his wife had worked it out immediately. "I assume it was meant for number twenty-eight?" she whispered.

"Yep."

The couple left the two ladies deep in conversation as they made their way to the bedroom.

"I had a call from Nick just after I spoke to you. I don't know all the details, but it seems our beloved daughter has stirred up all sorts of bother."

"She's told him then?"

"Told him what?"

"It seems Erin and her sidekick, Sam – you remember Sam?"

"Of course I do, game girl."

"Too bloody game. The two of them relieved some Russian Mafia boss of his ill-gotten gains."

"What? No wonder Nick's worried, he does most of his business with them."

"I think you're going to have your work cut out sorting this one, Big Man." Bridget was delighted to have her husband back. "I have every confidence you'll come up trumps. You can charm the birds out of the trees when you put your mind to it, Paddy Coyle. I'm sure this Russian oligarch will be eating out your hand before you leave."

"I wish I had your confidence, sweetheart," Paddy

replied, gently patting his wife's swollen belly. "Christ, what a bloody mess. I want you and Ma home, but even with this lot going on it's safer here."

"We're fine, a bit crowded, but hey, it's never dull," Bridget laughed. "There's one other thing I need to talk to you about while I've got you here."

"Go ahead, but it'll have to be quick."

"O'Farrell's been spotted."

"What! Has he been haunting the place?" Paddy scoffed.

"I'm being serious, Paddy, look." She handed him the photographs of Imelda.

"That's his sister, so what?"

"Errol and Sam have seen him and know where he's staying. The sister is in hospital."

"It can't be him, it's not possible. Trust me, I know what happened to the old bastard and there is no way he could be alive."

"Paddy, I've said the same thing but nothing will dissuade the boy. What do you want me to do?"

"Nothing, absolutely nothing. Keep this to yourself, Bridget. O'Farrell was well in with these Russians and it's going to be hard enough to persuade them to back off, without adding him into the mix. If it is him, and I don't believe it is, I'll sort him out later and trust me, he won't escape a second time."

"Okay, take care, I'll make sure they back off. Keep me up to date."

"Will do." And Paddy left for his meeting with Nick.

# Patricide

"I fucking hate him. I swear to God, I detest the old bastard," Junior ranted as he paced furiously back and forth in the flat the two pals shared.

"For fuck's sake, mate, keep the noise down. You'll have the neighbours on our case."

"So fucking what?"

As a rule, they followed the old villain's code when it came to their home: never attract attention or keep anything incriminating indoors.

"I'm telling you, Genaro, I've had it. I won't be spoken to like I'm some kind of chav. I had hoped that when the time came we could just pension the old fucker off, send him to the Costas and let him enjoy his time in the sun. But he's gone too far this time, making a pure cunt of me."

"So what do you suggest?" asked Genaro. "Don't forget he's a tough old fucker, and what about the boys?"

"Fucking boys, are you having a laugh? The youngest is pushing sixty. Thankfully, he's had to recruit a new, younger squad to deal with the Coyles and as long as they're getting paid they won't give a fuck who's in charge."

"Why not pay the Russians to off him?"

"No, it has to be me. He told me himself the only way to gain control was to take it."

"So, when and how?" asked Genaro.

"Very soon."

For the first time in years there was serious discord in Davey Thomson's camp. Between the threat from the Coyles and Junior's massive fuck-up, there was a real possibility of a mutiny.

"You better watch your back, Davey," warned Jimmy MacAfee, Thomson's right-hand man. "I'm worried about Junior. He's got some temper on him and that pup he hangs around with is a bad influence."

"He's got a temper alright, but no balls. Don't you worry, he'll be sitting indoors right now crying his eyes out that Daddy was mean to him. He needs to toughen up, Jimmy, there's no room for nancy boys in this game."

"Well, I've warned you," MacAfee shrugged his shoulders and left. His gut instinct told him there would be repercussions over this.

"Hi, son, how are you this morning?" Michael Coyle asked the hero of the hour.

"Not too bad. It's some mess isn't it?" Tommy surveyed the damage done to number twenty-six.

"Nothing that can't be fixed, thanks to you. Peter's making a brew, fancy a cup?"

The three of them sat round the table in Lizzie's kitchen as if it was an everyday occurrence.

"Paddy about?" Tommy asked tentatively.

"No, son, he's away, won't be back till the weekend. Is there anything I can do?"

"It's about the fire. I think I know who did it."

"Go on," pressed Michael.

"I don't think it was the Russian dudes. I'm positive

it was Junior Thomson and Cortellessa, and I think they were looking for me."

"Why would they be looking for you, Tommy?" Michael appeared puzzled.

"Cos they reckon I owe them." Tommy hung his head.

"You owe them? How did that come about?" Michael's tone changed completely.

"I got a loan from them a few months back, when I had all the trouble with the Russians. I couldn't get hold of anyone, my ma had gone on the trot and I was desperate."

"Have you paid the loan off?" Michael asked.

"Weeks ago, but a condition of the loan was that I would inform on you and Paddy."

"That wasn't very clever, boy. So what exactly have you told them?"

"Nothing. Let's face it, Michael, what do I know? They were on the hunt for me all day yesterday, so I'm assuming they wanted me as a lookout or something."

"Are you sure you've not passed on anything to them?"

"Honest, Michael, what could I tell them?"

"Well, you've certainly done them no favours."

"There's something else, I take it you know my ma's in rehab and Paddy's footing the bill?"

"Yes, how is she?"

"She's clean and almost back to her old self. The only chance of keeping her off the shit is to get her as far away from here as possible. Every day she's reminded of our Billy. I need a proper job and somewhere to live. I was hoping you could help me."

"What about your pitch?"

"I can hardly keep her off the stuff if I'm punting it.

161

I've had enough, Michael. My mam was never like this before our Billy went missing."

Peter and Michael looked at one another, both thinking the same thought. Sean.

"I can't promise anything, but I'll do my best. What about your pitch for now?"

"I can't afford to throw in the towel so I'll work it till she gets out. But I'm worried those two might pay me a visit."

"Don't worry, lad, these two boys will do their best for you. Look what they're doing for me and Theresa," assured Peter.

Both he and Michael were well aware that it was because of Sean Coyle that the Rileys' lives were in pieces.

"Thanks, both of you."

"Any sign of trouble, phone me and I'll get it sorted."

True to his word Michael had the pitch under surveillance that morning and thankfully there was no sign of the two mates.

# Comrades in Arms

$P$addy had to admire Nick the Greek's standard of living. A beautiful front-line villa, only metres from the beach, set in magnificent gardens. His daughter had certainly fallen on her feet with this guy; if it lasted, of course. Nowadays there were few as fortunate as he and Bridget. What was it they called it, soul mates? Whatever, there was no-one else for him. He'd had a few distractions in the past, but nothing serious. Of course with the new baby on its way he would be as good as gold.

What the hell kind of mess was he walking into here, though? There was no doubt about it, Erin was definitely her father's daughter.

"Grandee, Grandee," squealed the chubby toddler throwing himself at Paddy who promptly scooped the boy up in the air amidst further squeals of delight.

"Someone's pleased to see me," laughed Paddy. "My God, look how much he has grown."

Paddy settled on one of the big, over-stuffed sofas with Ryan climbing all over him.

"Hi, Dad," his daughter kissed him and, grabbing hold of Ryan said, "C'mon, buster, you'll see grandad later." She left the two men to get to grips with the business in hand.

"Okay, what's going on?" Paddy got right to the point.

Almost word for word, Nick relayed exactly what Bridget had said. "Business-wise, I guess I'm finished with him. I can't say it won't hurt, but we won't starve. Unfortunately, that's unlikely to be the end of it, you know how these guys operate."

"An eye for an eye, yes I know."

"How are we going to protect her and Sam? They have no idea how serious it is. Erin thinks she can write them a Get Well Soon card and that'll be the end of the matter."

"Does Romanov know for sure it was them?"

"I think so, there's been someone on their tail for days."

"Let's face it, Sam had to have the combination to take what she reckoned she was owed."

"Mm, stands to reason she's the main suspect. I don't suppose if he gets the contents back he'll leave it at that?"

"No chance, no matter where they go, the assassin will find them."

"Surely we can appeal on their behalf? There must be something we can do?"

"Yes there is. Either you or I take their place."

"Look, arrange a meet. We've got nothing to lose and if the situation remains the same, we'll take him out."

"For fuck's sake, Paddy, have you any idea what you'd be taking on."

"Well there's no way I'm giving up on my daughter. If it's too much for you, just say, because if you have any doubt, this is where you get out."

"Of course I'm not out, but this will be the hardest fight of your life."

"Look, son, let's see if we can do this amicably. Get him on the phone."

# Family Ties

"So you've crawled out from whatever stone you were hiding under," Davey Senior sneered at his son and his mate. "Would you mind telling me what the fuck he is doing in my house?"

"I'm pleased to see you too, Davey," answered Genaro sarcastically.

"It's Mister Thomson to you, boy."

"Shut up, old man. You want to know why he's here, why I'm here. Because we have had enough of your shit and the way you treat us, giving us no respect. Just who the fuck do you think you are?" Junior raged.

"Who do I think *I* am? You've got that the wrong way round, boy. I'm your father, that's who. Head of this family and don't you forget it. As for respect, you have to earn it, not like that sniffling coward standing next to you. The one who let Coyle walk in and take over what his father had worked years to build up. The one who's dripping poison in your ear, sucking you dry and sponging off you, but still you put him before your family."

"If you'd helped when I asked we wouldn't be in this situation."

"And what situation would that be?" Davey grimaced at Junior.

"This one," Junior snarled as he pulled out a gun.

"For fuck's sake, laddie, put that away and don't be so fucking melodramatic, you're not capable of shooting me."

"You think not? You know nothing about what I'm capable of. Nothing!" Junior boasted.

"I know you two are nothing but a pair of bum boys. Ask yourself, Junior, if things were the other way round, do you think Sir Galahad here would ride to your rescue? Would he fuck! If I'd helped you with that piece of shit, he'd still not have a pot to piss in. He's a loser. His father knew that. Why do you think Coyle took over so easily?"

"Shut up! Who do you think did Michael Coyle's woman? Not the Russians. It was us; the two gunmen at the funeral? That was also us. Everyone thought we were the bee's knees, Paddy Coyle was throwing himself at our feet in gratitude."

"What was the point in killing that wee lassie? Have you not learned a thing? Women and children are always out of bounds, that's the rules."

"Whose rules? Not ours," sneered Junior.

"Try explaining that to the Coyles when they come knocking. Because they will, after you two idiots tried to torch their home. It's the worst kept secret in Glasgow," his father scoffed. "You're a laughing stock, I'm ashamed to call you my son."

"You're ashamed? That works two ways, old man. I'm ashamed of you and the league of pensioners you call your mob."

"Get it over with, Junior," urged Genaro.

"What did I tell you?" interrupted Thomson's right-hand man. "Didn't I warn you about them?"

Cortellessa spun round to face Jimmy MacAfee.

"I fucking knew it. I knew this pair of lairy young arseholes would try their hand," he growled as he easily relieved Junior of the gun. "That's why I've been watching your back since we had that conversation."

"I know you were, Jimmy. I just didn't want to admit my son was a treacherous lowlife." Thomson looked every one of his sixty-odd years.

"So what are we going to do with this pair of cunts?"

# Blood is Thicker Than…

"So, the famous Paddy Coyle, we meet at last," the Russian shook hands with the two men. "And Nick, we seem to be seeing much of each other lately."

"Always a pleasure, Sergei."

"So what can I do for you gentlemen? It wouldn't have anything to do with a certain robbery?"

"It would, I'm sorry to say," replied Coyle.

"Go on," said the grim-faced Russian.

"Do you have children, Sergei?"

"I do, two boys and a girl."

"A princess?" Paddy queried.

"You're right, a princess. Twelve, going on twenty-two."

"She is the apple of your eye, is she not? You would gladly lay down your life for her?"

"Without question, but what has this to do with the theft of my property?"

"I also have a daughter," answered Paddy. "Fathers in our profession have to face the possibility that any one of our enemies may use our families against us."

"Agreed."

"Since the age of eight Erin has paid dearly for the privilege of being my daughter. She was so traumatised by an attack on the family she lost the power of speech for years. She regained it when she witnessed the same man about to murder me. She has been kidnapped and lost the father of her child in a car crash as he was attempting to abduct their son."

"Not an uneventful childhood, but I still do not understand the relevance."

"Together with an accomplice, she was responsible for the theft of your property."

"I know," replied the Russian. "I have known since the day it occurred."

"Well, you'll know why I am here. I don't for one moment condone what they did, however, she is a brave, headstrong young woman, who because of her past, lives for the moment with no real thought of the consequences of her actions. This was simply an adventure, the money for her was incidental."

"So what are you asking?"

"I am asking for leniency and understanding." Paddy faced the Russian without flinching. "I will not permit any harm to come to my daughter."

"Is that a threat?" The Russian was terse. "I do not respond well to threats, do I Nick?"

"Paddy wasn't threatening you, Sergei. He merely stated a fact. I agree with him. This would never have arisen if the two goons had paid their employee what she was owed and not tried to penny-pinch."

"What do you mean?"

"Sam was apparently an excellent negotiator and had worked without payment for months. A few pesetas here and there, but never what she had earned. She was desperate and thought she had no alternative. So, rightly or wrongly, she took what she reckoned was owed to her."

"You told me yourself the safe contained significantly more than a couple of months' salary."

"It did, and when she heard the two had been arrested, temptation took over. The police actually asked if she knew the combination to the safe. You could argue that they did us a favour. Who knows what else would have been uncovered."

Nick looked at the Russian knowingly. "It still remains that those two fools left themselves open to be robbed. If they had followed procedure, they wouldn't be languishing in a Spanish jail. And our money, remember, I'm a victim too, would still be tucked up safe and sound."

"So what is it you want me to do?"

"If the police had managed to open the safe, the contents would have become the property of the state and we would have said goodbye to it. However, the contents are in a safety deposit box in the Bank of Seville."

"So I should be thankful to these two women for stealing from me? Perhaps offer a reward?" the Russian replied scathingly.

"Of course not, but no real harm has been done, Sergei. The contents will be returned and both Paddy and I will be in your debt."

"You are forgetting one thing. The contract is out. We Cossacks, once the sabre is drawn, it cannot be sheathed without blood being spilled. If not his enemy, then his own."

# Good Neighbours

Oblivious to the crucial talks taking place only a few miles from their luxury apartment, the two old friends chatted away.

"So what's the story about the Canon's sister?" Theresa quizzed her friend. "She's the last person I'd have expected here, miserable old bugger."

"True. She's got a face that would curdle milk," Lizzie laughed. "As for why she's here, God knows. We've all seen her with the old man and honestly, Theresa, you would swear it was the black-hearted fiend himself, except for one thing. It's not only his heart that's black. Same look, same voice, same everything, but, like I said, he's as black as Newgate's knocker."

"Then it's not him. It can't be. Are you sure it's not a disguise?" questioned Theresa. "Anyway, I thought he drowned."

"Paddy and Michael are convinced he did and they were witness to that, so they should know."

"I thought we might visit her in hospital. Take her some flowers, make sure she's got everything she needs, neighbourly-like," Theresa said, watching Lizzie out the corner of her eye.

"I don't see how it would do any harm, she knows we're all out here. After all, it was Errol who caused the accident."

"Well then," agreed Theresa. "We should see if she needs anything."

"Aye, and get the lowdown on what's going on. You can't kid me, you fly old bugger," Lizzie laughed at the indignant look on her friend's face.

"Oh, Lizzie, I've missed you. It's not been the same with you and Bridget away."

"Get a move on or she'll be cured by the time we get there."

"What are you two up to?" questioned Bridget.

"Nothing dear, nothing, we're just off for a stroll."

"Wait, I'll come with you. I'm going stir crazy in here."

"No, you stay here, Paddy might come back." Lizzie pushed Theresa out of the apartment. "See you later, bye." The door closed behind them.

Those two are up to something, Bridget thought to herself, peeved at not being included.

Imelda Gavin couldn't believe her eyes. Bold as brass, marching up the ward, armed with a large bouquet of flowers and checking each bed as they passed, were two of her most hated acquaintances. That damned Coyle woman and her nosey neighbour. What in God's name were they doing here? Surely they weren't coming to visit her? She pulled the covers over her head in an attempt to hide from them.

"It's this one," Lizzie picked up the chart at the bottom of Imelda's bed.

"Shh . . . she's sleeping," whispered Theresa.

"I don't care. We've not come all this way in that infernal heat for her to be sleeping," Lizzie's strident voice echoed around the ward.

"Dear God, woman, you'd waken the dead," Imelda came from beneath the sheets to face her visitors.

"See, I told you she's not sleeping," said Lizzie smugly.

"No chance of that," the patient muttered. "What are you doing here?" Imelda asked ungraciously.

"Well, that's no way to greet visitors. We came to see how you were and if you needed anything, I don't suppose your brother will have been of much use?"

"My brother?" Imelda shot back at the two. "What are you talking about? You know fine well my brother died last year at the hands of your family, so go away. I want nothing from either of you." She pulled the sheets back over her head.

Completely ignoring the outburst Theresa wandered off to find a vase and Lizzie sat down by Imelda's bedside.

"Now what's happened here?" she asked the mummified form. "What was broken? Your hip?"

A muffled response was her answer.

"Don't be ridiculous, woman. I'm not going away so you might as well come out from under the covers. We know your brother is somewhere about, but that's nothing to do with us. He can settle his scores with our Paddy and Michael later."

"What's up with her?" Theresa returned carrying the vase. "C'mon dear, I've a nice bunch of grapes here, see." She shoved the bunch, or what was left of them, under the sheet.

"She's not very sociable is she?"

"Maybe not, but I'm not sitting here talking to a mummy." Grabbing the sheet, Lizzie tore it from Imelda's grasp.

"Nurse, nurse!" Imelda called.

"You're wasting your time, dear, there's no one about. What do you think we're going to do to you? Look, me and Theresa would never see a buddy stuck, especially not here, the place is full of foreigners. But, neither are we a pair of hypocrites. We know there's no love lost between us but, you tell us what you need and we'll get the nuns to sort you out. Agreed?"

"Agreed," the woman muttered.

"Now what's going on with Canon O'Farrell? How the hell did he survive and what's with his skin?" spouted Theresa, all in one breath, unable to keep quiet any longer.

"I knew there would be a catch, you lot are all the same."

"Theresa! You and your big mouth," Lizzie admonished.

"I've no idea what you're talking about. I appreciate your help but I want you to go." Imelda was not going to be an easy nut to crack.

"We all know he's alive and kicking, Mrs Gavin, there's no point in trying to deny it."

"I don't know what you think you know but my brother, Canon Francis O'Farrell, is dead."

"Who's the black man then?" asked Lizzie. "Nat King Cole?"

"Don't be facetious, it's none of your business," she replied, pulling the sheet back over her head in an attempt to end the conversation.

She hadn't reckoned on the tenacity of the two Glaswegian buddies.

"We'll find out, but in the meantime we need to get you seen to. Are you in pain? Are they giving you proper painkillers? What about food, can you eat that foreign muck?"

"I'm fine. The pain is under control and the food is edible. I just want out of here and home."

"Home here or home Ireland?" Lizzie enquired.

"There's only one home for me and it's not here."

"Well, we'll be off, and hopefully you won't be in for much longer. If you need help, here's our number," Lizzie handed the patient a scrap of paper. "I would tell your brother, or whoever he is, not to let my sons catch up with him or it's black and blue he'll be."

The two friends left the ward

# Breakdown

Back in Glasgow, Marie handpicked her most trusted guys: Tiny, James, Archie and Bill, all hard, capable soldiers and exactly the ones to have by your side in a situation like this. All of them had worked for Paddy and Michael for years and would defend the Coyles to the bitter end.

Marie relayed the phone conversation verbatim, watching for the men's reactions. "So what do you think?" The young woman looked around the table.

"You sure you don't want to wait till Paddy gets back?" Tiny asked.

"No, I don't. You heard what the caller said, they won't hang around for long, so if we want a capture we have to act fast. If we're not capable, we shouldn't be taking a wage." Marie knew she would be hitting a nerve here.

"Of course we can sort this out, I just thought . . ."

"With all due respect, Tiny, leave the thinking to me."

"They're holed up in a remote country farm, about twenty miles north of the city," reported Archie. "It's the perfect place for a hide-out. The building is at the end of a mile-long dirt track, across open terrain. Anyone approaching will be easily visible from the house."

"What do you suggest?" Maria asked Archie, who, together with Bill, had checked out the area.

"We'll have to approach on foot under cover of darkness. Everyone okay with this?"

"No option," replied James, the least fit of the group.

"What about staging a breakdown further back, along the main road?"

"I don't think our two pigeons are terribly chivalrous. They would most probably drive straight past."

"Not if it was you flagging them down."

"They might recognise her," ventured Bill.

"Not dressed like this," Marie pointed to her denims and hoodie. "It's certainly not the garb of a successful club owner."

"It could work," agreed Tiny. "Archie, you could wait and when their vehicle passes, call us. Marie can then get out and play the damsel in distress."

"We could have a long wait."

"Not as long as we've waited to make them pay for what they did to Margee."

"Michael is not going to thank you for this, lass."

"He will one day," replied his sister. "Remember, these guys are professionals, we'll only get one chance."

"A breakdown it is then. We'll leave here at ten and get into position. Remember, no prisoners."

It was just past midnight when the lone vehicle passed their first checkpoint.

"I'm not sure if it's them. I couldn't see inside the vehicle, but it will be with you in a couple of minutes."

Within seconds Marie was in position, bonnet of the car open and desperately waving a white scarf, determined to flag down the speeding vehicle.

As the vehicle screeched to a halt, Marie ran towards the driver's side.

"Thank God, I've been stuck here for hours. You're the first car to come along."

The occupants of the 4x4 seemed reluctant to leave the safety of their vehicle.

"We're not mechanics," answered the driver.

"Please have a look, my kids are on their own and I have to get home."

Speaking in their native tongue, they agreed to look, but were more interested in getting her back to the farmhouse, where she could demonstrate her gratitude. They would go through the motions of checking the car out.

Bent over the engine, tugging at various cables and pipes, the two were laughing, describing how she would show her rescuers how grateful she was. It took a few minutes for them to realise the woman was backing away from the car, retreating along the road.

"What the fuck?" called out the driver as he hit the ground, his body twitching violently as it was riddled with bullets.

His partner had no time for any words.

The bodies, peppered with bullets, were found early the next morning by a farmer on his way to market.

A victory for the Coyles and a stark reminder to those who would dare challenge their authority.

Michael Coyle was taken aback to find his young sister asleep on the sofa the following morning. He was even more taken aback when he discovered the reason.

"Why, Marie? Why did you take it on yourself to deprive me of the satisfaction of putting those bastards to death? To make them suffer the way they made Margee suffer. To know it was me taking revenge," Michael ranted and raved. "I promise you, Marie, I'll never forgive you for this. I told you, all of you, I wanted them brought in alive. It was up to me to decide how they should die. They had to pay and you've taken that from me. I'll never rest, knowing I failed."

"The last person who would want you to have blood on your hands is Margee," his sister spoke gently. "I know you're angry and probably hate me right now, but I would do the same again, Mikey. I couldn't let you stoop to their level. You could never be like those animals and that's what you would become. I know, over the years, you've had to take guys out, but you are not and never will be a cold-blooded murderer. One day you will be glad it happened this way.

Through gritted teeth Michael snarled at his sister, "Get out. I don't want to ever lay eyes on you. Sister or no sister, you're dead to me."

"Calm down Michael, calm down. I don't understand what you're saying," Paddy answered the call from home. For a dreadful moment he thought the Russians had killed their sister. Michael was raging, drunk and totally incoherent.

It took several minutes before Paddy sussed the situation. Marie, together with a posse of their guys had ambushed and disposed of the two Russian fugitives despite the fact that Michael had made it known that he was to mete out the punishment. He was threatening all kinds of retribution.

From day one his brother had been determined he wanted the pair brought in alive; he and only he was to execute the bastards who had defiled his beloved Margee. Paddy could well understand Michael's anger and frustration, knowing he would be equally as furious with their sister, but he also understood Marie's reasons for her actions. But, in order to move forward, Michael had needed to seek revenge and his sister had denied him this.

# Denial

"It's not fair, Granny." Young Errol was furious at finding out where his gran and Theresa had spent the afternoon. "It was me and Sam who tracked her down. You didn't even believe me when I told you."

"I know, son, but there was no chance you'd get in to see her. Who's going to throw two old doddery ladies out?"

"Speak for yourself," retorted Theresa. "Lizzie's right, son, she wouldn't open up to us to begin with, so you would have had no chance."

"What did she say?" asked Errol.

"Not much, denied everything. Then this one," Lizzie pointed to Theresa, "barged in with both feet as usual, which didn't help."

"We could have sat there till hell froze over, no way was she telling us anything we didn't already know."

"We learned one thing though, she's going straight back to Ireland as soon as she's discharged, with or without her illustrious brother."

"Did she admit it was the Canon?" asked Errol.

"No, son, but she didn't deny it," replied Lizzie.

"Seriously, what harm can he do now?" queried Theresa. "He's an old man, not in the best of health, would we not be better leaving well alone?"

"Don't be taken in, he's an evil old bastard," interrupted Bridget, entering the room. "Who was involved in the biggest paedophile ring in Europe as well as trying to kill my husband? He deserves everything coming to him. Believe me, your sympathy is wasted there."

"Maybe so," answered Lizzie. "But Errol here needs to stay well out of it."

"Well, here's hoping he pays more attention to your son than you do," answered Bridget, not best pleased with her mother-in-law or Theresa. "I knew as soon as you two got together there would be trouble. Stay away from the woman. In fact, stay away from both of them."

"Auntie Bridget, that man has been hanging about outside again."

"What man, son?" Bridget felt a cold shiver down her spine.

"The one in the video, the one Uncle Paddy showed us."

"When was that, son?" asked his aunt.

"This morning, just after you left, I noticed him from the balcony. I didn't realise it was him at first but when I heard the lift stop at this floor I knew it was. I think he was going to break in."

"Why didn't you phone one of us?" Bridget asked, looking worried.

"I pretended there was someone else in the apartment. I called Nick's name, making out I wasn't alone, then I heard the lift go down. He was there for quite a while."

"Wait a minute, there was a tall, shifty-looking character hanging about the entrance when we came back," volunteered Theresa.

"I didn't notice anyone," answered Lizzie. "Why didn't you say?"

"How was I to know he wasn't kosher? I only thought he was shady when he turned away as we went forward for the lift. I don't think I'd recognise him again."

"Don't worry, ladies, it's probably nothing more than a coincidence," Bridget laid a reassuring hand on Lizzie's arm. "Let's have a cuppa and you can tell me all about Imelda Gavin."

# Plan B

O'Farrell had spent most of the day dozing as the Lady Di cruised the Med. He was so different from the lively, demanding passenger he'd been on previous trips, but it was his skin that Simon found difficult to get used to. From a distance he looked like any other elderly black man, but close up, his skin looked anything but natural. He looked like he'd been burnt to a crisp.

"Where do you want me to berth for the night?" Simon called to the old man.

"I don't mind. How far are we from Palma?"

"No more than an hour's sail," the skipper answered.

"Fine, let's head for there. I have to make a few calls. After that I'll retire for the night."

"Have you any plans for tomorrow?" Simon enquired.

"Depends on the calls, but I'll let you know."

O'Farrell was anxious about his sister's whereabouts. He pretty much knew for sure that she hadn't returned home to the apartment since she had not responded to the note he'd left her.

He had to find her. Apart from Imelda he had almost no contacts now, certainly none he could trust. He racked his brains and finally hit on the idea of enlisting the help of Sylvia Smith.

The Smiths were the family Bobby Mack had hired

to look after Ryan. Despite the fact that the child had almost died, thanks to her husband's greed, O'Farrell was confident that for a fee she would do as he asked.

There was also the question of Sergei; there was no doubt he had upset his Russian friend. He knew only too well how dangerous and foolhardy it was to have threatened the Russian with their past association. He thought it would also be useful to get the skipper ashore for a while, give himself time to explore the yacht. Years ago, Pete McClelland had shown his son Bobby and the Canon a concealed hideout which could be used to store contraband or human cargo. It had been built into the yacht on its construction and, despite several raids, had remained undetected. Even though Simon had free run of the yacht, it was unlikely, unless he too had been shown, that he would discover the hiding place by himself; this could prove vital if things didn't go to plan.

Sylvia Smith shuddered. Someone had just walked over her grave at the precise moment the phone rang. Dear God, it was a voice from grave.

"Sylvia, is that you?"

The woman shuddered again. "You! I thought the world was rid of you."

"Not yet, my dear, but soon I think, soon."

"Not soon enough," the woman spat.

"I have a job for you," the ex-priest ignored the venom in the woman's voice. Money would soon sort that.

"No chance. Whatever it is, forget it."

"There's good money in it and it's nothing illegal."

"Well that's a first. How much?"

"Five hundred pesetas."

"No way."

185

"I'm only a few miles from you. Why don't I meet you in the morning and we can discuss your fee then?"

"I'll think about it." The line went dead.

O'Farrell had no doubt she would do as he wanted. His next call was to his Russian friend.

"Sergei, it's Francis."

"What game are you playing, my friend? You call me in trouble and when I send help, you have flown. What is wrong with you?"

"I couldn't wait, the Coyles were almost knocking on my door and I took fright. I apologise. You were right, I need to move to a safe house until we can sort these mongrels out."

"Where are you?" The Russian asked, although he knew from Simon's call earlier, exactly where the priest was located.

"I've chartered a yacht and I'm on my way to Morocco."

That lie sealed the old man's fate. Enough was enough. Sergei now knew he couldn't be trusted and was a fool if he thought he could outsmart a Russian of his standing. He'd speak to Simon in the morning; the priest would not return from this sailing trip.

# Takeover Bid

"What do you want me to do with them?" Jimmy Mac asked his boss again. The old man was certainly slowing up, that was the second time he'd had to ask. He wanted shot of these cocky little bastards.

"C'mon, Dad," jeered Junior. "Tell him. Tell him he has to do both of us, c'mon," his voice rose with each taunt. "Don't be shy."

Junior Thomson had no regard for either his father or his right-hand man. Another fucking dinosaur, Jimmy Mac, scourge of the Southside. Christ, he could hardly bend down to tie his shoe laces, the man was well past it.

"Okay, old guy, you gonna try to take us both out? I don't think so." Genaro joined in.

"Old guy? I'll fucking old guy you." MacAfee attempted to pistol-whip the young dude.

That was a big mistake. Allowing the pups' taunting to get to him, he lost concentration, only for a second, but that was enough.

Genaro Cortellesso whipped out his trusty 'Stanley' from his inside pocket and went on the attack. He frantically sliced and criss-crossed the man's face and arms until he was unrecognisable. There was nothing MacAfee could do to protect himself from the blade. Blood streamed down his face and into his eyes. His mouth was now a gaping hole where Genaro had carved the infamous 'Glasgow smile'. Completely ignoring the man's screams, and his pleas for mercy, Cortellesso went for his eyes. Gouging them out he kicked them like golf balls across the floor, laughing maniacally.

Davey Senior, hard man, who had taken out God knows how many men over the years, had never witnessed anything so barbaric in his life. The boy, for that's all he was in Davey's eyes, was a fucking lunatic and Thomson was rooted to the spot.

"Look at him, Genaro," Junior laughed, pointing at his father. "Look at big bad Davey Thomson drooling like a baby."

What the fuck was he talking about? Davey was puzzled, what did he mean drooling like a baby?

"You wouldn't want someone to spoon feed you, or wipe your arse would you?" taunted Junior.

Davey didn't understand what was happening, what were they laughing at? He had to get away from these animals, but he couldn't move. Years of over-indulgence and the sheer terror of the past hour had taken its toll.

"Look at him, the old fucker's had a stroke."

It was then that Thomson Senior understood what was wrong.

"What're you thinking, Junior?" his mate asked, still on a high. "We have to cover this lot up."

"How about a nice bonfire? See if we've got any better at it."

"Fucking brilliant. There's a can of petrol in the boot of my car, I'll fetch it."

"Remember the back door. All good arsonists worth their salt start at the back door."

188

Laughing at the terror in the eyes of his old man, Junior struck the match.

It was all his now. Or was it?

He'd run like fuck as far away from the house as possible and was now emptying his guts on the pavement. Tommy Reilly couldn't believe what he'd just witnessed, it was fucking brutal.

He'd arrived at Thomson's gaff only minutes after Jimmy Mac had surprised Junior and that other headcase. Tommy could see right away there was something serious going down. There was no way he was going to get mixed up in any family feud. He knew how easily these situations could flip and the bystander become the victim.

The trouble was, though, he couldn't escape without alerting them to the fact he'd seen and heard everything. He was the only eye witness to the brutal murder of Jimmy Mac, and Davey Thomson being left to burn to death in his own home.

Why the fuck had he come here? How stupid had he been, putting himself in the frame and getting caught up in things best left well alone?

It had been at the suggestion of Jimmy Mac, who was an old pal of his ma's, that Tommy had gone to see the old man. He'd try anything to get Davey's son and his mate off his back.

It was all well and good for Michael to assure him he was safe, but he'd suffered not so long ago as a result of the Coyles' promises and he had no intention of spending the next however many years looking over his shoulder.

# The Truth

As Paddy promised, Michael pulled out all the stops. He'd called in many favours and work was already under way on number twenty-six, with Peter as the self-appointed clerk of works. He was in his element, brewing tea, going for supplies and gossiping. Christ, thought Michael, he could give Theresa and his mother a run for their money.

It wasn't only the repairs to his house that were of interest to Peter. The latest gossip and goings-on circulating about the Thomsons appeared to fascinate him.

"I'm telling you, Michael, young Tommy witnessed the whole thing. That Italian bugger slaughtered Jimmy Mac and then, would you believe it? Junior torched the house with his old man still alive inside. Pair of mad bastards. Thankfully they have got their comeuppance. It seems the crew have turned their back on the son and want nothing to do with him. All that terrible business and they've ended up with fuck all."

"Terrible, Peter, terrible," Michael answered, not paying particular attention to the man's drivel. Anxious to get rid of him and get on with the day's work, he continued, "If you'll excuse me . . ." he made an effort to end the conversation.

"Aye, it's terrible alright, but that's not all," interrupted Peter. "Now, I need you to sit down and promise me you won't go off on one. Fuck, I wish your Paddy was here, he's much better at these things than me."

"For God's sake, Peter, get on with it, I've got work to do."

"Well, it's about Margee."

Peter saw the man's jaw tighten.

Michael Coyle stood up and lifted him bodily out of his seat. "You better not be fucking around, Peter, or trust me, you'll not leave this room alive."

"Michael, I wouldn't do that, we're neighbours. It wasn't the Russians, it was Junior and Cortellessa. Honest, son, I didn't want you hearing it from someone else. Seemingly they've been bragging about it."

Michael didn't hear the rest of Peter's story; he'd already raced off.

# Trust Issues

"I don't trust that bugger," Paddy confided in Nick after their meeting with his ex-business partner. "Do you really believe he's called his man off?"

"I hope so. We worked well together for years, but it's all about face with these guys."

"So what do you suggest?" asked Paddy.

"Return his property. That at least shows respect and that we're upholding our side of the deal."

"I'm not sure I agree. While we still have it, we have some manoeuvrability."

"Don't kid yourself, Paddy, that money is petty cash to him. He could lose that much on the turn of a card and not bat an eyelid. The longer we stall, the more likely something could go wrong."

"Maybe so, but the documents and the gun must be of some value?"

"Gun, what gun?" Nick asked, annoyed that yet again he'd not been told all the facts.

"Along with the currency and documents there was a gun and a box of ammo, and I'd stake money that's what he wants back."

Shit, what else was she keeping from him? Nick thought. Erin obviously didn't trust him, but why? He'd never understand women. It looked like he had been sadly mistaken about Erin Coyle. What did he have to do to earn her trust? He'd put his life on hold to find her boy. He'd risked everything and it still wasn't enough. Now, because of her stupid antics, he stood to lose his business partner, money and his reputation and still she withheld information. Information that could get them all killed, and yet here he was, trotting behind her father like some lap-dog, willing to do whatever necessary to keep her safe. How big a fool was he? Once this fiasco was over, it was back to the single life for him; he should have known better. However, first things first, he had to recover Sergei's property and do whatever was necessary to smooth over the situation.

"Why didn't you tell me about the gun?" Nick asked Erin as she was getting Ryan ready for bed that evening.

"Gun? Oh Lord, Nick, I forgot all about it. I wanted to leave it behind in the safe. You know how I feel about weapons, but Sam insisted we keep it. It's still on the Lady Di. I'm sorry."

She looked like butter wouldn't melt, but he wasn't going to be fooled this time, "How could you forget about a weapon?" Nick asked incredulously. "First thing tomorrow we're going to collect it."

"We can't, she's out on a charter and won't be back till the weekend."

"Call Simon," Nick demanded.

"A few more days won't make any difference and we don't know who's on board. Look, Sam will sit with Ryan tonight, why don't we have dinner out?"

"I have plans, don't wait up," Nick snapped as he made for the door.

Erin fought back the tears. Things were going from

bad to worse. Their relationship was floundering, and they were like ships that passed in the night. He'd even taken to sleeping in the guest room on the pretext he didn't want to wake her or the boy when he came home late. Was there someone else? She didn't think so, but damn him, she wasn't waiting around to find out, she'd make him realise what he was missing.

"Sam, it's me. Fancy a night out? I'm going stir-crazy in here."

"You don't have to ask me twice, but what will Nick say?" her friend asked. "He doesn't like you going out on the town without him."

"Well, maybe he should take me out instead of going on his own."

"If you're sure, see you in an hour." Sam hung up.

Now all Erin had to do was persuade Bridget to babysit. "Mum, can you have Ryan tonight? He's all ready for bed so I can bring him over now if that's okay?"

"Of course, sweetheart. It's time you and that man of yours had some quality time."

No way was she telling Bridget of her plans – there would be hell to pay.

# Laid to Rest

The results of the post mortem came as no surprise to any of Davey Thomson's crew. It was the findings of the procurator fiscal's office that David Thomson aged sixty-six had suffered a severe ischaemic stroke with smoke inhalation being the primary cause of death. The second body recovered from the burned-out shell was that of James MacAfee. MacAfee had died from multiple stab wounds and since there was no evidence of smoke inhalation, the fire was not deemed to be the cause of death.

The fire was a deliberate act of arson carried out by person or persons unknown and a full murder investigation was underway.

Things had certainly not gone to plan for Junior and his sidekick. On hearing the news of the fire, Davey Senior's workforce, the same workforce that the two young pups had branded as old and useless, refused the summons to swear allegiance to his successor. Without exception the men had refused the call, both old and new recruits. Junior may have inherited the turf but he had no way of working it. So, like Cortellessa, he was out in the cold.

"This was not how it was supposed to be," Junior ranted. "They have to work for me. It's the way it is, the way it's always been."

"It didn't work for me," Genaro reminded him.

"Don't take this the wrong way, mate, but no way could you have taken on Coyle."

"And you think you could?" Cortellessa angrily faced up to his mate.

"Hey, we'll never get anywhere if we start fighting between ourselves," Junior slapped him on the back. "A united front is what we have to be."

"You're right, Junior, but enough with the cracks," mumbled Genaro.

"I need to organise a funeral. Once he's planted they'll come round, you wait and see."

"I wouldn't be so sure," answered Cortellessa. "Why not make it a private do, family only and don't tell anyone where the service is to be held?"

"Good idea. I'm damned if I'm going to stand by shaking hands with a bunch of Judases. They can all go fuck themselves."

As lavish as Mario Cortellessa's passing had been, Davey Thomson's was nothing short of a pauper's. There had been no obituary, only the cheapest of caskets and no floral tributes or mourners. However, the local undertaker, who had served the family both legally and illegally over the years had put the word out. Once more the two idiots had underestimated the loyalty of the old-school villains.

Standing by his father's grave, David Thomson Junior was subjected to the most humiliating experience of his life. In single file, each man passed by, stared him straight in the face and spat at his feet; the ultimate insult. He was persona non grata. With the exception of one man, Rab McAfee, brother of Jimmy; he was last in line and, marching up to the heir-apparent, he faced Junior, eye to eye, hawked from the back of his throat and spat straight in the son's face.

As Junior was about to pounce, Cortellessa grabbed him. "Not now," he whispered. "Keep calm, it's almost over."

"You're a dead man," stated McAfee. "Enjoy today, boy, it may well be your last."

Wiping the spittle off his face Junior turned to face his protagonists. "You think that scares me?" he laughed. "Make the most of this? If you thought my dad was bad, you've seen nothing yet." he shouted.

This was met by the sound of the many spectators slow hand clapping as the two made their way through the throng. They were finished.

What had gone wrong? Genaro Cortellessa puzzled. Why had the Thomson crew blackballed Junior, turning their backs on him? The old adage: 'The King is dead – Long Live the King', was the code of the underworld and it was Junior's right to succeed. If Davey Senior had been unable to withstand the coup, then he had no right to the position of general, but his men were having none of it. They hated and mistrusted Junior and had done since he was a kid; a spoiled, treacherous brat, tolerated only because of his father.

"I'm telling you, I'll get the fucking lot of them, every shitfaced one," ranted Junior.

"Of course you will, but not right now. What we need to do is lay low for a bit, let things cool down. The cops have been sniffing around and though we're cast iron, it would do no harm to put some distance between us," advised Genaro.

"I'm not running away," roared Junior. "I'm not scared of any of those old fuckers."

"I didn't say run away, but we do need to figure out how to get back what's rightfully yours."

"Spain, we'll go to Spain. The old man has a place in Marbella. He always maintained it was his bolthole if things went belly-up. God knows when he was last there. A few of his mates have used it from time to time when they were on the run. I'd guarantee no-one would go looking for us there."

"Perfect, Marbella it is then."

# Opportunity Knocks

The club was still the hottest venue in the whole of Spain, always a full house. The Marbella Princess was a heaving mass of steaming hot bodies, the best DJs on the scene and the most fantastic, dramatic light show. The queue to gain entry was legendary, but not for Erin and Sam. They were escorted straight to the cordoned-off VIP area, where the crème de la crème of Marbella, professional footballers and many of Hollywood's A-listers hung out when in town. It was the place to be. The club, once owned and run by the Macks, the Coyles' most bitter enemies, was now the property of Erin's son. Ryan had inherited Bobby Mack's fortune, including the fabulous club.

Young, gorgeous waiters were delivering $300 bottles of Crystal, fused with sparklers and the atmosphere was electric. It was impossible not to feel it. Sam was already draped around some random guy at the bar. She certainly didn't waste time, thought Erin, not that she was short of admirers.

"Who's your friend?" she asked Sam on her eventual return.

"Lush or what? I met him a couple of nights ago, he's just arrived in town. Come to think of it, he's from your neck of the woods," Sam smiled at her friend. "So keep your hands off."

"He's certainly good-looking, but not my type. Anyway, I'm not interested and certainly not in someone from home. As soon as they know who I am, it's curtains, or they turn out to be some chancer trying to get an in with my dad."

Jesus, it was daylight. Erin blinked against the glare of the morning sun as they left the club. It was five a.m. and checking her phone, she found at least a dozen missed calls. The majority were from an increasingly angry Nick. The others were from Bridget, warning her Nick was on the warpath. She'd better not be up to any mischief, warned her mother, or woe betide her.

Giggling like a schoolgirl, Erin struggled with the lock. She was suddenly catapulted into the apartment as the heavy front door was wrenched open by a none-too-happy Nick.

"Where the hell have you been till this time?" He snapped.

"I've been checking out my son's investment, if you must know. Is that a problem?" she answered impudently.

"It's a problem when you're out until this time with no protection."

"Protection, what do I need with protection? I'm Paddy Coyle's daughter."

"We've already been through this. Paddy Coyle's name means nothing here, he's just another tourist."

"I'd love to hear you say that to his face," Erin argued back.

"Enough. I'll speak to you when you're sober," replied Nick as he stormed off to bed.

"I'd better go," said a contrite Sam. "I'll pick up a cab on the front."

200

"No, stay, he'll be fine," said an unsure Erin. "I have to get some sleep, just bunk down on the sofa. We'll sort things out in the morning. Oops, it is morning," laughed a still-drunk Erin.

It was years since Junior had last spent time in the Costas and surprisingly, little had changed. The whitewashed villa with its bougainvillea-covered walls, set in well-tended gardens and the inviting, sparkling pool, was just as he remembered it and the key was still under the pot at the front door.

Davey Senior had hired an elderly couple to take care of the place and they had certainly done a good job, it was immaculate.

"Christ, say what you like about your old fellow, he enjoyed the good life," complimented Genaro.

"Aye, he enjoyed it, but no other bugger did unless they were paying him a hefty wedge to hide out."

"Well, whatever, that was in the past. It's all yours now and it's about time we had some fun. Sand, sea and shagging, what do you say?" Cortellessa dumped his case. "Let's get some grub and suss the place out."

The two mates marched off to survey their new playground.

"Do you see who I see?" Genaro shouted over the noise of the music, pointing to the VIP area.

"Oh! It's that big blonde I met a couple of nights back."

"No, you tosser, look who she's with."

"The red-haired bird?"

"Yes, don't you recognise her? That's Erin Coyle."

"Fuck me, she'll know us right away."

"No she won't. I'm pretty sure she doesn't know me, and how long is it since you set eyes on her?"

"You're forgetting the funeral, she was there."

"Okay, but the mate doesn't know us."

"Christ, here she comes."

Sam had left the cordoned-off area and was making her way to the bar, having spotted Junior from above.

"Hi, beautiful." He could charm the birds off the trees when he had a mind to. "Can I buy you a drink?"

"No, you're okay, I've got one upstairs."

"Upstairs? Either you're stinking rich or extremely well-connected, if you have a VIP pass for here."

"Who says I'm not both?" Sam laughed. "Want to join us?"

"Thanks, and don't take offence, but we're fine here," he nodded to his mate. "We're not stopping long. How about giving me your number and we can meet up somewhere a bit less noisy?"

The blonde seemed delighted with the idea and he stored her number for future reference. He wasn't sure how she would figure in their plans but if she was well-connected, it could do no harm. She must be well in with the Coyles for a start, Junior thought as he watched her weave her way back to the VIP area.

"As long as I make sure I don't bump into the Coyle bird, we should be okay."

"Is it not a bit dicey? Christ, there are thousands of good-looking birds, why her?"

"She's a connection to that fucker Coyle and you never know, she could come in handy. It won't do any harm as long as I'm careful. I'm just Dave from Scotland, here to look at business opportunities, nothing shady about that."

# On the Trail

Sylvia Smith came out to meet the Lady Di as Simon tied her up on the jetty. O'Farrell noted how careworn the woman looked since they'd last met.

"Is it really you?" Sylvia Smith asked, taken aback at O'Farrell's appearance.

"It's me alright, have no fear on that count."

"God works in mysterious ways," Sylvia muttered to herself.

"No guests?" O'Farrell enquired.

"Business is slow," the woman replied tersely. "You've not come all the way here to enquire about that, so what is it you want?"

"A light refreshment, maybe some tea?" The old man teased.

"State your business or leave, I'm a busy woman."

"Come and sit down, Sylvia, and listen to what I want you to do for me. My sister is missing and I need you to find her."

"Me find your sister? How on earth would I do that?"

"I'm pretty sure she's met with an accident, so I want you to come with me to Marbella and check out a few places."

"Why can't you do it yourself?" she asked.

"It's complicated. There are a few people who would

dearly love to get their hands on me, therefore I can't move about as freely as I would need to, and my health is failing. It's fairly straightforward. She left our apartment last Sunday morning to attend mass at the Santo Christo church. That was the last I saw or heard from her."

"How do I know it's your sister you're after and not some poor soul you have a vendetta with?"

"She'll confirm who she is when you find her."

"How much? And you can forget a couple of hundred pesetas." Sylvia got straight to the point.

"How much do you want?" the priest replied.

"Well, it looks to me like I'm your only option, so I think a thousand pesetas would make it worth my while."

"Dear God, woman, that's ludicrous," the old man spluttered. "You should only be away overnight."

"Maybe so, but I have to pay someone to look after the children. So take it or leave it, and I want it up front."

"You're a hard woman, Sylvia Smith."

"No, I'm a widow, thanks to you and your partner, so what's it to be?"

"Like you said I've no option."

The Lady Di sailed back into her usual berth in Marbella. The skipper and Sylvia immediately went ashore, leaving O'Farrell time to investigate on his own.

Sylvia's first port of call was the church where Imelda had been heading that morning. Fortunately the priest taking communion was the same who'd spoken with Sam and Errol.

"Goodness, so many people looking for this poor woman."

"What do you mean, Father? Who else has been looking for her?"

"A boy and a young woman were the first to come, then two elderly ladies spoke with the nuns about her, and now you."

"Where is Senora Gavin now?"

"She was admitted to the General Hospital, just out of town, but I don't know if she is still there."

"Thank you, Father," she headed back to the car.

"Right, Simon, she was admitted to the General Hospital."

O'Farrell made his way to the master stateroom. Within minutes he had located the hiding place where Sam had planted the gun, however this was not what he was looking for. The room which was used by the previous owner, Pete Mack, to carry illicit cargo undetected, had an ingenious, concealed entrance. Unless you knew where it was, as he did, it was almost impossible to detect and yet could easily hide two average-sized men when closed. The door mechanism was so cleverly incorporated into the fittings; no-one would ever guess what the wardrobe and wall panelling concealed.

Opening the panel, O'Farrell had a rush of déja-vu. The times he had helped Bobby and his father stash contraband while next door, in the main salon, the chief of police had been partying alongside half the town council, not suspecting a thing.

He was positive the room had not given up its secrets to anyone. The small fridge was still stocked with drinks and there was bedding to make passengers comfortable. Lying undetected for all that time was a package. By the look, size and weight of it, it didn't take much to figure out the contents.

O'Farrell heard footsteps. There was someone on

board. Damn, who could it be? Now was not the time to take a chance as he stepped back into the hidden room and slid the panel back in place.

He had no choice, he would have to bide his time until the coast was clear. What if they knew about this hiding place? O'Farrell was thankful he'd picked up the gun.

# Flown the Coop

The BMW roared into the yard and screeched to a halt. Michael sprang from the car, leaving the engine running and crashed into the office. Rummaging for the keys to the gun cupboard, he scattered everything in his wake until he found them. He grabbed two semi-automatics and flew back out the door and down the stairs to his car.

"What's up, Michael?" His way was barred by Harry, the yard foreman.

Harry was a giant of a man, standing at six foot five. As a rule, he and the boys never interfered with the comings and goings of the brothers, but Paddy had tipped him the wink regarding Michael. If there was anything out of the ordinary he was to act as he saw fit.

The normally amiable Michael carrying enough fire-power to take out half of Glasgow could be considered out of the ordinary.

"Fuck off, Harry. It's nothing for you to get involved in. I've got a bit of business to attend to."

"It wouldn't have anything to do with Thomson and Cortellessa perhaps?" The foreman reached into the car and pocketed the keys.

"What's it got to do with you? Don't fuck around, give me back my keys."

"You're too late, Michael, those two have flown the nest. Paddy would have a better chance of catching them than you."

Harry had been expecting a visit from Michael, having heard the rumour the previous night that it had not been the Russians who'd murdered his fiancée but the two morons in question.

"I said, get out of my way." Michael snarled.

"I can't do that, boss. I can't let you leave here tooled up and ready to blow some cunt's head off. Now give me the guns."

"Don't make me repeat myself, Harry. Get out of my way."

Michael took one step towards him and was laid out cold. Harry slung Michael over his shoulder and dumped him unceremoniously on the couch in the office.

"Sorry, boss, but it was for your own good." Harry half-expected to be fired on the spot as Michael came round.

"Tell me what you know." Michael demanded, nursing his bruised jaw.

"Look, I don't know much, but the word is that those two murdered Thomson and MacAfee and were overheard bragging about Margee. They also set Marie up to get rid of the Russians. They've been busy boys by the sound of it."

"If they're not in Glasgow, where are they?"

"I don't know for sure but again, rumour has it they've hightailed it to Spain."

"Okay, Harry, you can go now, I'm alright. I won't go after anyone, well, not here anyway."

"Are you sure, boss? Paddy would have my head on a plate if I let you get yourself into a mess over this. You'll have your day with them, just not today."

"Trust me, Harry, I won't do anything stupid. Put these back for me and lock up."

Harry wasn't convinced Michael would leave things alone, but at least for today he'd managed to avert disaster.

So the bastards are in Spain, Michael thought to himself. What was to stop him from paying the family a visit? Christ, the whole mob was there apart from him and Marie. His feelings towards his sister had changed since he'd discovered that Margee's murderers were still on the loose. Christ, he could have killed Marie when he thought she'd denied him his rights.

He had to have revenge, it was the only way he could live with himself; it was what kept him going, gave him a reason to get up in the morning. No-one really understood, not even Paddy. Oh, Paddy would go after anyone who did him wrong, but his motives were not the same as his. Paddy's were all about saving face. Michael had failed to protect his woman, he'd let those two animals hurt and defile her so they had to pay. There was just one problem, his passport was at home and he had not set foot in the place since the day Margee died.

Driving along the familiar street Michael could feel the emotions welling up in his chest. He got as far as the front door when the panic hit him. His hands were shaking so badly he couldn't turn the key. He just couldn't do it; he couldn't cross the threshold of the once-happy home. Back in the safety of his car he decided he would have to get someone to collect it for him.

"Hi, sis."

Marie's heart skipped a beat, he'd forgiven her. Thank

God. She didn't show it often, but she loved her brothers dearly and would do anything for them.

"What's wrong? You must be in trouble to make this call."

"I need you to go to the house and collect my passport."

"The house? Your house? Why can't you go yourself?" Marie knew she was being tough, but it was the only way her brother would get back to normal, if that was ever possible.

"I can't, but if it's too much trouble, forget it." No way was he begging her, but she did owe him.

"I didn't say I wouldn't, I asked why you can't. Where are you off to, anyway, and who's going to hold the fort?"

"I'm going to Spain for a few days. Everything is under control; I just need to get away. I need to sort my head out, so will you do this for me or not?"

"Of course, I just need keys."

Thank goodness things were good between her and Michael again. It was a shame she couldn't get away for a day or two. It would be nice to have all the family together.

# Liar, Liar

There was no doubt it was the Lady Di, moored in her usual spot. Erin had been emphatic she was out on a charter and yet here she was. Another lie. Nick parked his car and made his way on deck. The cruiser appeared to be deserted; there was no answer to his call. No point in wasting the opportunity, he thought, quickly forcing open the door to the main salon. Nick knew from Erin's description where she and Sam had secreted the firearm. He located the hiding place, only to find it empty. No weapon, no ammunition, nothing. Had the skipper found the gun? Simon would know the vessel inside out, so it was likely he had removed it for safe-keeping. If not him, perhaps someone on the charter? Such hiding places were common on board these yachts.

Yet again his girlfriend was involved in some duplicity for which he was being held responsible. He was going to have come up with a damned good reason for the delay in returning the goods. Romanov was getting mighty impatient and, frankly, so was he.

Imelda Gavin watched the woman walk through the ward, checking the patients' name charts. She was looking for her; she knew it as she huddled down under the sheets.

"Mrs Gavin, Imelda, don't panic. Your brother sent me to find you."

This could be a trick, thought Imelda. "I've no brother, missus. My only brother died last year."

"Well, if he's not your brother you won't want this." Sylvia waved a letter tantalisingly under Imelda's nose. "You won't want to know what plans he's made."

Imelda immediately recognised Francis's handwriting. "Give that here," she said, grabbing the letter. "You've delivered it, so don't let me keep you."

"Listen, madam, I detest your brother with all my heart, but I've been paid to find you and make sure everything's in order, so read the letter and I'll go with pleasure."

Imelda opened the envelope and sure enough, it was from her brother.

*Dear Sister,*

*I am sorry to say it is unlikely we will meet again this side of life. You have been a great help and comfort to me over the years, both in my ministry and for 'The Cause'. You have sacrificed more that any one person should.*

*I don't know how much time I have left, but I know it is not long. So with this in mind I have made provisions for you. The apartment is yours to sell or keep and the deeds are held in a safety deposit box in the Banco Seville, here in Marbella, together with a considerable amount of money. The key is hidden in the apartment. Think of St. Jude's and you will know where to look.*

*Please take this money and enjoy what is left of your life, my dear sister, and don't think too badly of me.*

*Fondest regards*
*Francis*

For the first time in many years Imelda Gavin felt remorse. If she hadn't been so stubborn she could have been with her brother, not trapped in a bed at the mercy of others. She had to get to Francis; she would stay and care for him as she always had.

"Where is my brother?" she asked the woman.

"At the moment he is in the marina, on board a fancy sailing ship, but as soon as I return with news of you, we set sail. After that I have no idea."

"I'm coming with you. Nurse, nurse!" the invalid called. "Nurse, bring me my clothes. I'm discharging myself."

"She hasn't a clue what you're saying," laughed Sylvia. "If your brother had wanted you to join him, he would have said. You need to stay here and get well. Do you have a message for him?"

"Just tell him thank you."

Imelda turned away from her visitor, not wishing her to see her tears.

# Unexpected Guests

"What the hell are you doing here?" Paddy almost choked on his coffee. The last person he'd expected to see was his brother Michael.

"You all seemed to be having such a grand time, I thought I'd join you for a bit."

"That's all very well, but who's taking care of business?"

"Everything's under control, I only expect to be here a few days. A week at most."

Paddy's reply was cut short by Lizzie and Bridget's arrival.

"Michael, oh Michael, it's good to see you, son. Why didn't you let us know you were coming?"

"It was a spur of the moment thing, Ma. I just caught a flight and here I am."

Bridget knew from Paddy's face that he wasn't taken in by his brother's explanation. There was more to Michael turning up than he was letting on.

"Where are we going to put you?" Lizzie fussed over her son.

"Don't worry, Ma. I've booked into the hotel across the road. I'm sorted."

"It's a bad job when my own can't get a bed and we're

giving what we have to feckin' strangers," the old dear glared at Sam.

"I'll go back to my own place," the girl offered. "It should be safe enough now."

"You will not," Bridget insisted. "Michael's a big boy. He'll come to no harm in a luxury five-star hotel, situated not a hundred yards from here."

"Humph." This came from Lizzie, who had never bought the story of the boyfriend from day one. Sam was just a freeloader as far as Lizzie was concerned.

"So, what's the real reason for your visit?" Paddy challenged Michael, as they sat in a bar overlooking the marina. "You don't for a second think I'm buying that bullshit?"

"I take it you know about young Thomson and his sidekick? We were all duped by them. The Russians had nothing to do with Margee, or anything else for that matter. While we were chasing halfway round the country looking for Rasputin and his mob, that pair were sitting back laughing at us. They've been taking the piss from the start and I'm here to finish them."

"I had my suspicions, but why are you here?" Paddy queried.

"When his father's crew dumped them and McAfee's brother threatened them in public, they took off. Old man Thomson has had a place here for years."

"If they are here, we'll find them. You can be sure of that."

"Maybe I should move back? I'm going to have to soon anyway," Sam said to Bridget.

It was cramping her style being in such a crowded

apartment. It hadn't bothered her to begin with, but she really liked this new guy, Dave, and it was a bit awkward not being able to take him back at the end of the evening, not that he seemed bothered by that.

He was certainly keen – she'd had lunch, a couple of drink dates and he was constantly calling to see what she was up to. Unlike most blokes, he seemed really interested in her, wanted to know about her past, her life here in Marbella, in fact, everything. He was so easy to talk to, a complete gentleman and gorgeous to boot.

"How long have you stayed with your mate's family?" he asked as they were enjoying cocktails in the Polo House.

"It's been a couple of months now, but it's getting a bit crowded. I'm thinking of moving back to my old place."

"I hope you don't mind me asking, but why did you move in with them?"

"A jealous boyfriend broke into my apartment and trashed the place." Sam had tripped this story off so many times she was beginning to believe it herself.

"Is he still bothering you?" Junior asked.

"Who. . .?" Sam was confused for a few seconds. "Oh, you mean my ex?"

"Of course, who else would I mean?" Junior picked up immediately there was something not quite right. "Trust me, you don't have to worry on that score. I'll take care of him or anyone else who gives you grief, for that matter."

Sam had often wondered what it must be like to be Erin Coyle. To know someone cared enough to protect you day and night. All her life she'd had to fend for herself. Sam had spent so many years ducking and diving, it had become second nature. Maybe Dave was the one? But,

216

as much as she liked him, it was still early days, so she'd carry on with the charade for the time being.

"He's always around somewhere, but he doesn't bother me. It's probably safe enough now but living with the family has its advantages."

Junior knew it would be safer for him if she didn't live with the Coyles, however she was a mine of information about their comings and goings.

"I'd give it a bit longer just to make sure."

"You must come and meet them, they're quite a crew. And now Michael's arrived, that's the whole family together."

"Not quite, there's still the sister, Marie."

"How do you know about her?" Sam was immediately on her guard.

"I'm from Glasgow, everyone over the age of five knows the Coyles," Junior recovered quickly, realising his slip-up.

"Are they that famous?"

"Infamous is more like it. You're fraternising with the elite of the Scottish underworld. As for meeting the family, I'd rather not, if you don't mind. I'm way out of their league." I should have been an actor, Junior smiled to himself.

Sam was falling for him. Junior knew it, but to him she was just a means to an end.


"This is our chance. We might never get another opportunity like this again."

The two mates were lazing by the pool, discussing the information Junior had gleaned from his date the previous night.

"I agree, but how? We can't go in all guns blazing."

"Why not? I'll find out from the bird what they're all doing and take it from there. She's already invited me to meet the family."

"Shut up!"

"If Michael has arrived on the scene, I'll bet my life it's because he knows we're here. We'll have to be vigilant."

"They're bound to go out for dinner together some time. Old Lizzie won't be able to resist showing off her boys. That's when we strike."

"I'd better keep in Sam's good books then. She's got some mad ex stalking her, that's why she's staying with the Coyles."

"That could work in our favour, take the heat off us. See what else you can find out. It could be useful."

"Right, it's time we did a bit of gardening," joked Junior.

"Gardening? Fuck off! I thought the old chap did that?"

"He does, but we need to do some digging."

"Digging in this heat? You're having a laugh." Cortellessa was not amused.

"C'mon," Junior made his way to the lean-to where the old Spaniard kept his tools.

Sweating profusely, they uncovered Davey Senior's armoury: a large, steel box, so heavy it took both of them to drag it to the house.

"You didn't think he'd keep this lot under the bed, did you?" laughed Junior.

"Of course not," Genaro gasped at the contents of the trunk. "Thanks to him we're well provided for. There's enough in here to equip even the most respected terrorist," he joked.

# Disappearing Act

Where the hell had the old bugger gone? Simon was positive there had been no one aboard the vessel when he and the woman returned, and he was pretty sure the glass door had been forced. He'd searched the Lady Di and found no sign of life. The old man had said nothing about going ashore, in fact Simon didn't consider him fit enough to be out in this blistering heat. Just as he was about to report the situation to Romanov, O'Farrell strolled into the stateroom, quite unperturbed.

"Where have you been hiding? I've been searching high and low, in fact I was getting rather worried," Simon asked, annoyed.

"Hiding? I wasn't hiding, I was in the shower, cooling down. I didn't think that would be such cause for alarm."

"Of course not, but I looked there," Simon answered, somewhat puzzled and a little embarrassed. "I was worried because it looks like someone has forced the lock on the main door, it won't close properly."

So there had been an intruder, the old man ruminated. He hadn't meant to stay concealed for so long, but neither had he wanted to risk being caught. He must have dropped off, something he was succumbing to more and more these days. One thing he'd learned, however, the skipper had no idea about the hidden room

"Well, how did things go?" he addressed Sylvia.

"You were right about her having had an accident. She was on her way to church when she was knocked over."

"By a car?" the old man asked anxiously.

"No, a kid on a skateboard," replied the woman.

O'Farrell knew right away who had caused the accident, the same menace who'd been tailing them this past while.

"She was admitted to hospital with multiple fractures and required surgery."

"Surgery?"

"Yes, a new hip. But she's recovering well and expects to be home in the next few days. She attempted to discharge herself in order to look after you."

"She's a game old bird, my sister, but I don't want to be a burden to her. I presume you delivered the letter?"

"Of course. She told me to thank you. Now, I've done what you asked. I want to go home to my family"

"Surely you don't think you earned a thousand pesetas just by visiting my sister in hospital?"

# Out of Time

"It's time I shipped that lot back home." Paddy pointed to his womanfolk sitting out on the balcony. "I want Bridget back in plenty of time before the baby's due. This heat's killing her, and a houseful like this is far too stressful.

"Don't kid yourself, they're all having a whale of a time. In fact, I'm pretty sure they've forgotten why we sent them out here in the first place." Michael tried hard not to sound bitter, but the family appeared to be on their 'jollies', showing no consideration for his loss.

"I'm not happy," Paddy continued. "If those two are out here then the women would be safer at home, although I'm beginning to wonder if your information is sound. No-one's seen them and let's face it, they're not hard to miss."

"I was sure they'd be out there, giving it large, making contacts, establishing themselves and letting everyone know two new big shots were in town."

"Me too, but there's been nothing. Maybe we got it wrong, maybe they're still holed up at home, lying low till things die down?"

"I know this sounds daft, but I know they're here, I just know it," replied Michael.

"Look, we'll give it a week. If we don't flush them out by then, I'll take the girls home and you can stay on a bit, how does that sound?" Paddy clapped his brother on the back.

"That sounds good to me. I'm off to have a scout in the old town and you never know, I might get lucky."

Theresa had just got off the phone with Peter and was regaling the ladies with the progress on number twenty-six.

"The living room's finished, all beautifully papered and painted, but listen to this. I've only got a brand new fitted kitchen. What do you say to that, Lizzie? It's almost worth getting killed for. I never thought I'd see the day when Theresa Murphy had an all mod cons, fitted kitchen."

"Listen to me, my friend, you're worth all the fitted kitchens in the street for looking after my boys. Isn't that right, Bridget?"

"Who has a fitted kitchen?" Bridget hadn't been paying attention to the chat, she was more interested in what was going on outside.

"Theresa, is that the guy you saw hanging about earlier in the week?" Bridget pointed to a tall figure lurking in the shrubbery at the entrance to the building.

"Mm . . . I'm not sure, he does look familiar but from where, I couldn't say."

At that moment Sam roared out of the underground car park on her way to town. Alexei sprang into action and was soon hot on her heels.

"He's following Sam," Bridget called to her husband. "That guy who's been hanging around. You'd better go after her."

"How do I know where she's off to? She could be going anywhere." Paddy answered, annoyed at being caught on the hop. "Phone and warn her she's being followed. Tell her to go straight to Nick's, I'll meet her there." The man of the house made for his car.

Racing into town, the wind in her hair and a smile on her face, Sam was off to meet Dave. She paid no attention to the message alert beeping on her cell phone. It was Bridget, whatever she wanted could wait; Sam wasn't putting off her date. She probably wanted her to pick up something from the store, or collect her dry-cleaning. Not today. Today she had a date with destiny, she laughed to herself.


Alexei Petrov was exhausted. He felt as though he'd been following these females forever, and he was no nearer to success. How had he got into this situation? He wasn't an assassin; he picked locks and opened safes for a living. The only thing he had ever killed in his life had been a mouse in a trap, years ago, and even then he'd had to get his wife to dispose of the creature.

This was so out of his comfort zone. Why hadn't he refused at the start, stood up to the man? Who was he kidding? He was a coward, that's why.

His time limit to regain the goods for Romanov was well up, even the phone calls had ceased. He was on his own, out in the cold. He had failed and the Russian boss didn't accept failure. It was highly likely that he was now the pursued, with a bounty on his head.

It had proved impossible to get near Stasinopoulos's woman. She never left the house without security, and the villa was constantly patrolled. Despite his best endeavours he had been unable to get anywhere near her.

He had, therefore, concentrated all his efforts on the tall blonde. She had been quite lax in the beginning, and he had just missed capturing her on a couple of occasions. Now she had taken up with this new boyfriend she was proving just as elusive.

Today was the day, Alexei decided. He couldn't take any more. He would either capture her or throw himself at the mercy of Romanov. He had to be worth something to the oligarch; there was no-one who could open a safe as well as he could.

As usual, Sam was running late. Dave, already seated at the best table in the restaurant, smiled as she approached.

"Sorry, I got held up," Sam apologised as she sat down opposite her date.

"That's okay. You look beautiful," Junior complimented her.

Blushing, she thanked him. He certainly knew how to charm a girl.

"What have you been up to today, anything exciting?"

"Not really, I spent most of the day with Erin. She's having relationship problems, not that I'm much help in that field," smiled Sam.

The two chatted amiably over dinner, although Dave seemed a little distracted.

"Is everything okay?" Sam asked.

Please don't let him go off me, she thought to herself, convinced she was punching way above her weight.

"That guy on the other side of the street," Dave pointed out the locksmith to Sam. "Do you know him? Is he the ex-boyfriend? Every time we're out together he's been hanging around."

"No, he's not my ex, but come to mention it, I have seen him before."

No way could she admit to being tailed by one of the Russian Mafia because she had relieved them of a significant amount of dosh. As understanding as Dave might be, she was sure he would draw the line at dating a thief.

"Interesting," he deliberated. "So you have no idea why he would be following us?"

"Could it be you he's interested in?" she asked.

"I shouldn't think so. We've only been in town a short while. Nobody knows us. At least, I don't think they do. Anyway, he's only about when I'm with you." Junior knew damned well there was every possibility it could be him the dude was after, but he couldn't blow his cover. "There's only one way to find out." He called for the bill and the two left the restaurant and headed towards Sam's car.

Turning into a quiet residential street, Junior suddenly stopped dead, spun on his heels and raced back the way they'd come, leaving Sam perplexed at his actions.

He pounced on the man following them and grabbed him by the throat, pinning him against a wall.

"What's your game, buster?" Junior snarled at his captive.

Whatever language the guy spoke it wasn't English. Struggling, attempting to free himself, the tall Russian knew he was in trouble and implored Sam to help, which of course, meant nothing to her.

"Leave him, Dave, you've scared him enough. C'mon, let's go before someone calls the cops."

But her date was on a mission, raining blow after blow on the locksmith, relishing each punch. Sam, no stranger to fights, or violence, recognised this was no 'warning off'. This was murder and it scared her witless. This guy wasn't going to stop, despite all her pleading, until his victim had drawn his last breath.

Suddenly the battering ceased, the locksmith dropped to the ground and Sam saw the glint of steel in Junior's hand. Fuck, he'd stabbed him. She ran to where the man lay in an ever-increasing pool of blood. Junior grabbed her by the hand, dragging her back to the crowded main strip.

Sam drove in silence for some time, still shocked at what she had just witnessed.

"You do realise I saved your life back there?" Junior spoke first. "I did it to protect you, you do understand that, don't you?" He had to make sure she would back him up. "No-one scares my woman."

"What if someone saw us, someone from the restaurant?" Sam stuttered.

"No-one saw us, the street was deserted and he has no identification on him. I made sure of that," Dave pulled out the blood-stained wallet.

"He's Russian," Junior looked through the contents. "Why would a Russian national be tailing either of us?"

"It's not me," Sam stated, not sounding particularly convincing.

Fortunately, under the cover of darkness, Junior didn't notice his dinner date turn decidedly pale.

Deep down, she knew Dave's actions were not that of an ordinary Joe; he had enjoyed the confrontation too much. This guy could more than handle himself and he was well armed. It certainly wasn't the first time that knife had seen the light of day. What if he decided she knew too much? She could end up on a slab in a Spanish mortuary next to tonight's victim.

# Return to Sender

"I want you to deliver a package for me," the old man said, smiling.

"I told you, I've done what you asked. Job done," replied Sylvia. "It's time to head for home."

"We won't be setting sail until this delivery is made. So make your mind up. Of course, you could always charter a boat to take you home, but it'll cost."

Furious, but seeing no alternative, Sylvia agreed to the old man's request.

"It's quite straightforward. All you have to do is deliver this to Sergei Romanov personally. As soon as you leave the building, call me. Is that understood?"

"Of course, but what if this Sergei person is not there or he refuses to accept?" Sylvia asked.

"Bring it straight back. Remember, it is vital you call me the minute you leave."

"What's in the package?"

"That doesn't concern you."

"It does if it puts me and my children at risk."

"That's a chance you'll have to take. The sooner you go, the sooner we set sail."

"Who sent you?" Romanov demanded.

"The old Irishman," replied the woman. "I was to

deliver it to you personally, with this," she handed a handwritten note to the Russian.

The note simply read:

*The last delivery from the Lady Di,*
*regards Frank.*

"You can tell the old man, if he wants to live, not to cross my path again."

"It's been delivered," Sylvia reported back to O'Farrell as instructed.

Señor José Rodriguez, Marbella's chief of police, had been astounded to hear from the Irishman, one-time associate of his old friend, Pete Mack. He was sure he had been reported missing a while back, but whatever the case, O'Farrell was back in the land of the living with a few scores to settle and the means to do so.

Top of Rodriguez's most wanted list was the Russian oligarch, Sergei Romanov; there was no scam that man didn't have a finger in. The chief was well aware of his activities but he was untouchable, or he had been up until now. If the information from the old man was legit, Señor Romanov would find himself behind bars before the end of the day.

The chief watched as the courier left Romanov's den. She made a brief call before speeding off in a waiting cab. A few minutes later the chief got the green light, the raid was on, and for once the man in question had no advance warning.

Sergei Romanov was charged with possession of Class A drugs with a street value of 100,000 pesetas. Of course he'd been set up and of course he knew by whom. How could he have been so easily taken in, and by a man of that age? He certainly wouldn't get any older. A few bars would not deter Romanov from running his empire and the old priest was first on his hit list.

O'Farrell chuckled to himself; everything had gone exactly to plan. Romanov was spending his first night in Marbella's jailhouse. The old priest knew that with Sergei's contacts and wealth, it would be a short stay. However, for the moment he was safe.

"I know you'll find this hard to believe, my dear, but I had no grievance against your husband. It was greed that was his downfall. Now take the money and go back to your family. It is unlikely our paths will cross again."

"You don't look like you'll last more than a few days. You're a dying man and I hope to God you suffer every hour till you're taken."

"I'm sure you do," the old man muttered.


Simon had tried most of the day to contact Sergei, with no luck. His cell phone was going straight to voicemail and the landline remained unanswered. Unusual as this was, like all Romanov's men, he never questioned the boss's orders.

No prisoners, Romanov had commanded. The old man was not to step ashore. The reality of the situation was that, given a few more days, his passenger would probably die of natural causes. However, the skipper daren't take that chance. Anyway, he would be doing the old fellow a favour, a few pills in his evening drink would do the trick, and he'd send him off to a watery grave. There would be no returning from the dead this time.

Where the hell was he? Simon had gone to wake his passenger from his afternoon siesta, but the old man was nowhere to be found, he'd disappeared again. The skipper searched the length and breadth of the Lady Di without success. He had last seen him when the woman disembarked and they'd set sail for home. Where was he? There was no way he could have left the vessel without being seen. He must have fallen overboard, there was no other explanation.

Safely tucked up in his hiding place, O'Farrell was amused at the dilemma he was causing the skipper and how he had upset his plans. He'd known what his fate would be from his first night on board. It hadn't taken much to decipher the gist of the telephone call between Simon and Romanov. It seemed that this was to be his last journey. That may well be true, but he intended to take a few of his enemies with him. He'd already ensured Romanov was out of the picture, now he just had to wait. A family party, most of the Coyles in the same place, he couldn't have planned it better.

# Second Sight

"What's up with her?" Lizzie moaned to Bridget as they were preparing lunch.

"Up with who? Sam? Nothing that I know of. She's a bit jumpy, but I suspect that's because of the guy who was following her yesterday."

"Jumpy? She nearly cleared the feckin' balcony when I said good morning. It's got nothing to do with anyone following her. I hope she's not up to any nonsense because I'll bray her if she's involved that other daft mare."

"That's no way to talk about your granddaughter," Bridget laughed.

"No wonder. The pair of them together couldn't make a half-wit. But seriously, they are up to something, mark my words."

"Whatever is wrong with Sam doesn't involve Erin, trust me."

"It's going to be some party with that pair mooching about like a couple of wet Tuesdays."

"Party, what party?" Theresa chose that moment to descend on the kitchen.

"Who's having a party?" Lizzie smartly turned the question back on her friend.

"That's what I asked you," Theresa replied.

"Asked me what?"

"Oh, forget it. She's getting worse," Theresa whispered to Bridget, not seeing the grin on the old one's face.

Bridget had a job to stop herself laughing out loud at her mother-in-law's antics.

Errol was bored. Everyone was out or occupied, except him; he'd been warned to stay put, not to wander far from the apartment. The uncles had given him quite a stern lecture yesterday. All to do with a load of Russians and some guys from home who were after the family. What did they expect him to do? Hide under the bed? As if! There was no way any Russian dude would capture him, he was way too fast. Anyway, what would they want with him? He was only a kid – he didn't know anything. So he was reduced to skating back and forth from the apartment, along the busy seafront to the marina.

"Wow!" he exclaimed.

The Lady Di was back. Errol loved the luxury cruiser and would spend hours aboard, cleaning and polishing – much to the chagrin of his gran, who was often caught bemoaning the fact the youngster failed to keep his bedroom in such good order. In Errol's eyes this was different, this wasn't woman's work. Errol loved the smell, the gleam of the chrome and the highly-polished decks. Simon had promised he would allow him steer the next time they went out and Errol intended keeping him to his word. The youngster would live aboard the Lady Di if he could.

From his position, he watched as the skipper collected his belongings, locked up and placed the keys in the door safe. Yes! He air-punched. That was the rest of his morning sorted, he thought, as he keyed Ryan's birthdate into the pad and released the keys. With his shoes off and skateboard put aside, he got to work.

Stiff, and in excruciating pain, O'Farrell quietly slipped open the panel to his makeshift accommodation. Confident the skipper would be ashore for several hours, he would take this chance to stretch his legs.

It was almost a year since the old man had been diagnosed with prostate cancer. He'd already outlived the prognosis he'd been given by several months, but he knew his time was imminent.. If he could just hang on for another twenty-four hours, then c'est la vie, it would all be over. He was tired and there was nothing more he had left to do. He had taken care of Imelda and after this trip the brothers would reign no more. It was this thought that had kept him going.

The sound of footsteps above startled the old man. As quick as he was able, he stumbled back into the open space, closing the panel behind him. Had he been seen? The old man had no idea, but he could hear fumbling on the other side of the door.

Errol didn't know what he'd seen, but he'd seen something. One minute there had been a strange figure standing in the gloom by the wardrobe and the next it had vanished. Maybe it was the ghost of the previous owner? Come to warn him off his beloved boat. Naw, he didn't believe in ghosts. Anyway, they don't appear in the middle of the day, he argued with himself. But what else could it have been? Opening the wardrobe door, he peered inside, fumbling with the hinges. There was nothing unusual, it was just a wardrobe. What had he expected, Narnia? All the same he was spooked. No way was he hanging around here on his own, just in case.

There was still no trace of their prey. Despite both brothers contacting most of their associates here on the Costas, no-one had any news of Thomson or Cortellessa.

"I think we're wasting our time, Michael. I'm not convinced they're here. Somebody would have spotted them. Neither one is exactly low-key. But, as we agreed, you stay on for as long as you see fit. I've got to get back. I must get Bridget settled back home and there are other things that need our attention."

"Of course. How is number twenty-six coming along? Is it ready for Theresa's return?"

"Another couple of days will see it finished. Wait till you hear this, though. I had a call from Peter last night. It seems there was a bit of bother in one of the shops. Don't panic, it was nothing to do with what's been going on here. Some punter decided he hadn't been paid out what he was due and wasn't having it. So he came back with an air gun and shot the manager."

"What? Was he badly injured?" Michael asked.

"No, he was bending over and copped a load of pellets in his arse," said an amused Paddy. "Anyway, Peter then goes on to tell me that he and wee Riley took it upon themselves to sort things out and are running the shop as we speak."

"Unbelievable," Michael laughed. "We've nearly two hundred men on our books and we have to depend on our next door neighbour and the local drug dealer."

It was a while since either brother had had much to laugh about.

"Christ, Peter will be looking for a gaffer's job next."

"That's not quite all. They've only hired Tommy's ma, Sandra, to clean up after the builders and generally look after things."

"Maybe you don't have to go back so soon? It seems like they've got everything under control," smiled Michael.

# Unsuspecting

"Is everything arranged, and are you sure she definitely doesn't suspect anything?" Erin asked her mother.

"Yes I'm sure, and Lizzie has taken her off to buy something posh to wear. She thinks you've invited us for an evening cruise before we head for home."

"Theresa would never think for a moment that anyone would go to the trouble of celebrating her birthday. She's such a funny old trout, but Gran would be lost without her."

"You know, Erin, I'm dying to get back to my own house. It's getting too near my time to be away from home and although it's been exciting, I just want a bit of peace and quiet."

"You've been great through all this, but I understand why you need to get home. With the all the carry-on Sam and I stirred up, I'm sure you'll be glad to see the back of us."

"Don't be daft, lassie, I could never want to be rid of you. You do know this baby will never take your place?"

"Mum, I'm a bit long in the tooth to be jealous of my baby brother or sister," her daughter laughed.

"It's good to see you smiling. You've not done much of that this past while. Is everything alright? I've not seen much of Nick lately."

"Me neither," answered Erin. "I think it's over

between us. We never see each other and when we do, we have nothing to say."

"Oh, darling, I thought he'd got over all that nonsense with the Russian. Your father thinks he has, shall I get him to have a word?"

"No, Mum, definitely not. That's part of the problem. He thinks I put my dad before him, which is ridiculous."

"Not really, he's a proud man and it may sound old-fashioned, but men like Nick and your dad have to feel they're in charge. You just have to learn how to let them."

"It's too late. I'm pretty sure I'll be coming back with you."

"That's such a shame. You know I was quite against the two of you at the beginning. There's the age difference for a start, but I like him and I would have put money on him being the 'one'."

"Well, you would have lost," her daughter said sadly.

# By Invitation

He'd been ringing since early morning and although Sam wasn't ready to face last night's dinner date, there was no avoiding him.

"Meet me at the Family News Stand in half an hour," Dave insisted. "We can grab a paper and see if anything's been reported."

Sam read out the report stating that the unidentified body of a man had been found the previous evening. No witnesses had come forward and the Gardaí Civil were looking for a group of youths, thought to be German, seen in the area.

"I told you no-one saw us, so stop worrying. I did it for your sake, remember. If I hadn't sorted the situation it could have been you."

"Stop worrying? I've not slept a wink and I can't get the poor man's face out of my head."

"Poor man? For God's sake, he wasn't hanging about for nothing. Forget it, you're safe now, don't give it another thought."

"Are you mad? You killed a man, how can I forget it?"

"Ask your mate. Her family are responsible for half the murders in Glasgow. She'll tell you it's a dog-eat-dog world nowadays. I'm sorry you had to witness that but I'd rather you be a witness than a victim."

"The family know something's wrong with me. Both Paddy and Bridget asked if I was feeling okay. I just can't get it together. I'm terrified I'll blurt something out."

"You'd better not. You have to keep quiet, we don't want them poking their snouts in."

This female was becoming a liability, Dave thought. She was going to have to go before she landed them both in the shit. She'd just about outlived her usefulness. What the fuck was she prattling on about now?

"There's a family party on board the Lady Di tomorrow. I don't think I can face it on my own. A couple of drinks and God knows what I'd say."

"I'd come with you and hold your hand, but I've got an important business meeting which I can't renege on."

"Couldn't you come after, just for a quick drink? The family are keen to meet you."

"I'll do my best."

By that time, he smirked to himself, they should be no longer be a problem.


"A family party on board the cruiser couldn't be better," Genaro clapped his hands.

"Are you thinking what I'm thinking?" Junior grinned.

"Would it have anything to do with a quantity of plastic your old man had the foresight to provide?"

"It would. There's enough in there to sink the QE2. Certainly enough to make their party go with a bang."

"How are we going to play this?" Genaro asked his mate.

"We're going to dispose of the bastards all in one go."

Both Junior and Cortellessa were well used to

explosives, having used and experimented with them since they were teenagers.

"We can hire equipment from one of the diving schools on the beach and charter a speed boat from the guy we used before. We'll plant the explosives tonight around midnight. Tomorrow we intercept them on their way back to the marina. Get close enough to detonate the explosives, making sure they recognise us, but be far enough away so as not to be caught in the blast. BOOM – party over," Junior laughed.

It was almost 3am when the two conspirators finally rolled home. No way would the Lady Di survive the blast they had engineered, both agreed. With the plastic placed strategically below the water line she would sink quickly, and hopefully without a trace.

# Just Another Day

"I'll miss this place," said Theresa thoughtfully. "It's been grand, but I'm dying to see my house, and Peter, of course."

"He seems to have come into his own while you've been away," remarked Lizzie. "The lads are quite impressed. It seems he's running one of the shops until they get back."

"I told you there was more to Peter than folk gave him credit for."

"Oh aye, kidding you on for all these years while he was out painting the town red, that's certainly commendable."

"That's in the past, Lizzie. I don't want to fall out with you, not on my birthday."

"It's your birthday?" kidded Lizzie. "Why didn't you say? We could've had a wee party."

"Not at all, you've all done enough. Anyway, I'm looking forward to tonight. I've never been anywhere so posh. The nearest I've ever been to a cruise is the Renfrew Ferry," exclaimed an excited Theresa.

"Away you go and get ready, we'll be leaving soon and you know what Paddy's like about being on time." Lizzie was beginning to find it difficult keeping up the pretence.

It had been murder for the two young bucks to stay out of circulation; they were used to being players. But everything depended on them lying low and not alerting the Coyles to their presence. That would all change after tonight; Marbella would soon know who the new faces were.

"According to Sam it kicks off around five," said Junior. "Drinks on board, a short cruise along the coast to Gibraltar for dinner and then back around ten." Junior reported.

"We'll take a trip to Gibraltar this morning and suss out a good spot to set off our fireworks," Genaro laughed at his mate. "I've waited a long time for this opportunity, after tonight, Glasgow is ours for the taking."

"Michael, that was James Urquhart on the blower," Paddy called to his brother.

"Who?"

"James Urquhart, the bank robber from Stirling. He's just after telling me he spotted Cortellessa this morning leaving a charter shop down by the marina."

"Was it definitely him?" Michael queried.

"Positive. Urquhart had a run-in with his old man, Mario, a few years back, over some job that went wrong. There's been bad blood between the families ever since. He didn't know we were looking for the dude or he would have contacted us earlier." Paddy was annoyed at the delay. "Shit, we'll have to leave it for now. Bridget will skin me alive if we let her down tonight."

"I don't suppose another day will make much difference," replied his brother.

"At least you know for certain they're in town."

Erin and Sam had spent the previous two hours decorating the Lady Di with bunting and floral displays in honour of Theresa's birthday.

"What's up with you? You've hardly said two words all afternoon." Erin questioned a very subdued Sam.

"Good God, can a girl not be quiet without the Spanish Inquisition?" Sam snapped.

"Not when that girl is as gobby as you are normally. So c'mon, 'fess up, something's bothering you. Has the boyfriend dumped you?"

"No, but you're right, something did happen the other day and I can't get it out of my head."

"He hasn't harmed you, has he?" a concerned Erin asked.

"No, not me."

"So he's harmed someone?" Erin was trying her best to elicit the reason for her friend's mood.

"You know the Russian who's been on our tail?"

"Of course. My dad and Nick think he's been called off."

"He hasn't, he's dead."

"Dead? How do you know?" Erin exclaimed.

"Because I was there when it happened," the girl admitted.

"Good God, Sam, how?"

"It was Dave, he killed him."

Sam relayed the evening's events to a shocked Erin.

"And he insisted he'd done it for me. Honestly, I pleaded and pleaded with him to stop. Then he knifed him."

"We need to speak to Nick and my dad. I can't say I'm sorry, he might have got lucky and one of us would have copped it."

"Funny, Dave said you would say something like that."

"Did he now? How very astute of him, I can't wait to meet him properly," an indignant Erin replied.

"I'm not sure if he's coming tonight, he has an important business meeting that can't be put off."

"How very convenient. But, if not tonight, I'm sure we'll cross paths very soon. He's right about one thing, Sam. The deed's done, there's nothing you can do to make it different. You have to put it to the back of your mind and get on with life."

"If we last that long," mumbled Sam.

How ironic, Erin thought to herself, if only she could take her own advice. She'd hardly seen Nick since her night out on the town and how she regretted her smart remarks. But, she was her father's daughter and no matter how hurt she was, she would keep face. Her man was out until all hours, often not returning until the following day and sleeping until noon, meaning their paths seldom crossed. Erin knew the longer this lasted, the less chance she'd have of recovering the situation. Her best chance was this evening: a romantic cruise with a few drinks and, hopefully, she would be able to prise her man away from business. She had to give it her best shot.

# Blast Off

The guests were assembled, awaiting the VIPs' arrival. Together, along with the family and Nick, Bridget had invited an elderly couple the ladies often met for coffee on their morning stroll and a gentleman, originally from Glasgow, who it turned out was a retired art dealer and sometime forger they had been introduced to at one of the many tea dances the two enjoyed. Making up the numbers were the young couple from the apartment block whom Bridget had become friendly with.

"All for me?" the birthday girl repeatedly asked, "All for me?" between bouts of tears. "Wait till I tell them all at the bingo. Imagine me having a party on a big boat like this. Lizzie, make sure you take plenty of pictures." Theresa was completely overwhelmed.

It was a lively group who set off on their evening cruise to Gibraltar. No one was at all interested in the powerful speed boat on their tail.

"This thing can shift," Genaro shouted over the noise of the engine. "We should get one back home, it would be fucking fantastic for pickups. It could definitely outrun those 'puddle jumpers' patrolling the river just now."

"As long as it can keep up with today's target," Davey roared back.

"Leave it to me," Genaro watched the Lady Di disappear over the horizon.

"For fuck's sake, stop mucking about and get within sight of her. This is the only chance we'll get to take them all out."

"Calm down, I know what I'm doing. It's a shame we have to sacrifice such a beauty. She really is a magnificent beast."

"Listen, when we take over you can have all the boy's toys you want. Let's get this over with first."

The cruiser was back in sight and Junior calmed down considerably.

For two of the most sadistic killers of their time, Thomson and Cortellesso lived by their own peculiar, moral code. They were not the stereotypical hard-drinking Scotsmen, indulging only occasionally in an American-style beer. And although drugs were freely available, an odd line of coke was their only weakness. They got their kicks from a far deadlier source. However, this evening was a special occasion. Tonight they would take out Glasgow's most powerful family. So a line of the purest and most expensive coke available had them banging. They were on top form, ready for anything.

"I can't wait to see the expressions on those bastard's faces, especially the Big Man's. When he realises it's us, he'll shit himself," gloated Junior, who could barely contain himself, almost shaking with excitement. Watching the Lady Di through his binoculars, he muttered, "Shouldn't be long now."

What the fuck was going on, what was happening? Junior couldn't believe the scene that was unfolding before his eyes'.

"Have you had a look at your mother?" Lizzie asked her granddaughter. "She looks awful, I'm quite worried about her."

"She says she feels a bit seasick," answered Erin. "But look, the water's as calm as a mill pond."

"I think we should get her checked out, get the skipper to call ahead for a doctor or an ambulance to meet us, what do you think?"

"Better to be safe than sorry. It's probably nothing, just the heat, but it won't do any harm," Erin agreed with her gran.

"Don't say a word, she'll get even more agitated. You know what she's like about causing a fuss."

"I agree, you go and sit with her, try and get her to lie down. We're not far from Gib, I'll arrange for someone to meet us. What about my dad, should we tell him?"

"Just tell Paddy she's feeling a bit off colour, we don't want him running about like a headless chicken. You know what he's like," stated Lizzie.


"Erin, can I have a word please?" Nick pulled his girlfriend aside.

He'd been trying to gain her attention since he'd come on board. He had to admit she looked fantastic – breathtaking – wearing a pale lemon dress, which set off her deep, golden tan. And her hair, definitely her crowning glory, actually glistened in the early evening sun.

"Sorry, not now, Nick. I need to see to my mother. Later, we'll talk later," she dashed off.

"Too late," he muttered to himself, "much too late."

He'd hoped, just for once, she'd put him first. But no, he was way down the pecking order. Why on earth had he come on this trip? he asked himself. His business with the Coyles was all but finished. All that was left to deal with was the return of the contents of the strong box. Now he was back in Sergei's favour, and the Russian who had been tailing the girls had been taken out by Sam's new boyfriend, there was nothing more to keep him involved. He was sure Erin intended returning home with her family later in the week. It was a pity they hadn't lasted long, but he'd live, he was much better as a single man. She had been the first in a long time to tempt him.

"Simon, I need you to call ahead and arrange for an ambulance to meet us. I'm worried about my mother and I want to make sure everything's okay."

"Sure, I'll do it now. I have to alert the port authority before we arrive anyway. They can arrange for medical attention."

"How long before we get there?" asked Erin?

"ETA forty minutes," replied Simon.

# Old Scores

"Sir, what do you make of this?" Naval Officer Jones called over to his senior.

The officer was about to go off duty when he received the call. Desperate to get home, he toyed with the idea of passing it on to the nightshift but he knew how his boss felt about this particular vessel and its crew. He couldn't risk missing a capture.

"Good God," was the astounded response. "I never expected to see her again. It must be two years or more since she last ventured into these waters."

Officer Jones could see his early night disappearing. "What action do you want me to take? What do I do about the request for medics to be in attendance?"

"We stick to the usual procedure with suspected smugglers, Jones. I'm damned sure their request for a medic is merely a decoy. Which crew is in the vicinity?"

"The HMS Scimitar, sir. They are approximately three miles south of the target."

"They'll be the first responders. I've been waiting a long time to capture this bunch."

Bridget was relieved to get out of the heat, she'd felt nauseous most of the day and her back was agony. It was time she was home and no matter what objections he might have, she intended telling her husband the next day.

Lizzie had gone off to make some tea, leaving Bridget alone in the deliciously cool stateroom. For the first time that day she was comfortable. Lying in the darkened room, she drifted off to sleep. She was in that semi-conscious state, between dreaming and wakening, when a grating noise, like a door opening, brought her back with a start.

Peering over her was a grotesque figure. Was she still dreaming? It took Bridget a minute to recognise the black man. The one everyone had mistaken for Canon O'Farrell. Why was this person at her bedside and where were her family?

"Well, well, Bridget, long time no see."

Hail Mary Mother of God, it was him. "What are you doing here?" she asked the gnarled creature. "If Paddy Coyle sees you you're a dead man."

"Again? I don't think so," said the old man waving a pistol.

Further conversation was cut short as Bridget was gripped with an intense pain. God, no! Surely she couldn't be going into labour? It was far too soon.

"Get Lizzie for me," she shouted at the old man.

"You have to be kidding," chuckled O'Farrell. "I came here to get rid of the Coyles, not assist in another one entering the world."

"Get someone, please. My baby's coming, I need help."

Voices outside the door prompted O'Farrell to return to his hiding place.

"Lizzie! Thank God it's you. Canon O'Farrell was here. He's going to shoot Paddy."

"What? Jesus, where did he go?"

"He's in the wardrobe," insisted Bridget.

"He's in the wardrobe?" repeated her mother-in law-incredulously, almost laughing out loud. "Oh, lassie, you've been dreaming. Here, have a sip of this," she handed a cup of tea to Bridget.

"I'm telling you, he's in the wardrobe, hiding. Look if you don't believe me." Bridget realised how stupid she sounded but she still insisted the man had been in the room.

"He's got a gun, he says he's going to shoot Paddy," she gasped, gripped by another contraction.

All thoughts of black men with guns went out of both women's heads; there were more serious issues at hand.

# All Aboard

Errol had spent most of the cruise on the bridge with Simon. He'd been well warned by his gran and Uncle Paddy to behave, not to be a nuisance. He was in his element and when the skipper let him take control of the powerful vessel, he couldn't believe his luck.

"Keep in a straight line, don't deviate or change course and keep a lookout for other ships. Any problems, I'll be in the galley."

Unknown to Errol, Simon had set the cruiser on automatic pilot. Although he was confident enough in the young lad's capabilities, like his cousin, he was a natural at the helm, but you couldn't be too careful.

"Visual contact reported – over," the radio operator of HMS Scimitar called into base.

"Roger, Scimitar – over."

HMS Scimitar was one of two fast response vessels patrolling the waters around the Rock and was advancing on the Lady Di at full speed.

"This is Royal Navy Gibraltar squadron – identify yourself – over. I repeat, this is the HMS Scimitar, identify yourself – over. No response, sir," the officer reported.

Errol was in his glory, he had a ringside seat. The naval boat must be after someone, smugglers maybe?

The only other vessel in sight was a speed boat which had just made a swift turn and was going back the way it came. Suspicious, thought Errol. This was exciting, far better than being with the oldies.

The radio suddenly burst into life. "Lady Di, this HMS Scimitar."

This was brilliant, the young lad thought as he picked up the mike. "Hello. This is Lady Di – over."

"Lady Di, be prepared to be boarded – over," replied the patrol boat.

"Okay – over." Errol was having the time of his life, but thought he'd better fetch Simon if sailors were coming on board.

"Lady Di, did you understand? Prepare to be boarded," the radio crackled.

"Understood – over." This was cool, thought Errol.

"Simon, you better come, there's a navy boat coming alongside."

Simon, returning to the bridge, couldn't believe his eyes; he was aghast to see a Navy Patrol vessel approaching.

"What the fuck?" shouted Simon. "Why didn't you call me?"

"I'm sorry. I didn't think it was anything to do with us."

"Go get your uncles fast," ordered Simon.

The sound of a loudhailer had the guests peering at the patrol boat pulling alongside.

"Lady Di, turn off your engine and drop anchor, we are coming aboard."

Simon had no alternative but to obey.

"What's going on?" demanded Paddy, "Why are they interested in us?"

"I've no idea but we better do what they say. Please tell me there's nothing I should be worried about on board. You don't have anything incriminating on you, do you?" Simon quizzed the brothers.

"No – for Christ's sake, my wife and mother are on board. Of course I haven't got anything."

"Michael?"

"Ditto."

"How about you, Nick?"

"How stupid do you think we are?"

"It's nothing personal, I have to know what I'm dealing with," replied the skipper.

The launch pulled alongside the stationary cruiser and the 'Rummage Squad' came on board.

"Get out of here," yelled Lizzie at the two young sailors attempting to search the stateroom.

"Sorry, ma'am," one replied, "but we have orders."

"Orders? I'll feckin' orders you," threatened Lizzie, just as Bridget let out another unholy scream, frightening the two young lads half to death.

"Who's in charge?" demanded Lizzie. "Is it you?" she pointed to the captain of HMS Scimitar, who had just arrived on the scene. "What the devil is going on? Why are we stopped?"

"It's just a routine investigation, ma'am, we're sorry to inconvenience you."

"Well, you better get your arse in gear, my lad. My daughter-in-law is in need of urgent medical attention. We have to get her to hospital immediately." Damn, she hadn't meant to alert Paddy to the seriousness of Bridget's condition.

"What did you say? How bad is she?" Paddy pushed his way into the stateroom where his wife lay sweating.

254

Bridget was in excruciating pain and in obvious need of help.

"She's bad enough, son, we have to get her to hospital."

"I'm sorry, but no-one is leaving this vessel until we conclude our investigation."

"Bollocks," Lizzie cried at the Captain. "If anything happens to my daughter-in-law, I'll hold you personally responsible. And he'll murder you, and I mean murder."

The captain had no doubt the old woman spoke the truth. It was clear that the younger female in the room needed help, and the expression on the husband's face confirmed he would carry out Lizzie's threat without a second thought.

At that precise moment Bridget let out an unearthly shriek, letting those on board know just how serious her condition was.

"For God's sake, man, listen to her," pleaded Lizzie.

Turning to his second-in-command, Captain Kelly ordered the inflatable to be launched.


"They've been stopped by a Navy Patrol Boat," reported Junior to his mate.

"What the hell for? They couldn't have detected the explosives, could they?" asked a worried Genaro.

"I don't see how, but we'd better stay well back. It could be just a random spot check."

"I don't think so, look." Genaro spotted a second patrol boat bearing down on the scene. "They're definitely looking for something big. It's more than likely to be drugs."

"I would never have believed Paddy Coyle would involve his family in a drug run."

"So he's not so smart after all. That doesn't help

us, though. I suggest we head back to Marbella. Wait a minute, what's happening now?"

"Someone's being stretchered onto one of those inflatables, but I can't tell who."

"The old girl's gone along too."

They watched as the boat sped off towards the harbour.

"Jesus, what's going on now? It's divers, they're sending divers down. We need to go! The first thing they'll find is the explosives. Get going before anyone spots us."

They were too late. As interested as the boys were in what was going on with the Lady Di, they were just as interesting to one of the passengers on board.

# Double Trouble

"Please, God, please don't take another one of my family," Lizzie prayed as she was being pummelled by the raft battering its way through the swell.

Bridget had lapsed into semi-consciousness which terrified her mother-in-law more than her dreadful screaming had.

"Please don't let her die. Have we not suffered enough? Take me instead," she begged.

Lizzie couldn't bear to think of life without Bridget. This baby was the blessing they'd all hoped for, but it was looking bad. Really bad. Holding her dear daughter-in-law's hand, she prayed as hard as she ever had.

Back on board, the partygoers were huddled in a group on deck, watching in silence while the 'Rummage Squad' trashed the beautiful cruiser, taking it apart, piece by piece. The exquisite hand-carved panelling was stripped and left lying in a heap, upholstery was torn and strewn all around in their hunt for contraband, and still nothing was found.

"What is it you're looking for?" Erin raged at the Captain. "Look at the state of my property. Somebody will pay for this."

All the while, Paddy paced back and forth muttering to himself, desperately afraid for his wife. No-one could console him.

"Calm down, Dad, she'll be fine. This will soon be over, we've nothing to hide."

Nothing except a bloody gun and ammunition, she thought to herself. A gun Sam had insisted they leave on board. Why the hell had she listened to her?

The squad had been in the stateroom since her mother had been stretchered off, they were sure to find it any minute.

"Are you okay?" asked Nick. "Don't worry. It'll be fine," he reiterated the words she'd used only a few moments ago to calm her father.

"Don't be so sure. The gun, Nick, the gun is still behind the panel, they're bound to find it."

"No they won't. It's not there. I checked a few days ago, it's been moved. Don't worry. I don't think that's what they're looking for."

"Oh, thank God. What do you think this is all about?" she asked.

"Personally, I think it's old scores. It was well known that the Macks used this cruiser to carry out their drug business, amongst other things. I think this is the first time the Lady Di has entered their waters since Pete met his maker. My guess is it flagged up on a list somewhere. The authorities weren't to know it was under new ownership. There's nothing to worry about."

"No? Well, something's up. The divers look as though they've found what they were looking for."

"Shit," said Nick.

"Attention, please." The Captain addressed the company. "We're going to move everyone across to the Scimitar. Collect your belongings and make your way to the gangway."

"Hold on," responded Nick. "Is the boat being

258

impounded? Are we under arrest?"

"No, the investigation has been suspended for the time being."

"Then we should be free to carry on with our journey. This man needs to get to the hospital to see his wife," Nick pointed to Paddy. "And in case you haven't noticed, a few of the guests are not in the first flush of youth. It's getting dark and we want to be on our way."

"The investigation is still on-going, but for safety reasons we have to vacate the vessel. I'll explain once you're all on board the Scimitar."

"No way. I'm not going anywhere. Either we're free or we're not," Nick argued back. "I'm staying put."

"I'm afraid I can't let you do that, sir. A situation has developed and I must insist you follow orders," commanded the Captain.

"No chance. It looks to me like you've fucked up, big time. Look at the damage your men have already caused. You want us shipped off so you lot can plant evidence. No way."

"It's not that simple, sir."

"Oh, but it is," Michael joined in.

"It's routine procedure to send a team of divers down to examine any vessel suspected of smuggling."

"What makes you think anyone on board is engaged in illegal activity? This is a family party and so far you've found nothing," sneered Michael.

"Not exactly. The divers didn't recover what we suspected the vessel might be carrying. However, there is enough explosive attached to the hull to take out a vessel ten times the size of this one. We have to go, and go now. It could blow any minute."

Turning to Erin, the Captain continued, "You have

some serious enemies, Miss Coyle. Believe me, whoever planted the explosives were making sure there would be no survivors."

The passengers were transferred to the naval patrol boat and immediately taken ashore.

"What will happen to the cruiser?" Michael asked the Captain as they disembarked.

"The bomb disposal team will examine it and decide whether it can be disarmed or not. Meanwhile, we have cordoned off the area."

Desperate for news of his wife, Paddy refused to wait for the formalities and stormed off with Erin hot on his heels. Leaving Michael and Nick in charge of the group, he headed straight to the hospital. Please let her be alright, the Big Man prayed silently. He'd never forgive himself if anything happened to Bridget or the baby.

On identifying themselves at the hospital reception, they were ushered immediately to the Intensive Care Unit, Paddy dreading what he would find with every step he took.

"Oh, son! Thank God you're here. What a time she's had," sobbed Lizzie. "She had to have an emergency caesarean section. Oh Lord! It was touch and go for a bit. Paddy, I was so frightened, she kept calling for you and there was nothing I could do. Thank the heavens Bridget's a fighter, the doctors are pleased with her, she's going to be fine. She needs lots of rest and the babies are doing well."

"Babies?" Paddy repeated perplexed.

"Aye, son, babies. Twins. One of each. They're small, but perfectly healthy. They're in the baby unit just now. Go and see them while Bridget's asleep. She's exhausted, she's had a hard time, Paddy, but she'll be alright."

"Twins? Two of them? I can hardly believe it." The Big Man, overwhelmed by the news, headed off to meet the new additions to his family.

# Best Laid Plans

"For fuck's sake, mate, take it easy. You'll get us both killed at this rate."

As soon as the Naval Patrol vessel had appeared on the scene Genaro took off in a fury. Driving at full speed, crashing against the waves, bouncing and rolling dangerously, he headed back the way they'd come.

Junior had no fear of speed but this was crazy; excessive, even for them. "Calm down, I know you're pissed off, but capsizing the boat won't help."

Reluctantly Genaro took heed and reduced the speed considerably.

"There was nothing we could have done," said Junior relieved that his mate had slowed down. "How the fuck could we have foreseen the navy turning up? Let's face it, those divers couldn't fail to discover the explosives."

"True, but neither can they prove who planted them or when."

"Maybe not, but I want to put as much distance between us as we can."

Pulling into the Marina they dumped the hired boat and legged it out to the main drag.

"I don't know about you," said Junior, "but Christ, I need a drink."

"Me too," agreed his mate. "I could get well and truly bladdered," replied Genaro, as they headed into town.

The club was heaving as usual, as they stood at the bar lost in thought. Absorbed in their disappointment, neither felt the need for conversation. Quietly and determinedly they downed round after round of shots, still churning up inside, angry and frustrated over the night's fiasco.

"How the fuck could we have foreseen that?" Junior was eventually ready to talk.

"Just bad luck, mate. Nothing we could have done."

"Well, they're not getting off scot-free," stated Junior. "Maybe it's time to send them another message."

"You don't mean the blonde, do you?" said a grinning Genaro.

He refused to call Sam by her name, always referring to her as 'the blonde', not without a twinge of jealousy. Junior had never shown a preference for either sex, male or female. Although Genaro knew Junior had no feelings for these bitches, that didn't stop him hating them and the desire to hurt and inflict pain was always present.

"Got it in one," his mate answered. "She's more than outlived her usefulness. It's definitely time for her to go."

"Why don't I go back to the villa and prepare for our visitor?" Cortellessa couldn't hide the delight in his voice. "You have a couple more drinks, then invite her back."

The night may not have turned out as they had anticipated, but something could be salvaged from it. This might not hurt the Coyles in the way they'd planned, but they'd get the message. The game wasn't over yet, not by a long shot.

The guests had not had such an exciting night in years.

"I wouldn't be surprised if those boys hadn't arranged

this as some kind of entertainment," laughed the old forger. "I'm just sorry I missed my dinner."

"Even Paddy Coyle can't hijack the British Navy," Nick interrupted sarcastically, "however, he can provide dinner. There's cars waiting to take you all back to Marbella and dinner has been laid on."

A couple of phone calls was all it had taken to arrange.

During dinner word reached the partygoers that all was well with Bridget and the proud father. It was only right they should wet the babies' heads, time and time again.

Just after midnight Michael saw the last guest depart. Nick had gone to meet a business associate, Sam dashed off to meet her new boyfriend and Theresa and Errol had been safely dropped off home.

What a bloody night, Michael deliberated. Why had they been the subject of an almost full military operation? He knew from past experience that raids on that scale were never random, they were usually the result of a tip-off, but he didn't think that was the case here. They had no record of drug dealing in this area and few people knew of his connection with the cruiser. What was even more sinister was the fact that someone had planted explosives. The Captain was right, whoever it was, they wanted rid of his family. They had quite a few enemies, but he knew who his money was on. He needed a drink, in fact he needed several.

Sam ditched the oldies as quickly as it was polite to do so and made for the Marbella Princess. She was sure Dave would be in the hottest club in town. She was more than a little curious about his movements tonight and wanted a few questions answered.

Earlier in the evening Sam had been scanning the horizon when she spotted a high-powered speed boat heading in their direction. As it drew nearer her stomach flipped in excitement when she recognised Dave. She was delighted he had decided to join her.

What the fuck? Sam had thought when she had seen the naval vessel approaching and then spotted the speed boat disappearing into the distance again. Why would Dave and his mate scarper like a bat out of hell just because a patrol boat was alongside the Lady Di? What did she really know about him, what kind of business was he in? If he was just an ordinary businessman, as he claimed, then why had he about-turned and left faster than he'd come? She was being paranoid, but the navy had found explosives attached to the hull of the Lady Di. Someone was determined to take the Coyles and their associates out of the game. They all could have been feeding the fishes right now! She wanted answers.

"Well, at least being born in Gibraltar, they'll be British," Bridget smiled at her husband.

"Of course, I didn't give that a thought. I've been so overwhelmed by there being two of them."

"Why should you be surprised? Don't twins run in our family?" said Lizzie, cradling her new grandson.

"He's an absolute brahma." Paddy tickled the baby under his chin, "And his sister is Erin's double."

"Where is she, by the way? I know she's here, I heard her a few minutes ago," asked Bridget.

"Just checking on your other grandsons," declared Erin as she came into the room. "Errol's home with Theresa and my little man is staying overnight with Bea, Nick's housekeeper. So everything's fine."

"What was the raid all about?" asked Bridget. "What were they after?"

"I've no idea, sweetheart, but whatever it was they didn't find it," replied her husband.

Bridget didn't need to know about the threat to the cruiser right now, he thought. No doubt the presence of the explosives would come out, but not at this precise moment.

"Not even Canon O'Farrell," laughed Lizzie. "You were positive you'd seen him and he was going to shoot Paddy."

"I can't really remember much except that he disappeared into the wardrobe. I must have been hallucinating," the new mother agreed. "It seemed very real at the time."

"Well if it was him and he's still in the wardrobe, he's on his own in the middle of the Med, once again."

"Let's give this lady some peace. We'll see you in the morning." Paddy kissed his wife and ushered the others out.

# Shock Horror

Most of the bars were closing for the night and it took a hefty tip to the doorman to propel Michael to the front of the very long queue gathered outside the Marbella Princess. As expected, a few leery young guys expressed their annoyance at this preferential treatment. A belligerent look from Michael soon quelled their protests.

The large scotch he downed in one barely touched the sides. Ready for another, Michael was trying to catch the barman's attention when he spied Sam at the far side of the bar. Great, he thought, someone to wet the babies' heads with, as he made his way to join her. As he got nearer he saw that she was draped all over someone, oblivious to anyone around her. Perhaps this wasn't such a good idea, he thought – he had no intention of playing gooseberry. He stopped suddenly, feeling as if he had been shot. He could hardly breathe. The last person he expected to see, and certainly not with Paddy's houseguest, was the man Sam was currently canoodling: Junior Thomson.

Jesus Christ, he could hardly believe his eyes. That fucking treacherous, double-crossing viper, who his brother had housed this past while, was wrapped around the deviant fucker he'd spent the last six months looking for: the bastard who was responsible for Margee's death, changing his life forever.

Keep calm he told himself repeatedly, keep calm. He wanted to rip them apart, tear them limb from limb, especially Thomson.

He couldn't believe the duplicity; he hadn't felt rage like this since the day the murder took place. To think that bitch had slept under his family's roof, sat at their table and all the while she was feeding that bastard with information. Backing away, melting into the crowd, he had to be careful. He had no weapon or back up. With Paddy very much occupied he would have to call on Nick.

"Okay, Michael, you're sure it's him?"

"Of course I'm sure. I'd recognise that ponce anywhere."

"And you say he's on his own, no sign of his mate?" asked Nick.

"Yes, which is unusual as I thought the fuckers were joined at the hip. In fact, gossip back home has implied they're a couple of benders. I didn't expect Junior to be shagging a bird."

"Don't let them out of your sight. I'll be with you in the next half hour. If they leave, follow them and call my cell phone." Nick hung up.

Sam was surprised to see Dave standing at the bar on his own; for once, there was no sign of Genaro. She usually spent most of the time trying to prise the little cockroach from his side. There was something decidedly creepy about Dave's mate and there was certainly no love lost between her and Genaro.

"No sidekick tonight?" she quizzed her date.

"No, he's hooked up with some exotic dancer and taken off."

"Really, that surprises me," answered Sam. "How did your business meeting go, by the way?"

"It dragged on for hours, hence the reason I didn't make it to your party."

Why was he lying? He could have said he didn't want to come, she wouldn't have minded.

"How did your evening go? Anything exciting happen?"

This was weird, he knew what had happened, he was there. Why all the subterfuge?

"Nothing out of the ordinary – the cruiser was only hijacked by the Gibraltar Navy. It seems they thought we were drug runners. Then Bridget was stretchered off and rushed to hospital, where she gave birth to twins. Just another day at the office, wouldn't you say?" she asked sardonically.

"Good God, are you all okay? It must have been terrifying."

Dave's reaction to her revelations seemed so genuine. Maybe she'd been mistaken, maybe it hadn't been him and his mate following them, but she'd been so positive at the time. Could she have been mistaken? she asked herself again. Why would he lie? She wasn't the clingy type. Despite her doubts she was determined to enjoy the rest of the night with him. She'd have a word with Erin in the morning, see if she could shed any light. Meanwhile, she had him to herself and she was going to make the most of this gorgeous, sexy man.

She appeared to have bought his explanation, not that he gave a damn one way or another. She was merely a means to an end and the end had come. As soon as she went off to the powder room, he'd fix her drink. He'd acquired a couple of Rohypnol tablets from some guy in the gents and he intended to lace her next drink. Judging by his past experience with this drug, it took about half an hour to take effect.

# Wetting the Babies' Heads

Paddy, Erin and Lizzie arrived back in Marbella just after one a.m. Lizzie, exhausted and completely worn out by the night's activities, slept most of the journey home. Father and daughter, however, were buzzing, not ready to call it a night. And Paddy, of course, wanted to tell the world his news. He hardly believed it himself.

"Dad, let's go for a drink after we drop Gran off. There's no way I can go back to Nick's tonight and anyway, it's tradition to wet the baby's head, doubly so in your case. I bet Uncle Michael and Nick are out on the town, let's go and find them."

"Good idea," her father agreed.

The big man had secretly hoped she would suggest such a plan; he was still blown away at the arrival of his new son and daughter. Twins! More trouble, he chuckled to himself.

The queue waiting to get into the Marbella Princess had diminished a little, not that that made any difference to the two Coyles. They headed straight to the VIP lounge and bought champagne all round.

One of the features of the exclusive area was the 360-degree view of the club. Tonight, Erin was getting quite an eyeful. She could see her mate in a real state, falling all over the joint, making a proper show of herself. This was way out of character for Sam whose 'claim to fame' was that she could drink any man under the table. Yet there she was, completely smashed.

"Look at the state of her," Erin said disgustedly to her father. "I should go and rescue that poor guy. I've never seen her like this."

"Oh, leave her alone, she's a big girl and to be honest, I've had quite enough drama for one night," replied Paddy.

"How long will Mum have to stay in hospital, and how soon before the babies can make the journey home?" Erin asked, tearing her eyes away from Sam.

"A week, ten days maybe, but knowing your mother it could be tomorrow," laughed Paddy. "Twins, eh?"

"Double trouble," laughed Erin.

Talking about trouble, she noticed there was now no sign of Sam; the boyfriend must have taken her home, thought Erin. It was unlike her to get that drunk. In the past, when they had been out on bar crawls, often for hours, Sam would still be standing long after others had fallen by the wayside. Something wasn't quite right.

"I'll be back in a minute, Dad. I just want to check on Sam."

Erin left Paddy at the bar and sprinted down the long flight of stairs; she caught a brief glimpse of the couple as they were leaving the club.

"Sam, Samantha!" Erin called, but her cries were drowned out by the noise from the usual nose-to-tail line of cars sounding their horns. Unable to get through the crowds quickly enough, she couldn't reach her friend and watched helplessly as the young guy struggled to get her friend into his car.

This was all wrong, no way would Sam be incapacitated that she was virtually comatose. They had both been warned of incidents where girls had been drugged, raped and at worst, murdered. She knew she had to stop him driving off, but how? She had no purse, no phone; she probably wouldn't even be able to get back into the club to get Paddy.

"What the hell are you doing here?" Nick and Michael appeared before her.

"Thank God, I think Sam's been drugged. She's in that car with some guy, we need to stop him."

"Look, we haven't got time to discuss this, but no, I don't think she's been drugged, she's in cahoots with her boyfriend, Junior Thomson."

"Rubbish!" exploded Erin.

"Get your dad to follow us," said Nick as the two men took off in the customary black 4x4, the work horse of the criminal fraternity. Not a job for the Ferrari.

Where had the girl disappeared to? Seriously, she couldn't keep her beak out of anything, Paddy grumbled to himself. Sam was more than capable of looking after herself, why couldn't Erin leave things alone? He was ready for another drink, but supposed he would have to go looking for her. The queue outside the ladies would have daunted a lesser man, but not so Paddy Coyle, who had no such inhibitions. She wasn't there. Surely she hadn't left the club without him? Nothing would surprise him, he thought, as he made for the front door.

"I'm telling you my son owns this club! I came out to find a friend, a friend who's been drugged, by the way." Erin was giving it full tilt to the burly doorman and being cheered on by the clubbers at the front of the queue.

"You're trying to tell me that your *son* owns this club? You don't look more than a kid yourself."

"My name is Erin Coyle. You checked my pass when I came in earlier with my father."

"So you came in with your father, your son owns the gaff and your mate's been drugged? I've heard some tales in my time, but this takes the biscuit."

"It happens to be true, boy," said the Big Man, stepping in front of the doorman with his best 'don't mess with me' look on his face. "Her son *does* own the gaff, as you put it."

Taking the measure of Paddy, the doorman knew when he was out of his league. "I'm sorry, sir, but you have to admit it's original, and highly unlikely."

"You're right, son," laughed Paddy. "It's certainly original. Now, young lady, what the hell were you thinking, leaving me all on my ownsome?"

"Dad, we've got a big problem. Sam really does look as if she's been drugged. What makes it worse is she's with Junior Thomson. Nick and Uncle Michael are tailing him."

"Bloody hell, Erin, how many drinks have you had?" her father looked doubtfully at her.

"I'm telling you, they were waiting for Thomson to leave. Nick said I was to get you to follow on. You ring them while I grab a cab."

"Christ, that was a close shave," Junior breathed a sigh of relief. "Imagine Erin bloody Coyle turning up like that." He'd only just got away by the skin of his teeth, but he was positive she hadn't recognised him.

"She nearly caught us," he continued chattering to his passenger. "Get some sleep now, lady, because you won't get much later."

274

"It's a pity about the cruiser," he mused. "Bloody navy turning up like that. We couldn't have foreseen that happening, could we?" He vented his pent-up frustrations at Sam. "I'm talking to you, bitch," he shouted as he slapped her. A trickle of blood ran down the side of her mouth. "I said we couldn't have guessed the navy would turn up, could we?" He slapped the drugged female again.

Pulling into the drive, the villa ablaze with lights, he spotted Genaro waiting at the door in anticipation.

"Get her inside before anyone sees us," Junior snapped.

"For God's sake, it's two a.m. Who's going to be snooping about at this time?" asked Genaro.

"I'm not taking any chances."

"You're sure you weren't followed?" Genaro looked back along the street.

"Of course not. Stop yammering and help me move her."

Slinging Sam over his shoulder Junior made his way into the house and down the cellar steps, tossing her down on the stone floor.

"She'll not come round for about an hour," he said as he gave the prostrate figure a vicious kick.

Michael and Nick had kept a good distance behind Junior, keeping him well in sight but not drawing any unwanted attention.

As they travelled out to the exclusive Guadalmina Baja area, they watched him turn into a private road. And just at that point Michael's mobile rang.

"Michael, its Paddy, what's the score?"

"Thomson has just pulled into a villa next to the Guadalmina Golf Resort."

"Okay, I'll be with you directly. I'm just leaving the club now."

"So have they found them, right enough?" Erin quizzed her dad.

"They have. This is it, girl. It will all be over tonight, one way or another."

"Good. What about Sam, is she alright?"

"He didn't mention her, but she's obviously chosen which side she's on."

"I don't believe a word of it. She'd never betray us. Never. I'm coming with you."

"Indeed you are not. You'll get a cab back to the apartment and stay there till it's over," her father ordered.

"I'm not arguing with you, I'm coming."

"Look, this is wasting time. I can't take care of business and watch out for you at the same time. Erin, please, for once in your life do what you are told." Paddy climbed into the waiting taxi and sped off.

Erin was fuming. No way was she leaving Sam. She didn't believe for one moment that her friend had been deceiving the family. Anyway, she owed her big time for her help in the past.

She flagged down a taxi and jumped in. "Follow that cab." she told the driver. "I've always wanted to say that," she smiled.

The driver, looking at the crazy woman, asked "Where do you want to go?"

"I told you! Follow that cab, but don't let him know," she repeated, waving a bundle of pesetas at him.

"Let's have a scout round while we wait for Paddy," Michael suggested.

"Okay, but no heroics. We wait until your brother arrives so there are no slip-ups. Agreed?"

Michael nodded reluctantly, he couldn't wait to get

his hands on the bastards.

Keeping in the shadows, they followed the boundary of the property. The house was ablaze with lights and Madonna was blaring from speakers all over the house.

"They obviously don't give a fuck about the neighbours," commented Michael.

"Right. Paddy should be here shortly, let's get back to the car now we know the layout."

A sharp tap on the window of Nick's vehicle alerted them to Paddy's arrival.

"We've checked the place over," Michael informed his brother. "They were both in the lounge when we left five minutes ago."

"What about the girl?" Nick asked.

"If she gets in the way . . ." Paddy let the words trail off. He liked Sam, but as he'd told Erin, she'd chosen her side, so she had to take the consequences.

"Okay, boys, take your pick." Nick opened the boot of the 4x4 to display an array of weaponry. "You'll need these," he handed the brothers each a set of night vision goggles, "when I cut the power."

This guy was a professional, reflected Paddy.

Tooled up and ready to go, the three moved away from the car and silently made their way to the back of the house, unaware that someone was quietly following behind them.

Once Nick located the power supply, he immediately plunged the house into darkness, allowing them to enter via the kitchen, undetected.

"Fuck, another power cut. That's the second this week," called Junior, stumbling up from the cellar. "God knows how long this one will last."

"Shush, what was that? I'm sure I just heard something

outside." Cortellesso walked out onto the terrace to investigate.

"Look," he pointed to the villas on either side. "They still have power."

"How can that be?" asked a bewildered Davey.

"Get back inside," Cortellesso whispered. "Go. Now. I don't like this," he backed warily into the pitch-black villa.

"What the fuck was that?" Nick had also heard a noise. There was someone else out here.

Erin had been caught out when the villa was suddenly plunged into darkness and had fallen over a heavy metal bin. Scraping her shin, she let out a yelp. Where were her dad and the others? They'd obviously not made their move yet.

Since she was a kid, Paddy had instilled in her the need to be vigilant, never to leave herself open to danger. She knew she was in a bad place right now, too exposed. She needed cover till she could be sure they had things under control. Turning to retrace her steps, she ran smack into someone.

Unless the girl had escaped from the cellar and he knew there was no chance of that, then who the hell did he have here? Genaro wondered. It could only be one person, he smirked to himself, two birds with one stone. Grabbing the girl by the hair, he dragged her screaming and kicking across the terrace, towards the patio doors.

Fuck, where the hell did she come from? Fuck, Fuck, Fuck. Paddy cursed inwardly.

"Do you hear her, Coyle?" Cortellesso shouted into the blackness. "Do you hear your precious daughter?"

Although he was desperate to answer, Paddy, like the others, maintained his silence.

"Come out or I'll shoot her now, like the dog she is.

278

Or maybe we'll have some fun like we did with Michael's bird. What do you say to that?"

Still there was no reply.

Genaro was puzzled. Maybe she had come on her own. He found it impossible to believe that Paddy Coyle would stand by and allow anyone to abuse his daughter. He had to admit, she certainly had balls to take him and Davy on single-handed. Like the rest of the Coyles, she was a fighter.

Terrified though she was, Erin had recovered from the initial shock of being caught but she knew it was imperative that she get free. Cortellesso would do as he said, he would shoot her. Fortunately, years of self-defence classes had taught her a few moves.

She slumped against him, making herself a dead weight. Cortellesso stumbled and loosened his grip for a few seconds, which was all the time she needed to take him down. Erin grabbed his balls and with her talon-like nails, dug in until she drew blood, then twisted with all her strength.

Her captor fell to the floor, screaming and cursing, bringing Junior from his hiding place. Erin ran for her life, right into Nick's arms. "Go get them!" she shouted.

With the night vision goggles provided by Nick, there was no hiding place in the blacked-out villa for Thomson and Cortellesso. As they careered around in the dark, their every move was watched. The chase was short-lived.

While her dad and uncle were focusing on the two thugs, it didn't take long for Erin to find Sam, still unconscious on the hard cellar floor.

"I need help," she called. "Nick, I can't carry her by myself."

Coming immediately to her aid, Nick was still shocked at how affected he'd been when he feared Erin was in real trouble. He realised he would have been devastated if anything had happened to her. He couldn't imagine his life without her, but he wasn't sure his feelings were reciprocated.

Carrying Sam out to the car, he made Erin promise she would remain with her friend until the business in the villa was done. "Please don't come in. You can never unsee sights like these. It's bad enough you have to know that sometimes they're necessary."

Heading back into the villa Nick saw Thomson and Cortellesso naked and trussed up.

"Scared?" Michael asked. "Well, you fucking should be. The more you plead, the worse it'll be. I'll show you the same mercy you showed a defenceless woman, a woman who never did any wrong in her life. Her only mistake was believing you pair of evil cunts."

"You've got this all wrong," pleaded Cortellesso. "I had nothing to do with it. It was him," he nodded at his mate.

"You had nothing to do with it, is that what you're saying?" Michael growled at the ponce.

"That's right, it was him."

"You fucking liar!" screamed Junior. "It was your idea. You were the one who planned it all. You brought in the Russians. So don't give me that shite."

"You're both mistaking me for someone who gives a fuck." Michael stated menacingly.

Paddy began the proceedings with a hammer he'd picked out of a nearby tool box. After smashing kneecaps, splintering bone and shattering calves, he removed the expensive Italian shoes both men favoured, and hammered toes until they were reduced to pulp.

Writhing and screaming in excruciating pain, justice for Margee had begun.

"Shut the fuck up," snarled Michael, stuffing soiled rags into their mouths.

Gagging and choking, they suffered as their victims had. Unable to withstand the intolerable pain, Cortellesso passed out twice. No way was Michael letting him off that lightly, and each time he brought him round, spluttering, drenched in ice-cold water.

It was Nick who administered the next round of torture. He chopped off each of their fingers and tore the nipples from their skin. They still hadn't suffered as Margee had. She was an innocent, beautiful flower, crushed by these animals. Michael still wasn't satisfied as he delivered the final humiliation.

"Hold them still," the younger Coyle ordered. And using Cortellesso's trusty 'Stanley', he inflicted the ultimate degradation by slicing off each one's penis and forcing them into their mouths. The mark of a nonce.

Michael was exhausted. At last he had taken his revenge on the monsters who'd killed his Margee. He knew life would never be the same for him but he had at least salvaged his pride. Davey Thomson Junior and Genaro Cortellesso were no more.

The following morning the local paper's front page screamed:

*Mutilated bodies found!*

*The naked bodies of two unidentified males were picked*

281

*up by the crew of a fishing boat as it returned to port this morning. Thought to be the result of a revenge killing between warring gangs, anyone with information is asked to contact the Gardaí Civil.*

"It looks like there was some party last night," the villa's caretakers discussed the mess over their coffee.

They'd arrived just after eight, as usual, to find the normally well-kept villa in an utter state of disarray. Broken furniture and glass strewn everywhere, with no sign of the occupants.

"Youngsters nowadays," the old woman grumbled to her husband. "They've no respect for anything." As she went about her work she thought, these two were worse than most. Lazy, arrogant, nasty pieces of work. She would be glad to see the back of them. Surely their holiday was almost over?

# The Departure

"I've warned enough kids over the years about spiked drinks and I let it happen to me." Sam was still feeling woozy and somewhat disorientated from the effects of the previous night. "I'm glad I was unconscious while it was all going on."

"Trust me, Sam, you'll never know how lucky you were to escape unharmed from those two nutters."

"I know. If it hadn't been for you, God knows what would have happened. Mind you, it's hard to believe everyone thought I was in league with them."

"Forget it, it was a misunderstanding. Everything's sorted now, best put it behind you."

"That fine for you to say, there aren't that many like Nick around. It'll be a long time before I trust another man, I can tell you," Sam said wistfully.

"Don't be daft, you'll meet someone, you've just been unlucky."

"Unlucky! I'd say falling for a psychotic murderer surpasses that."

"Fair enough, point taken," Erin smiled at her friend.

"Have you decided what you're doing? Are you staying or heading back with the rest of the clan?"

"I'm pretty sure I'm going back to Glasgow," answered Erin. "There's nothing for me here."

"Really? Go talk to him. Don't give up at the first hurdle. He's mad about you, it's obvious to everyone."

"Well, not to me it's not. I'd rather go now while we're still on reasonable terms."

"Well, I think you're mad."

"You're probably right," Erin smiled sadly at her friend.

"I'm leaving in the morning," Michael informed his brother. "I've done what I came to do and it's time to get back to business. I've a lot of catching up to do."

"Take Ma and Theresa with you, they'll drive me up the wall otherwise," replied Paddy.

"You've got to be joking. I'll try, but I wouldn't count on it. Have you any idea when you're likely to be home, not that there's any pressure?"

"Hopefully within the week. There are a few things I need to tie up here. I have an idea concerning Thomson's villa and I need to sort out the Lady Di," replied Paddy. "Erin had a call from the Port Authorities to tell her it was cleared and ready to be collected."

"I hope she's going to send them the bill for the repairs."

"I don't think that would do much good. But what do you make of this? There was a report of a passenger being left on board."

"What? Impossible!" said an astounded Michael.

"He was seen by several of the team and the officer was adamant there was someone left on board. He wanted to know how it had happened, who he was and did she realise the old man could have been killed."

"Old man? Do you think it could be . . .?"

Before Michael could finish, Paddy interrupted, "Of

course. It had to be O'Farrell. What did Erin tell them?"

"Erin told them she knew nothing about any passenger, said it must have been a stowaway."

"So where is he now?" Paddy laughed.

"Well, that's the strange thing. The officer said he disappeared."

"And they just left it at that?" asked a baffled Michael.

"I don't suppose they had an option. Anyway, I'm taking Simon to Gibraltar with me later today. He'll bring the boat back to Marbella."

"Well, make sure there are no unwanted guests on board."

"I don't want to go home, Erin," said her young cousin, sulking at being told to start packing. "I love it here. Can't I stay with you and Nick? I won't be any trouble," he pleaded.

Errol had spent a fun morning with Ryan around the pool, diving and splashing, having a great time until Granny Lizzie put a damper on the proceedings and Errol's fantasy of staying in Spain went up in smoke.

"Your mum would never allow it, nor would Gran for that matter." Erin tried reasoning with the lad.

"You could ask them. Please," he begged.

"It's not that simple, sweetheart. I don't think I'm going to be here much longer," said Erin quietly.

"Why? Is Nick going back to London? I thought he had to stay away."

"Shush, keep your voice down. Nick's not going anywhere."

"Well, where are you going?" Errol demanded to know.

"Nick and I are not really together now and I've

decided I'm coming home. So you see, you can't stay, but you can spend your holidays here."

"What do you mean you're not together? You live here."

Erin had no intention of telling her young cousin she was only still in residence due to lack of space at their apartment. She'd barely seen Nick since they had returned home after that dreadful episode at Junior's villa. He spent all day in meetings and the evenings out and about, enjoying the Marbella nightlife. It was time to call it quits. And although she was desperately sad and unhappy, no way would she let it be known. As soon as Theresa and Errol left she would move into the apartment until Bridget and the babies were fit to travel.

"Tell you what, Simon is bringing the Lady Di back from Gibraltar this afternoon. Why don't you and I go for one last sail?"

# Homecoming

"How are my precious bundles this morning?" enquired Paddy, bending over the cribs.

"Oh! I'm just fine and dandy," retorted Bridget, smiling.

"I was including you," Paddy grinned. "Seriously, how are you feeling? You look much better today."

"I'm fine, Paddy, and I'll be even better when I get out of this place."

"What's wrong? Are they not looking after you properly?" asked her agitated husband.

"Of course they are, I just want home. And I mean home to Glasgow."

"Well, you'll have to content yourself for a bit longer. I've just spoken to your consultant and he reckons you and the babies need to spend another couple of days resting, to be on the safe side."

"I can just about cope with that." Bridget looked serious. "So what's been happening? And don't lie. I know you've all been up to something." Bridget knew her husband inside out; there was little he could hide from her.

"We finished what we came to do. The threat's over and it's time we all went home. You don't need to know any more than that."

"Is it definitely over?" Bridget looked him square in the eye.

"It is. Michael, Theresa and Errol are leaving in the morning. There was no way I could persuade Ma to go with them, she's determined she'll leave when you do."

"Now you've got rid of that pair, how will that impact on us, Paddy? What exactly does it mean?"

"It means you'll see even less of me than you do now," said Paddy, making light of her question.

"That's what I was afraid of. You listen to me, Paddy Coyle. Erin barely saw you when she was growing up and I'm determined that's not going to happen this time. I know you're a big shot now, but family comes first. Remember that."

"I know, and I promise that won't happen. It might be difficult for the first few months until things settle down, but Michael will step up to the mark. He's a changed man, Bridget. Marie will take on more than running the club, so don't worry. How could I ever become a 'big shot' with you and my mother keeping me firmly in my place?"

"You've come a long way since the night you came to tell me about my father. And I've had your back every step of the way, so don't you dare let me down now. These babies are a miracle, they deserve to have the attention of both parents."

"I promise," said Paddy gently kissing her cheek. "I promise."

"Is it not about time we gave these babies a name? We can't keep calling them T1 and T2." Bridget had said her piece; it was time to move on.

"What about …?"

Over the next hour, Mummy and Daddy argued back

288

and forth on the suitability of names suggested.

"I like Connor," volunteered Paddy eventually. "Connor Coyle sounds good."

"Yeah, not bad," said his wife.

"How about Caitlin for toots here?"

"I think we've nailed it, Daddy. Connor and Caitlin Coyle, welcome to the family."

# Watery Grave

"Can I come in?" Nick knocked on the bedroom door.

"Of course! It is your house, after all." she replied.

Ignoring the jibe, Nick sat down on the edge of the bed.

"We need to talk. You do remember there's something that has to be put right before you all disappear?" said Nick.

There was no doubt from that remark that he expected her to be leaving along with the family. "And what's that?" she countered, knowing full well what he was referring to.

"I still have to return Sergei's property. It belongs to the company."

"It's a scam, Nick. That money should be returned to all the poor devils who have been conned out of their life savings."

"How we came by it is no concern of yours. I don't want to go to Paddy to recover it, but I will if necessary," threatened Nick.

"It's got nothing to do with my father," Erin snapped back.

"You were quite willing to use your family to get

you out of the mess you'd caused, but now it's not their business? Are you forgetting a man died over this? And believe me, if Romanov doesn't get his property back, he won't be the last."

"Meet me at the Banco de Seville in Porto Benus, opposite the marina at three." Erin said reluctantly.

"Sam, it's me." As soon as Nick had left the room, Erin called her friend. "Nick's just left. He wants the money and I can't put him off any longer. I want you to get the key and meet me at the bank at three. Don't think about pulling any stunts. Do you really want to spend the rest of your life running from mad Cossacks?"

Erin rung off, not at all convinced Sam would do the sensible thing. However, she was convinced of one thing: her relationship with Nick was definitely over, there was no going back.

Emptying the contents of the safety deposit box into his briefcase, Nick snapped the locks shut and turned to Sam and Erin, saying, "Well, it all looks to be in order. We never did recover the weapon, but there's nothing I can do about that. Romanov has asked to see you, Sam. I don't know why, but it might be to your advantage."

"Me? He wants to see me?" Sam was perplexed by the invitation. "What could he possibly want to see me for? Unless it's revenge," the girl shuddered.

"Believe me, if he meant you harm you'd never know until it was too late. No, it was an invitation. Go and see what it's about, you don't have to commit yourself to anything."

"What do you think, Erin?" she asked her friend.

"I'm not sure I'd want to get mixed up with that lot."

"That's a bit rich coming from a Coyle," smiled Nick.

"I'll go if you come with me," Sam challenged Erin.

"I wasn't asked. You'd better go with Nick. He's right, you don't have to agree to anything you're not comfortable with. Go and see what he has to say."

"Okay, I will. Wish me luck.

Later that day, as Erin waited for Errol before their last trip on the Lady Di, she could see him flying along on his skateboard, heading for the marina. There was no way she was getting out of this trip, no matter how miserable she felt.

"It's not as bad as I expected," commented Errol as they boarded the boat, looking at the damage done by the search party.

"I think Simon did a fair bit work on it before he left. But it still needs a complete refit to bring it back up to the standard it was. I'm not sure what I'll do with her. Maybe put her up for sale," Erin confided in her young cousin.

"Please don't sell her, Erin, she's beautiful," said the youngster wistfully.

"Well, whatever the future holds, we don't have to make any decisions today. I'm going to put Ryan down for a nap then we'll be off."

The main stateroom was, as always, pleasantly cool and the little boy was soon fast asleep.

Erin was well aware she should wait for the skipper to return, but for all she knew he could have finished for the day. We won't go far, she thought, and we'll keep to the coastline. The sea was calm and still, perfect weather for a sail.

The old priest woke with a start. What was he doing in this small, cramped space, and why could he hear engines? He was quite bewildered. It took several minutes for his confusion to clear, for him to remember where he was. The Lady Di. He was aboard the cruiser. He had no idea how long he'd been asleep. The last he remembered was seeing naval officers aboard.

O'Farrell was sure one or two had spotted him, but they'd failed to locate his hiding place, so what did it matter? Where was the cruiser headed for this time? he pondered.

He stepped out into the stateroom and was immediately startled by a child's cry. There, lying on the bed, was a toddler. It was Bobby, his beloved boy. If he could have fathered a child, this would be the one O'Farrell wanted as his own.

It wasn't possible, it couldn't be. Bobby Mack had been a young man when he was taken, so who was this? The child had Bobby's bright, blue eyes, white blonde hair and a smile that would melt the hardest of hearts. Of course. Realization began to dawn. This boy had to be Ryan, Bobby's son.

The child was not at all impressed at being startled by this ugly old man and the level of his screams increased by several decibels. Picking the child up in an endeavour to sooth his distress, O'Farrell made matters worse and the screaming reached full pitch.

"Errol, nip down and check on Ryan. I can hear him crying," Erin bid her young cousin.

"Shall I bring him up on deck?" he asked.

"Yes, it doesn't sound like he's going to sleep."

Down below O'Farrell accepted his efforts to calm the child were worse than useless. "This isn't working," he muttered exasperatedly.

293

He had just laid the boy back down as Errol came through the door. "What are you doing? Leave him alone! Get away from him! Don't you *dare* hurt him!" yelled a terrified Errol.

"I'm not going to harm him, but you? You've caused me nothing but trouble since you arrived here. My sister is in hospital because of you."

"Is everything alright, Errol? What's all the shouting about?" Erin called down.

"Tell her everything's fine. Do it or I'll shoot," ordered the priest, brandishing the stolen pistol hidden by Sam.

"Everything's fine. I'm just playing with him," the lad called back.

"Well, come on up, I'll let you take over for a bit."

The old man shook his head, "Tell her you'll be up in a minute," he prodded Errol in the chest with the pistol.

"Now put the boy back down on the bed and go up to the bridge. Remember, I'm right at your back," the priest commanded. "Try anything and I'll shoot you both."

"So you changed your mind," Erin smiled at her cousin. "What's wrong?"

Errol stood to the side, allowing Erin full view of his captor.

"Where the hell did you come from?" she gasped. "So the captain was right. There was someone on board all the time they were searching. It was you."

"That's correct. I've been right under your noses all this time."

"What do you want? We've nothing of value on board, and very little fuel, so what's this all about?" asked Erin, totally bemused.

"It was actually Paddy I was after, but you'll do. After all, it was you who took my boy from me. If it hadn't been for you he would still be alive."

294

"I presume you're talking about Bobby? He wasn't your boy," Erin argued back.

"He was as good as," O'Farrell replied, "and you killed him."

"So it was my fault that Bobby ran off with Ryan? My fault he killed himself and his mother in a freak car crash, depriving his son of a father? Now you're going to deprive the same baby of his mother. That shows *real* compassion."

Watching the priest intently as she spoke, Erin could see how ill and frail he was. No way could he put up any sort of fight, but he did have a gun which evened the odds somewhat.

Meanwhile, down below, a bored little boy had climbed down from the bed and, crawling furiously, made for the open door and freedom.

He could hear his mummy. Mummy meant food and he was hungry. Chattering to himself, he followed the sound of Mummy's voice. There she was, straight ahead. "Mum, Mum, Mum," he babbled. "Errol, rol, rol."

Erin, sizing up the situation, had decided there was only one course of action. So intent was she on O'Farrell, she failed to notice the little visitor crawling toward her. Grabbing the ship's wheel, she spun it as hard as she could, turning the cruiser 180 degrees, causing the boat to roll dramatically and throwing everyone on the bridge off balance. The priest stumbled, dropped the gun and crashed painfully against the railings.

And then the world seemed to stop for Erin; everything happening in slow motion. She watched in horror as her baby slipped through the railings and fell into the wake of the Lady Di. Her baby! She had to save her baby!

In sheer terror, Erin launched herself over the side of the boat without a thought to her own safety.

"Shut down the engines!" the old man called to Errol and summoning strength he didn't know he possessed, he followed Erin over the side into the foaming waters.

He was determined he wouldn't be responsible for another death, and certainly not Bobby's son.

Despite the knowledge he was a fallen soul, O'Farrell prayed and prayed to a God he'd long forsaken, begging for help. He spotted the boy, floating face down on the surface, a few metres from him. Please don't let it be too late, he prayed as he struck out for the tiny body. His strength was failing as he reached Ryan and he struggled to keep them both afloat. O'Farrell was exhausted, several times his head disappeared and he swallowed water before managing to raise his head again – he knew they would both drown. He gave one last frantic kick and surfaced. There, in front of him, was the Coyle girl – the child's mother. And, how could this be? Swimming alongside her was his boy! Bobby had come to their rescue.

Suddenly he was alone. The child was safe, he thought as he drifted through the water, letting the swell carry him far away from the cruiser. The darkness descended swiftly upon him. This time there would be no coming back.

With Ryan firmly in her grasp Erin swam frantically to the cruiser, and with her last ounce of strength she managed to pull herself and the lad out of the water to safety. Unbelievably, the child seemed none the worse for his adventure, bouncing about the deck, intrigued by the life jacket which had no doubt saved his young life. He also appeared to have learned a new word – Daddy.

Where on earth had that come from? Erin puzzled.

The cousins were in a state of absolute and utter shock. What had begun as a pleasant farewell trip at the end of the summer had turned into a fight for their lives. Neither was in any doubt that the ex-priest would have murdered them without a second thought. However, if it hadn't been for him, Ryan would not be crawling about right now. He had saved the boy. Erin thanked her lucky stars that she had always insisted Ryan wore a life jacket at all times, even while napping. If she hadn't, the boy wouldn't have stood a chance – O'Farrell or no O'Farrell.

It was a very subdued pair who arrived back at the marina. Frightened and not knowing what he should do, Errol had called Paddy whilst the drama at sea was unfolding.

News of the Canon's drowning was met with derision from Paddy. "He's already risen from the dead once before so I won't count him out until I see the body. But thank God he saved the wee lad. For that alone we owe him gratitude, but I'm pretty hopeful we've seen the last of him."

"What were you thinking?" asked a furious Paddy when Erin had finished explaining what had just happened. "And why can't you keep her under control?" he attacked Nick whom he'd phoned as soon as he had received Errol's panic-stricken call.

"You don't seem to have done a particularly good job yourself, over the past twenty-one years," Nick argued back. "I don't believe it's up to me now."

"What do you mean, not up to you?"

"Ask your daughter," answered Nick, as he walked back to his car.

"Could we continue this discussion in private?" asked

a righteous Lizzie, herding everyone into the waiting cars.

"So what's all this about?" Lizzie cornered her granddaughter when they arrived back at the apartment.

"Don't ask," Erin snapped at Lizzie. "It's over between us. I'm going home with Mum," she announced. "Please, will you all just mind your own business?"

"I'll be damned if I will," murmured Lizzie. "What was it they said about the fat lady singing?"

# Big Changes

"**O**h my God, would you look at that? Where did you find this?" asked Theresa, darting from room to room, picking up new treasures and exclaiming over old memories miraculously saved from the fire.

It was the sight of her new, fitted kitchen that completely took her breath away.

"I can't believe it," she crooned as she ran her fingers tentatively along the shiny new surface. "I honestly can't believe it. I never imagined the kitchen would look anything like this," the woman was almost overcome with emotion. "My God, Peter, I never knew anyone that could get the likes of this this from the council."

"Don't be daft, woman, this has got nought to do with the council," bragged Peter.

"Oh, Peter, what have you done? They'll come and rip it out." Theresa could see her beautiful, white, shiny kitchen disappearing.

"It's got nothing to do with the council because Michael bought the house and we're going to pay him back."

"Dear God, I can't take on any more jobs to pay for a bloody house, what have you done?"

"I've got a job, that's what I've done. And when they

tart the rest of this estate up, this place will be worth double what he paid."

"Did you say you've got a job? What kind of a job? One that includes drinking and gambling, no doubt." Disappointment was written all over the poor woman's face.

"Sit down and listen. I'm taking over as manager of the bookies in Rutherglen, and wee Riley is my assistant."

"Wee Tommy Riley, the druggie? Aye, you'll make a fine pair."

"We will, he's a whiz with figures. And there's a flat above the shop for him and his ma. The move will take them away from all the drugs, now she's clean."

"How did this all come about?" Theresa asked doubtfully.

"Michael arranged it all. Be happy, Theresa, I reckon whoever set the house on fire did us a favour."

Ever the optimist, Theresa decided she'd enjoy her newfound luxury until it all went pear-shaped, because knowing her luck and Peter's reputation, it most definitely would. She'd deal with the fallout when it happened.

Tommy Riley was another who couldn't believe his luck. He watched his mother as she scrubbed the black and white lino until it positively shone, singing away to herself. He'd not seen her happy since before Billy went missing. She'd completed the rehab programme and was clean, for the moment. Tommy had no doubts that she would most probably fall off the wagon, but having removed her from daily temptation, he hoped he'd reduced the chances.

Tommy hadn't changed his mind about the Coyles. He was still sure that Sean Coyle was responsible for Billy's disappearance and he was equally convinced that the other two had covered up his crime, but he couldn't prove it. He had to hand it to them, though, they had done their best to make up for Sean's deed. Sandra would probably have joined her younger son if Paddy had not intervened. She'd certainly be back on the crack. The Coyles had earned his loyalty for that alone. The fire at number twenty-six had been a blessing in disguise for him also.

"Why did the Russian want to see you?" Erin asked her friend.

It was the first time the girls had had a chance for a catch up since Sam had moved back to her old flat. With the Cossack out of the way, there was no reason for her not to.

"Believe it or not, he offered me a job. Because of all the property scams it seems no one will trust the Russian developers any more. So they've decided to go legit and want a Brit to front their project."

"No disrespect, but why you?" queried Erin.

"He reckons I've first-hand knowledge of how they work, so I won't try to fleece them."

"That makes sense. Are you going to accept?"

"It's great money, Erin, I'd be stupid not to," answered Sam.

"Good luck then, I'm sure you'll do brilliantly."

"There's just one thing. I'm going to be working alongside Nick. Will that be a problem?"

"Why would it be? We're finished and I'm off home in a couple of days."

"Speak to him, Erin, he's as miserable as sin and so are you."

"It's too late, Sam, my mind's made up. I'll be back

later in the year to sort out the cruiser. Right now I want to put some distance between us."

"Well, I'll tell you what I told him. You're a pair of obstinate fools and need your heads banging together."

"What do you mean, what you told him? I hope you've not been discussing us."

"Of course I have. We *all* have," retorted Sam.

"Who is 'we all'?"

"Paddy, Lizzie, and I believe your mother had something to say on the matter."

"What about Nick, what's he got to say?" Erin tried hard to disguise the curiosity in her voice.

"Same as you, it's too late."

"Well then, there's no more to be said, so leave it be." Erin rose to pay the bill. "I don't suppose I'll see you before I leave, so good luck with the job and behave, if that's possible," she smiled regretfully

There had to be a way to get those two fools together, thought Sam, although she was fast running out of time.

A note, she'd get a note hand-delivered. It was an old chestnut, but right now she'd try anything. Rummaging in her bag, she found a pen and paper.

*Erin, I'm sorry. Meet me at the club house at 7pm tonight. We need to talk. Regards, Nick.*

*Nick, I'm sorry, please meet me at the club house at 7pm tonight. We need to talk. Love, Erin.*

The notes had been delivered, it was now up to them. There was no more Sam could do.

Erin read the note and thought, thank goodness, he's seen sense at last. An apology was all she wanted. Hopefully things were going to be alright, it was surely worth one last try.

Nick read his note, someone must have reasoned with her. He didn't ask for much, just a little respect. Maybe they could make a go of it. He could hardly admit to himself how much he'd missed her.

My God, he's handsome, Erin said to herself. With butterflies in her stomach, she crossed the floor to greet him.

She's a head-turner, alright, and tonight she looks particularly stunning, thought Nick.

The maître d' seated the couple at the best table in the house

"I was surprised to get your note," said Nick kissing her lightly on the cheek.

"What note?"

"The one you sent me!"

"You mean the note *you* sent *me*, saying you were sorry?"

"What have I to be sorry for?" said Nick, throwing his note on the table.

"Touché," replied his dinner date, producing her note.

"I think we've been had, and I can guess who by."

"So you're not sorry?" she asked regretfully.

"What for?" replied Nick.

"Well, this is a waste of time. Goodbye, Nick. I'm leaving in the morning. Take care of yourself." Erin left the restaurant, head held high and tears streaming down her cheeks.

She could murder Sam. How could she have thought a stupid, childish ploy like that would work? It was too humiliating, and to make matters worse, he hadn't come after her.

Erin cried herself to sleep that night. Thank God she was leaving in the morning; she never wanted to see him again.

Meanwhile, as Erin fumed in her apartment, Nick too, was agonising over their disastrous meeting. Why had he let her go? What a fool. Was it really so difficult to say he was sorry? But sorry for what? If he didn't know what he'd done then how could he apologise? For God's sake, he'd had enough women in the past to know it was easy to keep the peace, so why had he not just done so?

Maybe it was because this relationship really meant something? That they were beyond mere platitudes? They were equals and if she didn't see that then there was no future. For the first time in years Nick Stasinopoulos tossed and turned, sleep evading him.

"Morning, boss," Sam let herself in, hoping to find Erin at Nick's breakfast table.

She was met with a cold stare. "What the hell were you playing at last night? Have you any idea how stupid I felt? Any chance of reconciliation was killed dead in the water."

"I'm sorry, but I couldn't think of any other way to get you two back together."

"Don't, and I mean don't, *ever* meddle in my business again, or we part company. Is that understood?"

"Yes," said a defiant Sam. "If you get a move on you could be at the airport before they leave."

"Have you not listened to a word I've said?" Nick thundered.

"Not really. Come on! Move, or you'll be too late."

"Sam, enough. I'm not going anywhere."

"Well then, I'm not coming to work for you. I can't

work for a fool," the girl laid down the gauntlet.

"Did you just say what I think you did?" the hint of a smile touched his mouth.

"I don't know, what do you think? I said that you were a fool."

"Maybe you're right, maybe I am. But it's too late."

"Not if you go now. Go on, swallow your pride and show her what kind of man you really are."


The pilot of the private jet had gone through all the usual pre-flight checks and was almost ready to take the Coyles back to Glasgow. The family were all on board and he was awaiting clearance from the tower.

As she gazed morosely out of the window, Erin could hardly believe her eyes. Was it her imagination or was that a familiar, yellow Ferrari racing towards the aircraft?

She wasn't seeing things. It was Nick. He'd come for her, but the private jet was taxiing to the runway, ready for take-off.

Nick sped across the apron and raced alongside the jet, forcing the pilot to abort his take off. The jet slewed to a stop on the runway, much to the consternation of the passengers inside.

"What the hell is that damned fool doing? He'll get us all killed." yelled Paddy.

"I'll tell you what he's doing, he's come for me!" replied a deliriously happy Erin, grabbing her son. "We're staying!" she cried, as she made her way off the jet to her future.

"Can that lassie not catch a flight like normal folk?" moaned her gran as her granddaughter and great grandson left the aircraft.

# Epilogue

"Happy Birthday to you, happy birthday to you. Happy birthday dear twinnies, happy birthday to you."

It hardly seemed possible it was a year since that fateful cruise, thought Bridget, looking round the room at how her family had expanded. Erin, Nick and Ryan had flown in for the babies' birthdays.

They were such a happy, loving family. Nick was like a dog with two tails, fussing over his wife. His wife! Bridget was finding it hard to believe that her little girl was now married with a child and another on the way.

Michael had brought along his latest squeeze – a teacher, as different from Margee as it was possible to be. Bridget knew this wasn't a 'happy-ever-after' relationship. She'd be grateful for just a 'happy' time for her brother-in-law. But it was her husband who deserved the most accolades.

True to his word, and to give credit where credit was due, Paddy had done what he'd said he would. Despite the huge increase in his workload he had made time for his family. These babies certainly knew who their daddy was and, even at this early age, they could twist him round their little fingers.

Paddy Coyle was possibly the most feared and respected man in Glasgow: a big shot, as his wife called him, but at home he was just Daddy.

*

Lizzie and Theresa loved the white villa, as they called it. It was more their style than the big apartment once owned by Diane Mack. It was comfortable and within easy reach of their favourite cafés and shops. And they didn't have to lift a finger; the old caretaker couple kept it in tip-top condition.

No one had ever enquired into what had happened to the two young guys who'd disappeared overnight. No one was interested and Paddy had never divulged details of how he'd come into possession of the property.

As they reached their favourite café, the two ladies were disappointed to see their regular table was occupied. A very attractive, smartly-dressed woman, reading a magazine, glanced up as they sat down at the adjacent table.

"She looks familiar," Lizzie remarked to her friend.

"Mm, I was thinking the same."

"I can't put my finger on it, but I've definitely seen her before."

"It's the hair. I feel if she had a different hair colour or style, I might remember her."

"Whoever she is, she's a smart piece," admitted Lizzie, smiling.

"Good afternoon, ladies. It's been a while since we met."

"Holy Mary, Mother of God," exclaimed Lizzie, almost falling off her chair.

It was the Irish accent that did it. It was Imelda! Imelda Gavin. Gone was the insignificant drab of a woman and in its place was a smart, stylish lady about town. Well, thought Lizzie, that's a turn up for the books. Wait until the Catholic Mothers heard about this!